THE RISING OF 11 THE SHIELD HERO

Aneko Yusagi

Ren Amaki

Filo

Motoyasu Kitamura

S'yne

""Wahhh! Waaahhhhh!"
Motoyasu was bawling his eyes out.

"Maaaster! Heeeelp!"

Table of Contents

Prologue: To Market

"This way."

We followed, descending the stairway. My name is Naofumi Iwatani. I was a university student until I got summoned to another world to serve as the Shield Hero, and at the moment, I was with my companions in Zeltoble, the country of merchants and mercenaries. We came here to purchase additional slaves, which is why we were following a couple of slave traders to the underground slave market.

After the whole Spirit Tortoise ordeal ended, I knew we needed to increase our offensive capabilities before the appearance of the next guardian beast—the Phoenix—and before the next wave. I decided to establish my own village, so I had the Queen of Melromarc grant me a territory and the requisite noble title. That's when we ended up getting involved in the whole mess with Lurolona, the village Raphtalia was from.

Despite being citizens of Melromarc, the village residents had been forced into slavery in their own country and were being abused simply because they were demi-humans. Thanks to my efforts, the primary instigators of the demi-human discrimination—Trash and the Church of the Three Heroes—were dealt with and the queen issued an emancipation proclamation. But in a string of unlucky events, that proclamation came just a moment too late and the slaves ended up being sold off to another country, where they were being traded at ridiculously high prices. Numerous attempts were made to secure the villagers, but these worked against us. The result was that certain merchants, taking advantage of the situation, pushed prices up even further.

It was a truly miserable state of affairs. Rumors about my sidekick Raphtalia were apparently another reason for the skyrocketing prices, but whatever. Either way, a long string of unlucky events had resulted in the surging prices of the Lurolona slaves. As a result, we were forced to fight in the underground coliseums of Zeltoble to make money. And, well . . . we had a rough time, but we managed to win a tournament and successfully buy back the Lurolona slaves, fortunately.

"So you still want more people, little Naofumi?"

"I'm sure the numbers we have now won't be enough. You know we're rebuilding the territory, too, right?"

That woman hanging on to my arm was Sadeena. She was like a big sister to Raphtalia, and she had joined the coliseum fight tournament on her own in an attempt to rescue the Lurolona slaves. She was in her demi-human form now, but she could also transform into a therianthrope form that resembled a killer whale. As for her appearance . . . she was beautiful and had a certain Japanese air about her, while her expression hinted at being a carefree drunkard.

Even though Raphtalia, Filo, and I were currently in a weakened state due to the effects of a curse, I was sure we were still far stronger than your average adventurer. And yet Sadeena was strong enough that it took all three of us just to barely defeat her in the tournament. She insisted that she wasn't that strong and that it was because we had been debuffed while she had been buffed via support magic during the fight. But judging by her skills and fighting abilities, I was still sure she was quite formidable.

Oh, and there was a reason that she wouldn't stop hanging on to my arm, too. She had apparently decided long ago that her heart would belong to the man who could outdrink her. She started coming on to me when she saw that I was unaffected by eating rucolu fruit, which was kind of like highly concentrated alcohol.

"Oh? So you really are serious about rebuilding the village, I guess."

"Well, yeah. Just rounding up and securing the slaves isn't going to solve the problem."

There was also the incident of slave hunters attacking the village because of the skyrocketing prices of the Lurolona slaves. Fortunately, we had been training the villagers prior to that and they were able to turn the tables on the attackers. That was just it. We needed to make them realize that they couldn't keep holding on to naïve hopes of someone always being there to save them, and that realistically it was up to them to protect their own village.

The people of this world had a bad habit of depending on the heroes every time they were in trouble. If they actually took a moment to think about it, they might have realized how absurd summoning people from another world to fix their problems really was. Although, there were certain aspects of this world that made it feel just like a game, like the concept of levels and defeating monsters to raise your level.

"Oh, little Naofumi! You're so great! I think I'm falling in love all over again!"

"Get your hands off me! I told you I have no interest in that kind of thing!"

"Sadeena! Get a hold of yourself, please!"

That was Raphtalia that just reprimanded Sadeena. Raphtalia was a demi-human girl and a former slave who now fights by my side as my closest companion. She was chosen as the owner of the katana vassal weapon by the katana itself, which signified hero status in another world we had visited. She had proven her fighting prowess, and it fell upon her to actually defeat my enemies for me, since being the Shield Hero meant that I was unable to attack other people myself.

Raphtalia wanted nothing to do with romance or sexual relations, probably due to prioritizing her mission to save the world from the waves. I was repulsed by the thought of romantic relationships, too. Of course, it was being framed by that worthless bitch that had made me that way.

Raphtalia looked really, really good in miko outfits, by the way. But she refused to wear them because of her utilitarian nature. She was quite attractive, and her tanuki ears and tail provided the perfect accent, which was probably why the miko outfits looked so abnormally good on her. I would have been happy if that was all she wore, so I was secretly considering having a miko outfit with powerful effects custom-made for her.

"Oh?"

Lately, Sadeena had constantly been trying to get close to me and she always teased Raphtalia in the process. I really wished she would try thinking about what it was like always having to calm Raphtalia down.

"Fehhh . . ."

That was Rishia behind us that just made a really pathetic sound. There were times when she would step up to the plate—she could be a real force to be reckoned with when she got emotional. But she usually just stuck to handling the more intellectual side of things for us. It felt like her performance had been especially lackluster lately, even though she'd apparently been up to all sorts of things. Of course, having her fight at a place like the coliseum, while she was still a weakling, would have basically been signing her death warrant. So I guess she hadn't really had a chance to impress recently.

"Hmm?"

That was Filo cocking her head to the side with a confused look on her face. Filo was a little girl that was actually a filolial, which was a type of monster that loved nothing more than pulling carriages. Filolials exhibited a special pattern of development when raised by a hero that enabled them to transform into a human form resembling an angel with wings on its back.

Judging from her appearance, you might think she was just a cute little angel girl with blonde hair and blue eyes— until she opened her mouth. She was simple and innocent, but her instincts were impressive when it came to combat. Her performance in our most recent battle was still fresh in my mind. We'd found ourselves in a situation unable to use magic, yet Filo had managed to force our opponent into a corner by . . . singing. She'd learned a singing technique that was similar to magic while we were in Kizuna's world. I knew I could rely on her in combat.

"Rafu?"

That little thing sitting on Filo's shoulder and chirping was a shikigami—known as a familiar in this world—that I made using a lock of Raphtalia's hair. I named her Raph-chan. If Raphtalia had a therianthrope form that she could transform into like Sadeena, Raph-chan was what I imagined it would look like.

"Mr. Naofumi? You're thinking about something rude again, aren't you?"

"Oh! Little Raphtalia can understand what little Naofumi is thinking! I'm jealous!"

"Shut up."

Thinking about Raph-chan would restore some of my sanity that they had been chipping away at. Raph-chan was always up for a good time and would happily join in whenever I started making mischief. The cursed shield, which had been stuck to my arm since being summoned here, had abilities that let me make a familiar more powerful. Lately, though, I had been paying more attention to tweaking properties that had nothing to do with combat, like the quality of Raph-chan's fur. I wanted to get as close as possible to an ideal texture that would feel simply blissful when I pet her. But I had to make sure that Raphtalia, in particular, never figured that out.

Umm . . . I guess I got off track there for a second. Anyway, we needed more slaves to continue developing the village, and we were here to buy those slaves at a cheap price.

"We're here. Yes sir."

"Good. It's about time."

We had finished descending the stairway and arrived at the underground slave market. I looked around at the surprisingly fancy cages that the slaves were being held in. Sitting inside of one of the cages was a female demi-human that had horns like you might expect to see on an ogre. She had dark brown skin and a rather nice face. Her frame was a bit on the large side, and she had large breasts, too. I guess she would have been worthy of being called a rare beauty. She had a healthy complexion, too, which was odd. It made me think she had probably been eating well. But she wasn't the kind of slave I was looking for. She seemed like the type that would be traded as a sex slave or something.

"I'm not interested in sex slaves."

"On the contrary, this is one of the more combat-proficient demi-human types known as a kiki."

"*That* is?"

The slave was waving at me with a big, fake smile on her face that made me think she wanted to sell me something. Something about her really gave me the creeps. That face gave me the sudden urge to just punch it. But I was sure that wouldn't make anyone else here happy.

"She looks expensive. I'll pass."

When she heard my response, the slave's expression turned into one of being upset.

"Not at all. I'll give you a very good price."

"Even so . . ."

There was something about her I didn't like. Or rather, I

just didn't want her being one of my slaves. It wasn't like I had decided to only buy slaves that were children, so it wasn't an issue of standards. But something about her just seemed wrong. Then it hit me. It was because she reminded me of *Bitch*. Yeah, she looked like the former princess of Melromarc, who had falsely accused me of raping her just after I had been summoned to this world. Sheesh . . . I'd gotten tangled up in some real nonsense back then.

"Shall we move on to the next slave, then?" asked the slave trader.

"Yeah. Sorry, but I'll pass on this one."

"Oh? That's too bad!" said Sadeena as she pressed herself up against me in a rather provocative manner, making sure that the slave noticed.

"Why is that woman okay and I'm not?!"

The slave shouted at me angrily. I guess I had hurt her pride or something. Her behavior sure was confusing for a sex slave. But wait . . . why did she want me to buy her anyway?

"You're not the kind of slave I prefer. That's all."

"Sorry I'm not a cute little girl!"

Her outbursts sure were annoying. I glared at the slave traders.

Slave trading was a family business for the two slave traders standing in front of me. One of them handled the slave trade in Melromarc, while the other was based out of Zeltoble, and they were the spitting image of each other. If I were forced to come up with some kind of difference between them, the colors of their tailcoats would probably be the best I could do.

When I glared at them, they both suddenly shifted their gaze elsewhere. Whatever. They were doing plenty to help me out, after all. I glared at the slave.

"Cute little girl? It almost sounds like you might know who I am."

When she heard my response, the slave suddenly fell silent. Aha! I knew something seemed fishy.

"Oh? Do I really look that young?" teased Sadeena.

"How old are you, anyway?" I asked.

"Twenty-three. Tee hee!"

She was batting her eyes at me. I felt like throwing up. And besides, the way she was acting only made it seem even more like she was lying.

"I'm pretty sure that's the truth. I remember my father mentioning Sadeena's age before."

Raphtalia corroborated Sadeena's answer.

"I thought women were supposed to lie about their age."

"Some of them do, but several years ago father was talking about it being about time to have Sadeena start meeting potential suitors. Adding the number of years that have passed since then to the age that he mentioned would indeed make her 23 years old now."

"Oh? You remember that? Children have such impressive memories!" Sadeena exclaimed.

Saying things like that is exactly why I figured she was a lot older. Frankly, she usually sounded like an old lady.

Anyway, I didn't have any illusions about myself, despite how it might have seemed. Yes, most of the slaves I bought were children. And female. That's just how it had turned out, since I was focused primarily on gathering up the Lurolona slaves.

"Judging by her pronunciation and language use, I would say that slave is . . ."

I guessed Rishia had figured out where the slave was from. That reminded me of the fact that my shield had translation capabilities. Multiple languages were spoken in this world, just like in my own world . . . just like back on Earth. Conveniently for me, my shield could translate all of those languages for me. As for the official Melromarc language, I was pretty sure it was used in countries with . . . large populations of pure humans.

"It doesn't really matter, anyway. Just forget about it, Rishia."

"Oh, umm, understood."

"On to the next one."

"Understood. Yes sir."

"Why?! Why won't you take me?!"

I ignored the shouts of the slave and followed behind the slave traders.

Chapter One: Sacred Tree Elixir

"This is the next slave."

I looked inside of the cage that the slave traders had brought us to. It was another demi-human slave that looked healthy and well taken care of. This one was a child . . . and a female. She was waving at me with a big, fake smile on her face.

"Uhh . . . no thanks."

"What?!"

Just as I expected, she started complaining. Her response was slightly more childish than the last slave, but she was still way more chipper than she should have been. The slaves I knew all started out with lifeless eyes. They'd given up on everything. Even our fearless Keel had been terrified until she saw Raphtalia. This kid looked like a dreamy-eyed adventurer. There was no way she was a real slave.

I had the slave traders show me another slave. Once again, the slave complained when I showed no interest. I started to understand what was going on. I squinted my eyes and glared at the slave traders, who both started wiping the nervous sweat from their brows.

"Seriously?"

"It's unfortunate that none of our offerings seem to satisfy your preferences today. Yes sir."

I sighed.

"You've left me no choice. I didn't want to do this."

I beckoned to the slave that we had been brought to. When she got closer, I slowly reached out and grabbed her by the collar, and then started questioning her using my best threatening tone.

"Spit it out! Who's behind this? I'm the Shield Hero, you know. If you don't tell me, I'll destroy the country you came from."

The slave shrieked.

"D-d-daddy made me do it! He told me I had to marry the Shield Hero! They say the Shield Hero only associates with slaves, so daddy paid someone to set this up."

The slave explained while cowering in fear as I glared at her. She was just a child. This wasn't her fault.

"And is that what you want?" I asked.

"Huh?"

"Even if it *is* for your family's sake, you're being given as an offering to someone you don't even have feelings for."

Judging by the slave's appearance, she was probably a bit younger than Raphtalia was when I first saw her. The thought of someone using a small child like this to boost their own status filled me with disgust.

"Either way, I want you to go home. Tell them I saw through their plan. If that's not enough for them, tell them that the Shield Hero said he only helps demi-humans that are truly in need."

It was becoming clear that these kinds of slaves were being sent in groups.

"So that settles that. I kindly refuse your offer," I told the slave.

Siltvelt—the demi-human country—was obviously trying to set up an arranged marriage. They were disguising children of wealthy and noble families as slaves and sending them here for me to purchase.

"I'm pretty sure that country considers my word as gospel, right? I'm on the verge of personally notifying them in writing that it's going to work against them if they keep trying to force slaves onto me like this."

"Understood. Yes sir. I believe they will stop if that is what you wish. Yes sir."

"The Shield Hero does it again! Of course you would notice the slaves were fake! Such perceptivity sends tingles of excitement down my spine!"

"There's no way anyone wouldn't notice!"

It was as if they were practically shouting out that they were fakes! They could have tried to make it a little less obvious. Or they could have even sent slaves bought from some human-supremacist country or something.

"How deplorable . . ."

Even Raphtalia was losing her patience.

"There's no way Mr. Naofumi would be seduced so easily. It would save me a lot of trouble if it were that simple."

Huh? What was that supposed to mean?

"That's where I come in! Don't worry, little Naofumi, I'll cure you of your distrust of women!"

"Rafu!"

Sadeena's excitement rubbed off on Raph-chan, causing her to join in the ruckus. What an annoying woman. It was in my best interest to just ignore her.

"Oh? Your reaction must signify your approval! I won't let you down, little Naofumi!"

Huh?! She just interpreted my disregard however it suited her! Just when I thought this woman couldn't get any more annoying!

"Look! Boobies!"

Sadeena embraced me from behind and pressed her breasts up against me.

"Go to hell!"

"Mr. Naofumi! Calm down! Sadeena! Behave yourself, please!"

"Aww . . ."

Sadeena yielded, backing off when I protested. But she still had a grin on her face that was really getting on my nerves.

"Fehhh . . ."

"Can I rub up against Master from the back like Sadeena, toooo?"

"Permission denied!"

Filo seemed to think it was all some kind of game and started getting ready to grab me from behind in her filolial queen form. Damn it! If ignoring them didn't work, just what was I supposed to do?!

"Sheesh . . . Don't you have any other slaves? I'm going to be mad if this trip was all for nothing."

"We do, indeed! In fact, we've been saving the best for last."

"Every now and then you try to play tricks on me, don't you?"

Seriously. I really wished I didn't have to deal with these creeps.

"What is it that you're looking for then, Shield Hero?"

"Right now I could use some slaves that are good with their hands. Other than that, any slave that can fight will do."

I already had a few slaves back at the village that were good with their hands, but I needed more. What I really wanted was more slaves that had a natural aptitude for detailed work like Imiya, who I was teaching how to make accessories.

"I see. This way, then."

"You better not show me any more fakes."

"Of course not."

The slave traders took us to another section and . . . Yeah, I'd seen one of these before.

"Those are lumos, right?"

I walked over toward a cage filled with lumo therianthropes. Imiya wasn't originally from Lurolona, but if any of these lumos knew him already then it would probably make them easier to work with. Kind of like how having Raphtalia had made it easier to work with Keel. I figured it wouldn't hurt to ask.

"Do any of you know a boy named Imiya?"

"That's a common name. Which Imiya might you be referring to?"

A lumo that was slightly taller than Imiya responded. It was a . . . male, I think.

Hmm . . . So Imiya was a common name. This was useless if I couldn't say his full name. What was it again? I remembered it being abnormally long. Leu . . . Nope, I couldn't remember it. I gave up. It seemed like a good idea at the time, but whatever.

Oh, wait! Rishia was the brains around here, so maybe she would remember.

"Hey, Rishia. Do you remember that long name of Imiya's?"

"Fehhh . . ."

That meant she didn't.

"Oh well. We'll just have to bring Imiya back with us later."

Just when I was about to give up for good, Raphtalia spoke up.

"Mr. Naofumi, you know Imiya is a girl, right? Her full name is Imiya Leuthurn Reethela Teleti Kuwariz."

Raphtalia spouted off Imiya's full name like it was nothing. Just how good was her memory, anyway? Raphtalia was actually pretty impressive. Or maybe she was just good at remembering names.

"Just the other day you mentioned some dish with a rather long name, too, Mr. Naofumi."

"Oh yeah, I guess I did. *Faux* filets de sardines au basilic."

Sardines with basil, in other words. There were fish similar to sardines in this world, but they weren't quite the same. They didn't have basil here, either, so I just made do with some random herbs. Not long ago I'd cooked the dish for the slaves to celebrate their return, since we'd finally gotten the village's basic infrastructure in place. It was a French dish, by the way.

"Imiya's name isn't much more complicated than that."

"You think so?"

The name of the dish wasn't difficult to remember since each of the words had meaning. Imiya's name just sounded like some kind of foreign code to me.

"You mean that Imiya!"

The lumo male spoke up again.

"You know her?"

"She's my niece. Of course I know her!"

Oh? I guess we'd found one of Imiya's family members. It was our lucky day.

"Are any of these others from the same place as you?"

"Yes, some of them are from the same village."

"They'll do just fine, then. I'll reunite you all with Imiya."

I let the slave trader know that I would be buying the male lumo and his fellow villagers.

"Understood. Yes sir."

"And . . . might I ask who you are, sir?" the lumo asked me.

"What? Is it not obvious? I'm a slave driver."

I had a feeling slaves would come flocking over if I said the truth out loud while we were in this place. It'd save me a lot of trouble if I just glossed over it for now.

"There you go again with the lies . . ." interjected Raphtalia.

"Is Imiya . . . is she doing well?"

"She's doing very well. She's doing her best to help out at our village," Raphtalia reassured him.

Imiya was obedient. That was for sure. Perhaps a bit too timid, though.

"I see. I look forward to seeing her again."

I never would have thought that absurdly long name would turn out to be useful, but it sure helped us out today.

"Oh my! I have a feeling things are going to get even more exciting back at the village!"

Sadeena's mouth was moving again.

"Probably. By the way, I've been wondering . . . What's your relationship with Raphtalia, anyway?"

"I'm just a drifter that came from the same place as little

Raphtalia's parents. They took good care of me."

"Oh yeah?"

I'd just figured all of them had lived in Lurolona for generations. But I guess that made sense. The territory that I was governing now was a region that Eclair's father had worked to develop, and it'd been designated as a demi-human-friendly area. But once he died, there was no one around with political influence anymore and the region just fell into ruin.

"Well, I think that should do it for today."

My coin purse had been feeling pretty light ever since I'd paid Sadeena's debts off for her. I probably couldn't afford to buy any more slaves than this right now.

"I guess it's about time we head back," I said.

"Wait just a moment. Yes sir."

The Zeltoble slave trader spoke up.

"What is it? Is there something else?"

"We have a pair of slaves that we think you will find most interesting."

"If it's more slaves sent by Siltvelt then I'll pass."

"Oh no, certainly not. These two are . . . today's main dish, shall we say?"

"I'm just about all out of money, you know."

"A powerful drug can become a dangerous poison in the wrong hands. This is a pair that we believe you will know how to handle best, so we are prepared to offer them to you at a very reasonable price."

A powerful drug, huh? That sounded good, but it also meant I'd be dealing with a dangerous poison if I wasn't careful. Still, it wouldn't hurt to take a look.

"Let's have a look."

I followed the slave traders out of the room.

"This way."

We seemed to be in some kind of quarantine area for sick slaves. It sure didn't seem very sanitary. I wasn't about to start doing charity work, but this was just bad for my mental health. I walked over to a cage, pulled out a vial of medicine, and beckoned to the slave inside.

"Ugh . . ."

"Here. This is medicine. Drink it."

"Th . . . thank you."

I couldn't help myself. It was for my own mental health. The slave was suffering right there in front of me, so I gave it the medicine. I'd made a good portion of my money from selling medicine in this world, so I was confident that my medicine would make a difference.

"I'm sure you already know this, but—"

"Don't worry, we'll be sure to reimburse you with a portion of the profits later!" the slave traders cut me off.

"Don't speak in unison like that! It's creepy!"

The Zeltoble slave trader started skipping. Come on!

Seriously! He was creeping me out. Anyway . . . after all was said and done, it came time to meet the pair of slaves.

"Here we are."

We were standing in front of a cage with two demi-humans inside.

"Wh . . . what now?! I'm working like I'm supposed to, right? What do you want?!"

One of them was a young boy around 12 years old. He looked as healthy as could be.

"Oh? Is that you, little Fohl?"

"You're . . . Nadia!"

Huh? They knew each other? I pointed at the slave and Sadeena nodded.

"I saw him fighting in the coliseums every now and then when I first came to Zeltoble. I even saw him fight in the underground coliseums a few times."

So he was a slave and a fighter. I'd heard that some people in Zeltoble ended up as slaves and were forced to fight in the coliseums. I guess this Fohl kid was one of those combat slaves.

"And that one?"

I pointed at the other slave lying at the back of the cage.

"No idea," Sadeena replied.

It was hard to see since it was so dark, but I could make out someone lying on a bed of straw. Whoever it was didn't seem to be in very good condition.

Cough . . . cough . . .

I looked the Fohl kid over. The first thing that caught my eye was the color of his hair. It was black and white. I could tell from the colors and texture of his hair alone that he was more valuable than the other slaves. His eyes were blue, with pupils that were vertical slits, like those of a cat. Those slits, surrounded by blue irises standing out against the whites of his eyes . . . That alone gave him an air that felt almost intimidating. His face had a wild look to it. There was something in his eyes that said the whole world was his enemy. His ears were also a bit cat-like, but thicker and rounded. What really stuck out was his tail, with its black and white stripes. Could it be?

"Strange. Something about him reminds me of an opponent that we faced in Kizuna's world."

Raphtalia echoed my thoughts.

"What a coincidence. I was just thinking the same thing."

"Umm . . . the white tigers, riiight?"

Oh? Even Filo had noticed, apparently. She was right. Something about the slave reminded me of the white tigers that we had fought in Kizuna's world. It made me think of the half-human, half-beast enemies that Kyo had created. How should I put it? I imagined this slave was what the perfected version of those things would look like. He looked like a human that had been very skillfully combined with a white tiger. I'm sure he was just a demi-human, of course. But my prior experience with white tigers put me off.

"He seems expensive. Even for a kid."

"Factoring price in from the very first impression . . . My hat's off to your financial prudence, hero!"

Even Raphtalia seemed stunned by my verdict.

"Your focus on the bottom line is impressive, little Naofumi!"

Just ignore them all!

But actually, they did have a point. Maybe thinking about money before anything else wasn't such a good thing, after all.

"I mean, compared to the other demi-human slaves, something seems different about him," I said.

"You have good intuition. This slave is a hakuko. It's a type of demi-human with quite the reputation," the slave trader responded.

"Hakuko . . ."

"It's said that the very first holy heroes named the race in ancient times."

In Japanese, the character for "white" could be pronounced "haku" and "ko" was one of the pronunciations of the character for "tiger." When the two were combined to refer to the legendary white tiger they were actually pronounced "byakko," but if you didn't know that I guess you might mistakenly pronounce them "hakuko."

That meant it was a type of demi-human that had been around since ancient times. In that case, it might have been a good investment, but . . . what if he turned into some kind of monster like the Spirit Tortoise when he grew up and then ended up going on a rampage or something? That was not something I wanted to deal with.

And anyway, what was up with that name? Why did all of the past heroes seem to have such bad taste in these things? It was the same with the legends at the Cal Mira islands. Then again, I did name my filolial "Filo," so I guess I couldn't really talk.

"I see. And what are you planning to do with this one?"

"We would like to present him to you."

"He does seem rather strong, but certainly not what I'd call a 'powerful drug.'"

Even the White Tiger guardian beast in Kizuna's world hadn't been impossible to defeat. The shields that I had unlocked using materials from the beast had left an impression on me because they had some really annoying equip effects like support nullification. The same went for Raphtalia's katana, too. The equipment was really difficult to use well.

"Do you know his level and stats?"

"His level is written here."

I looked over the papers that the slave trader handed me. I'd had a hunch, but apparently the two slaves were siblings. Level 32? He sure looked young for a level that high. The slaves back at the village were all pretty grown by the time they hit level 30.

"That's higher than I expected. Does the fact that he still looks like this have something to do with his race? Or just individual differences?"

"He's still a child at this level. One special characteristic of this type of demi-human is that they cannot class up until level 50. They can reach level 60 without classing up, as well. Yes sir. Consequently, they can reach a maximum level of 120 after classing up."

"In other words, he'll be even stronger when he becomes an adult."

"Exactly."

Impressive. So this was some kind of special type of demi-human. Even Filo had to class up at level 40, so I could only imagine what kind of development these siblings might exhibit if I leveled them up. My interest had definitely been piqued. The boy's sister was level 1, by the way.

"The hakuko demi-humans are known for having used their exceptional combat prowess to repeatedly thwart the plans of Melromarc's legendary figure known as 'His Excellency, the Wise.' Yes sir."

Using Trash as an example wasn't going to help anything. Nothing about him impressed me. And that meant he'd used his influence to bring his tyranny all the way here.

"Using 'His Excellency, the Wise' as a point of reference isn't saying much . . ."

"If it weren't for that man, the name 'Melromarc' would likely mean nothing to other countries."

"You sure are talking him up."

"Regardless, the hakuko is one of this world's most prestigious races, not counting the heroes. Yes sir."

"I see."

Ignoring whether or not Trash was any more impressive during his prime, I guess it was safe to assume that hakuko demi-humans had exceptional combat skills. The ability to thwart an enemy's strategy using physical force was probably something I could use, considering that I was generally limited to defensive measures. Of course, that was assuming that these slaves truly had such potential.

The slave trader whispered in my ear, as if to avoid being heard by the siblings.

"By the way, even the supposedly unrivaled hakuko is no match for an orca in the water. Yes sir."

"Who are you talking about now?"

The slave traders both looked over at Sadeena.

"Oh?"

What?! Now they were telling me that Sadeena was a superior type of demi-human?! Then again, the Japanese character for "killer whale" was a combination of "fish" and "tiger," so I guess it made sense that they would be powerful animals. But anyway, we were supposed to be focusing on the slave siblings right now.

"As for these siblings, the brother is in perfect health, but the younger sister has a genetic disorder. She is blind, cannot walk, and does not have much longer to live. However, her brother cares for her more than anything else in the world."

So he was still trying to protect his dying sister even after they had become slaves. It sounded like the hero of some clichéd story. If this were some kind of manga or something, he wouldn't even need to be the hero. With that kind of conviction, he would be a popular character even if he were the villain or something. And he had the strength to actually stand by that conviction because of his race. He fit the stereotype perfectly.

"Oh yeah?"

"Perhaps you could separate the two. Put the brother to work. Tell him that his sister will be hospitalized, and then go leave her in a field somewhere. Of course, you would make the brother believe she was still alive. You have monsters that are good at imitating voices, right? Just let the brother hear her voice from time to time."

Did I have monsters that were good at imitating voices? There were only four things that my monsters did: dig up dirt, run around peddling, eat weeds, or fight. Did he mean Filo? I looked over at Filo.

"Whaaat?"

"Can you imitate voices, Filo? Can you do an imitation of Melty?"

"Yuuup! *Filo-chan, you're so charming!*"

Filo went straight into an impression of Melty. It was perfect. You would have thought Melty was standing right here with us. But what the hell? What kind of line was that?! *Charming*?! I'd have to have a talk with Melty next time I saw her. I motioned for the slave trader to continue.

"If you did that, the brother would continue fighting to the very end, all for the sake of his precious little sister, who would have actually already departed this world. All that would be left is for you to reap the benefits."

His plan was pure evil. It made me cringe. There were just too many ways it could backfire. I could just imagine someone like Itsuki showing up, rescuing the brother, and then teaming up with him to try to defeat me. That wouldn't even be funny. I'd win the fight, of course, but I wasn't going to go out of my way to create my own enemies.

"That's why you're useless at handling all but the simplest slaves. I'll show you how to do it the right way."

I told the slave trader to unlock the cage.

"Wh . . . what are you going to do?!"

"Just shut up for a second, you little brat."

"What?! I'm not a brat!"

"You sure look like one to me."

The brother was surprisingly aggressive, but I just ignored him. I went inside of the cage and approached his younger sister at the back.

"Stop! Don't touch Atla!"

The brother tried to stop me. I pulled some medicine out of my pocket and showed it to him.

"I'm just going to give her some medicine."

I'd made the medicine using my shield, by the way. I still couldn't pull it off on my own. That's how difficult it was to make. I'd learned how to make it from an equip bonus on the Spirit Tortoise Sacred Tree Shield. The bonus was called . . . miracle drug recipe.

Spirit Tortoise Sacred Tree Shield 0/40 C
<abilities unlocked> equip bonus: miracle drug recipe
equip effects: protection of the ancient flora, blessing of the sacred tree
mastery level: 0

I had no idea what the shield's effects did, although it was clear that they had something to do with plants. The miracle drug recipe had only taught me how to make one medicine. Even worse, it required a bunch of other medicines and potions to make: regular medicine, superior medicine, a healing salve, magic water, and soul-healing water. On top of that, you had to mix an extremely precise amount of poisonous materials, filter the mixture, and skim the top layer off to use along with . . . sacred tree sap, wherever that came from.

Just recently, I'd tried to compound the medicine without using my shield, but I failed. I went and asked the apothecary to try to figure out what had gone wrong, but he just scolded me and told me I was in over my head. That's how difficult it was to make. It was a priceless medicine that was practically impossible to get your hands on unless you just happened to have a legendary shield.

Its name: Elixir of Yggdrasil. It was the same medicine that the lively old Hengen Muso lady had used, so it went without saying that it was effective. Any gamer would know that something with "elixir" in the name was bound to be powerful. The name may have been my shield's translation, but it still included the name of the world tree, nonetheless.

". . ."

How did that old lady get her hands on such a priceless medicine? She must have been filthy rich. I wondered if maybe she had used the Hengen Muso style to rake in money while traveling the world. How did her son end up being so plain? The poor guy wasn't even worth mentioning.

Anyway, the elixir was a miracle drug that could cure any ailment in one go.

"You belong to me now. This is medicine that will cure your sister. You can pay for it by dedicating your life to serving me."

The apothecary mentioned that it had a ridiculously high

market value. Selling it wouldn't have made enough to buy up all of the Lurolona slaves, though, and my stocks were really limited. Very few cases were dire enough to actually require this medicine to save someone's life. Still, lots of people wanted it since it was so effective. Some said that it could even bring back the dead.

My funds were running low lately, so I'd brought it planning to rob someone blind, but this was the perfect chance to use it. Considering the coming battles with the waves, I needed power more than I needed money. I would use it to secure a powerful ally via an enormous debt that ensured allegiance.

"You better not be lying . . ." he said.

"Maybe you know the smell."

The brother sniffed at the medicine. Of course, if he'd smelled this medicine before, he probably wouldn't be here in this situation. He took a couple of really big sniffs before looking up suddenly and shouting.

"That's the Elixir of Yggdrasil!"

"So you do know it . . ."

What was he? A dog? Maybe being a superior race meant having a good nose, too.

"But . . . but . . . it could have poison in it!"

"Are you always this suspicious of medicines? Do you distrust every medicine your sister takes?"

"Uhh . . ."

"If you refuse to believe me then I don't have to give it to her. But will that save your sister? I'm buying you, either way. Whether your sister is suffering or not won't change that."

"Ugh . . ."

The brother let out a humiliated moan.

"Is somebody there?"

The girl coughed as she turned her head in our direction. She was blind, right? I guess she was relying on the sound of our voices as a guide.

"I sense the presence of someone who is incredibly strong, yet kind. Am I right, Brother?"

"Wh . . . who knows . . ."

"However . . . I feel great power . . . However . . ."

The girl slowly turned her head toward me. The brother hesitantly motioned for me to approach her. I moved toward this girl that he'd called Atla. She was in terrible condition. She was wrapped in bandages from head to toe. You couldn't even see her face. But I could still tell she was covered in sores. Judging from her appearance, it was surprising she was still alive. Her ears and tail were the only signs left that she was even the same race as her brother.

"However . . . what?"

She seemed to be referring to me, so I tried speaking to her. The first impression is always the most important, so I decided to go with my usual bigheaded attitude.

"I feel a deep sadness hidden within that great strength and kindness."

Deep sadness, huh? Memories of being consumed by rage after Bitch betrayed me came flooding back for a split second, but then faded almost immediately, being replaced by memories of my time with Raphtalia.

If I'd only just recently arrived in this world, I probably would have been drawn to this girl's act. Characters that spout off seemingly profound lines like this were common in manga and games. Not to mention, this was a young girl on her deathbed. It was all a bit too perfect.

"Umm . . . May I ask why you are here?"

"You know what kind of place this is, right?"

"Yes. I am being held hostage here in order to force my brother to work."

She understood completely, and yet . . . No, there was a sense of resignation in her voice.

"Man with the kind voice . . . Might you be so kind as to tell me your name?"

"Naofumi."

"Mr. . . . Naofumi."

Her pronunciation was impressive. Apart from the other heroes, this was the first time anyone had pronounced my name correctly here. Even in the other world, Kizuna had been the only one who could pronounce it properly. L'Arc and Glass could never say it quite right.

"Mr. . . . Naofumi. Please, take good care of my brother for me."

"Atla! What are you saying?!"

Wasn't it obvious? She knew she didn't have much time left, so she was asking me to watch over her brother.

"Sorry, but that's not a promise I'm ready to make."

"Oh . . . I see . . ."

"Because I plan to take care of you, too. Here. Take this medicine."

Atla started to say something in reply, but then simply nodded. I held the Elixir of Yggdrasil up to the young girl's lips. Unable to defy his younger sister, the brother stood aside with clenched fists and said nothing.

Gulp.

Atla drank the medicine without hesitation. Huh? In addition to the glow from my skill that increased the efficacy of medicine, there was another strange light radiating out. It was no small glimmer, either. I had unlocked the complete Spirit Tortoise series of shields thanks to Ost, so I did have a bunch of new skills. Maybe it had something to do with one of those. Whatever it was, it was obvious that it was increasing the efficacy of the medicine even further.

Pant . . . Pant . . .

The medicine was starting to work. She began to breathe more easily.

"What's . . . this? My body . . . suddenly feels lighter."

"Atla?"

"My skin . . . is tingling and . . . I can feel a warmth deep within my body."

"Well, it will probably take some time to feel the full effects of the medicine. I'll give you several doses over a period of time, so just rest for now."

"Understood. I'm afraid I will be useless to you, but I thank you for your kindness."

I stood up and stepped out of the cage.

"And your name was Fohl, right?"

The brother had been glaring at me but looked away when I spoke to him.

"I get it. You don't want to talk. I didn't want to wake Atla up, but I guess . . ."

"Yes! That's right! My name is Fohl!"

"And your last name?"

". . ."

He suddenly fell silent. Considering their race, they probably came from a good family. Maybe they had been disowned or something and could no longer use the family name. It didn't matter, anyway.

"That's fine. Either way, you're my slave now. Understood?"

"Yeah. Fine. That medicine seems to be the real deal, so I'll work until it's paid for. You want me to fight in the coliseums?"

Hmm . . . That wasn't a bad idea. But having this little brat fight in the coliseums in his current state would be a waste of time. I wanted to toughen him up a bit before anything else.

"I haven't decided if we'll do that yet, but I have different plans in mind for you, regardless. You don't need to worry about fighting in the coliseums for now."

"Then how am I supposed to make money?"

"I'll take care of the details, so you just do as I say. Don't worry. It's not like I'm going to short-change you."

I threw in an evil laugh there at the end and Fohl shot me an icy glare. This was how the relationship between owner and slave was supposed to be, right?

"That medicine is expensive, you know. It's on a whole different level than any Elixir of Yggdrasil you'll find on the market."

I threw in a bit of extra condescension for good measure. If I talked the price up enough, maybe I wouldn't have to worry about him trying to say he'd worked enough to pay for the medicine and running off. Although, it wasn't like I'd actually let him get away.

"I know! That's obvious from how peacefully Atla is sleeping now!"

Fohl was clearly unhappy, but his reply was an honest one. He seemed to have a pretty serious sister complex. Maybe it had just been the two of them for so long now that he viewed everyone else as an enemy. I could kind of understand where he was coming from. I saw pretty much everyone around me as an enemy for a while after being falsely accused by Bitch.

"But . . . there's no way I'll let you have my sister!"

"What's this kid going on about? Anyone?"

"You're ruthless, little Naofumi. You really are great!"

"Sadeena . . . If you think calling me great is going to make me happy, you're in for a rude awakening."

I wasn't Motoyasu, after all. I wasn't the kind of idiot who got excited over flattery. I preferred someone who would complain when I stirred up trouble, like Raphtalia did.

"Aww . . ."

I was busy trying to ignore Sadeena's sulky response when Raphtalia spoke up.

"He's just jealous because his little sister seems to like you," she said.

"Rafu!"

Raph-chan clearly agreed with Raphtalia. Hmm . . . So the kid was jealous. In that case, he definitely had the wrong impression.

"No! That's not it! What's that girl's problem?! You too, Nadia! Stop being so rude!"

Fohl pointed at Raphtalia and Sadeena while shouting. So this was what people meant when they talked about someone not knowing their place. I was going to push this brat harder than a Spartan soldier when we got back to the village. He supposedly had a lot of potential, after all. I was starting to look forward to his training. I'd given his sister the same medicine that cured the old lady, so I had a feeling she would get better, too. When she did . . . I was sure I could find something for her to do at the village.

"Don't worry. Mr. Naofumi is not that kind of person."

Raphtalia remained calm and smiled at Fohl.

"And little Fohl . . . my name isn't Nadia. You know my real name now, so use it, okay?"

I couldn't help but feel like things were getting a bit too lighthearted.

"We will perform the slave registration shortly. Yes sir."

"Sounds good."

And that was how I ended up taking the siblings off the slave trader's hands.

Chapter Two: Return to the Village

"Alright, I'll be taking you back to the village as we finish the registrations, so everyone line up."

The slave registrations were going smoothly. I took the slaves back to the village in groups using my portal skill as they were completed. Of course, we had to wait for the cool down to expire each time, so we were sitting around twiddling our thumbs a lot.

"It's too bad you don't have a more convenient teleport skill, Raphtalia."

"I could use Scroll of Return."

"Yeah, but it wouldn't do much good to send people to the dragon hourglass. Although, I guess we could have Filo pick them up and take them to the village from there."

It had a similar cool down time, though. The same was true for Kizuna's Return Dragon Vein. That reminded me . . . I guess Raphtalia could use Return Dragon Vein, too.

"By the way, I wonder where that seven star hero that's supposed to be in Zeltoble went," I mumbled.

I figured meeting up with Zeltoble's seven star hero would be no problem with the queen, the accessory dealer, and the slave traders all backing me. But the hero had gone off somewhere and was out of the country. Searching for the hero was too much trouble, so I'd had a message sent asking the hero to return. I wasn't sure if the hero had been summoned from another world or if it was someone chosen from this world, but this hero obviously didn't think much of the holy heroes. Then again, thanks to those other three idiots, people had come to the conclusion that I was the only one that wasn't a fake or just damaged goods.

"Still, at least we got to bind you to the hourglass here so that you can use Dragon Return Vein."

"Yes. But it would have been nice if we'd been able to meet and talk with the hero, too, for the sake of the world."

"Yeah."

Talking with the seven star heroes to learn about their power-up methods would boost my own stats, if nothing else. At least, that's what I'd hoped to see happen.

"Hey, little Naofumi. We've got some spare time, so how about you and I—"

"Portal Shield!"

I didn't feel like dealing with Sadeena, so I went ahead and sent her back to the village before the next group of slaves. Her flirting was getting out of hand and I didn't have the energy to put up with it right now.

"I can never tell if she's being serious or just messing around," I said.

"Sadeena never seems to be too serious about anything," Raphtalia replied.

"Yeah, I know. You have no interest in pursuing romantic affairs before this world is peaceful, right Raphtalia?"

"R . . . right . . ."

We went on chatting while sending people back with my portal each time the cool down expired.

And then, finally, it came time to send Fohl and Atla back. Atla was still recuperating, but Fohl brought her over and laid her near where we were all waiting. After he got her situated, he brought her a jug of water.

"Thank you, Brother."

"No worries. Are you feeling okay?"

"Yes. I feel very comfortable."

"That's good."

"Mr. Naofumi . . . When will we be departing?"

Atla turned in my direction when she addressed me.

"It's almost time."

"Understood."

"We should probably go ahead and give you one more dose of medicine."

I changed my shield to the Spirit Tortoise Sacred Tree Shield and gave Atla another dose of the remaining Elixir of Yggdrasil. She had already gotten a lot better, but her condition seemed to improve even more.

"Thank you."

"No problem."

I shot Fohl a patronizing look.

"Gununu . . ." he grumbled.

Hmm . . . Was it just me or did something about the way he said that sound just like someone else? Whatever. He was going to have to work hard to pay for this medicine. He was supposed to have some real potential, so I wasn't going to go easy on him. I'd work him like . . . a slave.

"Mr. Naofumi . . ."

Atla gripped my hand in hers.

"Please try to get along with my brother."

"We get along fine! Right?!"

Fohl threw his arm around my shoulder like we were good buddies. What was up with that attitude? I couldn't have him getting the wrong idea about our relationship.

"You too, Brother. This man is an extraordinary person."

"I . . . I know that!"

"I'm glad to hear that."

Atla seemed exhausted. She returned to her resting position. The medicine was working, but it was clear she was still sick. It only made sense she would be exhausted.

"I'm feeling a bit sleepy."

"The trip back to the village will be over in an instant. Then you can get plenty of rest."

"We'll all go fwoooosh and then we'll be there! I prefer running, but this is fun, too, so I'm sure you'll like it!"

Like always, Filo was terrible at explaining things, but I guess that was her way of describing my portal skill.

"The bird that pulls carriages is full of energy and . . . I sense a pure, untainted power within her. This bird . . . Her strength rivals even your own, does it not, Mr. Naofumi?"

Atla pointed in Filo's direction. Impressive. Her description of Filo was spot-on. She may have been blind, but it was clear that she was still sensing her surroundings somehow.

"What is it, Master?"

"This new slave that I just bought—Atla—is blind, but she says she can still tell that you're strong."

"Tee hee hee. I got a compliment!"

"It's clear that you spared no kindness in raising her, Mr. Naofumi."

"Yup!"

Filo puffed up her chest feathers proudly when she responded. Kindness? Me being kind to Filo? What was this girl going on about?

And then the time had come.

"Okay, my portal cool down has expired. It's about time we head back."

"Understood. We finally get to return at last," said Raphtalia.

"Yeah. That said, I'm going to have the slave traders

continue to search for Lurolona slaves, so we'll probably end up coming back to Zeltoble from time to time."

"The prices have stopped rising, but slaves . . . claiming to be from Lurolona are still being traded at high prices, after all."

I liked to think we had recovered the vast majority of them, but I couldn't say for certain that there were none left to be found. That's why we were continuing to search. It wasn't very likely, but it was always possible that a few had escaped slavery to become mercenaries or something. There could be other slaves out there that Sadeena hadn't been able to acquire. I never imagined that making certain none were left would be so difficult.

"Portal Shield!"

I used my skill to teleport us back to the village. I recognized the smell of the village instantly. It smelled like the sea. It was partly a fishing village, after all.

"So this . . . is Mr. Naofumi's village."

Despite being blind, Atla looked around the village.

"Can you see now?" I asked.

"No. But I can sense things . . ."

Sense things, huh? It was pretty impressive how little she seemed to be inhibited by her blindness.

"Anyway, you're still sick. We'll have you stay at the village infirmary. Fohl, take her to that building over there."

I pointed at the building that we were using for the infirmary.

We'd built it so that we would have a place to treat the slaves' wounds.

"G . . . got it."

Fohl put Atla on his back and began walking away.

"I'd like to talk with you again, Mr. Naofumi."

"I'll come check on you later, so just rest for now."

"Understood. Let's go, Brother."

"Okay."

Fohl eyed his surroundings nervously as he walked off toward the building with Atla on his back.

"Oh! Imiya!"

"Uncle! And everyone else, too!"

Imiya hugged her uncle, clearly happy to be reunited with family. I'd heard that her parents had been killed, so it was nice that she got to be reunited with her uncle.

It looked like the new slaves had already begun rekindling old friendships on their own. We'd just kicked off a little party at the village to welcome the new slaves. I decided to treat them all to some of my cooking for a bit of extra motivation. Before I knew it, the day had ended.

We began training the new slaves and monsters the next day. For the first few days, we just did a minimal amount of leveling while they got used to the village. I'd put Keel, Rishia, and Raphtalia in charge of the new slaves, and they were keeping them all busy with various tasks. Sadeena was helping level them, too. Despite how I felt about her at times, she was still ridiculously strong, after all. I'd heard that her group had been attacked by a bunch of monsters once and Sadeena had swiftly wiped them out with a magical attack.

Two days had passed since our return.

Chapter Three: Alps

It was night. I'd come to the village infirmary to continue Atla's treatment. She was complaining of itchiness, which probably meant the medicine was working.

"Mr. Naofumi . . . Umm . . . I'm sorry to ask this of you, but could you please change my bandages?"

"I can do that!"

Fohl jumped in front of me. There was that sister complex again.

"I have an ointment for skin diseases that we could apply, too. My hero abilities will make it more effective if I'm the one that applies it, but it's up to you."

"I'd like you to do it, Mr. Naofumi."

"Ugh . . ."

Fohl backed down upon hearing Atla's decision, so I stepped forward to treat her.

"Oh? The patches of skin that looked like burns before seem to be growing back new."

"Wh . . . what?!"

Fohl was staring at Atla's skin in amazement. Was it really that astonishing? I mean, she did seem to be healing surprisingly quickly, but still . . . I removed the bandages from her face to see if there was any change.

"Oh my!"

Raphtalia had been watching and gasped in response, clearly startled. I had expected there to be improvement, but even I was amazed when I saw Atla's face. Let's just say the result was more impressive than I had imagined.

The Atla I was looking at now was easily one of the most attractive among the village slaves. Her hair was shiny, and she had clear, pale white skin that seemed unfitting for a slave. Her brother looked like he might be 12 or 13 years old, so I'd figured she was even younger, but once the bandages were removed she looked even smaller than before. She was around the same size as Melty, I guess.

The slave trader's suggestion had certainly been evil, but with a slave this attractive he could've gone a whole different direction of evil and really cashed in. That was assuming her skin condition healed completely, of course. Still, I was at a loss for words. I could objectively say that Raphtalia and Filo would be considered attractive, but Atla's beauty belonged to a different category. She had a childish look, and yet there was a delicateness to her that reminded me of a fragile glass sculpture or something.

Fohl looked like he was crying.

"That feels much better. Thank you, Mr. Naofumi. Please apply the ointment whenever you're ready."

"Oh! You've grown into such a beautiful, young girl, Atla!

How time flies!" Fohl exclaimed.

He sounded like a father parting with his daughter before her wedding.

"Your progress is better than expected. I think we can skip the ointment."

"Is that so?"

The blind Atla placed her hands on her own face.

"My skin is smooth now."

"It looks that way."

"This is all thanks to you, Mr. Naofumi. Thank you."

Atla gave a small nod of appreciation.

"No problem."

Some of the other slaves were peeking in from behind the infirmary door. I could hear them whispering something about Atla being beautiful. Wherever the action was, those slaves could smell it from a mile away.

"Little Naofumi! Drinky time! Let's all get festive while looking at the cute girl!"

Not Sadeena, too!

"So there you are, Fohl. You know what this means, right?" I said.

"Yeah . . ."

Fohl snapped back to reality at the sound of my voice and gave me a regretful nod. I'd taken his younger sister from the verge of death to this. I was going to work him like a horse.

"Mr. Naofumi."

"What?"

"I'd like you to talk to me. I want to know more about the village. What is everyone doing here?"

Hmm . . .

"I'm making soldiers out of the villagers. Soldiers that will blindly follow my every command. In due time, you and your brother, too, will happily charge forth into the jaws of dea—"

"Mr. Naofumi!"

Raphtalia ruined the moment. I just wanted to shake Atla up a little bit. Raphtalia never seemed to enjoy my malicious shenanigans. Then again, I couldn't help but think my past behavior gave her good reason to be that way.

"The village, you say?"

I told Atla about all of the people in the village, and then Raphtalia helped me tell her about our plans for the future.

It may not have seemed like much, but having been able to bring a dying young girl back to good health made me glad that I had learned how to compound medicines.

We continued talking for a while until I realized quite some time had passed.

"Alright, let's call it here for today."

"Already? I want to talk some more."

"Don't be selfish, Atla," said Fohl.

Reluctant to part ways, Atla reached out to me quickly

when I stood up. Fohl lovingly intercepted her hand. But Atla had reached out so forcefully you would think she had been trying to leap at me, so when Fohl caught her hand she lost her balance and tumbled off the bed . . . and then caught herself on her feet.

". . ."

"Oh?"

Even Atla herself let out a gasp of surprise.

"And up . . . we go!" she said.

Using Fohl to help support herself, Atla then . . . stood up.

"Wow . . . So this is what it's like to stand up," she said.

"A . . . Atla! Atla is standing!" screamed Fohl.

It was like a scene straight out of *Heidi*. I was imagining Fohl in the Alps. Oh, damn. If I didn't already know Fohl's name, I probably would have ended up calling him that in my head. Kind of like Trash #2.

Atla slowly began walking with shaky legs, and then smiled.

"Thank you, Mr. Naofumi. Brother."

Fohl snuffled.

"Keep getting better, Atla!"

"I will, Brother."

To think she had gone from being a complete invalid to this in a matter of days . . .

"That's . . . amazing. That medicine of yours is amazing, Mr. Naofumi."

"I've cured your illnesses before, too, Raphtalia, so it's not that crazy."

"That's true, but still . . ."

But yeah, a young girl on the verge of death and who had never before stood in her life was walking now, right in front of our eyes. The Elixir of Yggdrasil really was something. First it was the old lady, and now Atla.

"Now then . . . What should the two of us do, Mr. Naofumi?"

"Well, I plan to have your brother fight for me. Fohl, you're leveling up with the others, right?"

"Yeah, that's my job."

"So he says," Atla poked.

"What do you want to do, Atla?"

Even if she could walk now, she was still pretty helpless.

"I would like to learn how to fight, as well."

"Atla! You don't need to fight!"

Fohl, a.k.a. Alps, blurted out in protest. I guess it only made sense that he would be opposed to his beloved younger sister wanting to fight.

"Even so . . . I've felt this way for quite some time now. I decided long ago that if I was ever able to move freely, I wanted to be able to protect others rather than always relying on others to protect me."

"B . . . but . . ."

Alps was having a hard time defying Atla's sense of determination. Hmm . . . If I kept calling him Alps in my head I was probably going to end up blurting it out eventually. I decided I'd better stick with Fohl.

"So, please, Mr. Naofumi . . . Teach me how to fight. Send me out with the others to level."

Hmm . . . It seemed like things weren't going to turn out quite like I had imagined, but that might not be a bad thing. After all, Atla was a hakuko, which meant she should be able to reach level 120.

"Alright. What about you, Fohl?"

"I'll fight, too! It's my job to protect Atla!"

"I like that eagerness. In that case, I have a proposition. Being the slave of a hero comes with all sorts of special benefits . . ."

I told Fohl and Atla about all of the boosts for slaves that came from being a hero. Ultimately, starting over from level 1 would likely result in being stronger in the end. Fohl had already gained a few levels and was level 34 now, so it might feel a bit like wasted time. But considering all of the little advantages, it was probably worth it.

"Oh? In that case, maybe I should start over, too?"

The drunkard woman butted in while leaning in through the window.

"You're strong enough already."

Where in the world did she even get that alcohol in her hand?

Sadeena was supposedly level 98 already. Raphtalia was level 87 now, by the way. Sadeena was strong to start out with, so there was no point in starting over for her. No, I couldn't actually say that. I had to admit I was curious to see how strong she would end up with all of my slave boosts, considering how formidable she was without them. But . . . the thought of an even stronger Sadeena making sexual advances—in a literal, physical sense—scared me.

"I want to be stronger, too! Let me start over, too, little Naofumi!"

Then again . . . Who knew what kind of trouble we might end up in if we started slacking. If it meant being stronger, she should probably do it.

"If you're that set on it, then why not? Alright then, I guess we'll reset your level sometime in the next few days."

"Let's do it!" she replied.

"There you have it, Fohl. If you really do want to be stronger, you should reset your level, too. What do you want to do?"

"I . . . I . . ."

"Atla might end up stronger than you in no time on just the boosts alone . . ."

I gave him a bit of a nudge. It would probably take Sadeena

a while to get back to her current level, but that wasn't true for Fohl. I could just throw him on Filo's back and have her run around killing monsters and he'd be back to where he was now in no time.

"I'd like to beat Brother."

"Ugh . . ."

Fohl looked over at Atla while trying to make up his mind. It would be pretty embarrassing if his precious little sister beat him to a pulp. He might never recover from that one.

"Fine. I'll reset my level, too."

"Alright. Now then, it's getting late. Go back to your assigned residence and get some rest. Atla, if you can walk then you can go with Fohl."

"Already? I would like to talk with you some more, Mr. Naofumi."

"It's night already. Go get some sleep so that you'll have plenty of energy tomorrow."

I couldn't rule out the possibility that Atla might only be able to walk while the medicine was in her system. It was probably best if she didn't overexert herself right now.

"Atla, I'll take you to our residence. We'll go slowly, so let's . . . walk together."

Fohl had a look of pure bliss on his face as he grinned and tugged at Atla's hand.

"But Mr. Naofumi! Brother! Let go! Let go of my hand! I

want to get better acquainted with Mr. Naofumi!"

These siblings were on completely different wavelengths. I sure hoped this didn't turn into a problem.

"Off you go! You're cutting into my nightly quality time with little Naofumi!"

"You go help Raphtalia put the other slaves to bed, woman!"

"Let's go, Sadeena. Some of the children still get scared at night, so we need to help make them feel comfortable."

"Rafu!"

Raph-chan jumped up on Raphtalia's shoulder and waved goodbye. I thought about how I hadn't been playing with Raph-chan nearly enough lately as I headed back to my own place.

Chapter Four: A Shield to Protect the Shield

Filo had gone to see Melty, and Rishia was in her own room trying to decipher the manuscripts we'd gotten from Kizuna and the others. I had the night to myself. Having some peace and quiet felt nice. I started compounding medicines to sell later, and after several moments there was a knock on my door.

"What is it?"

The door opened and standing there in the doorway was Atla. Yes, the same Atla that had just been practically dragged off by her brother to their residence.

"I, umm . . . I want to sleep with you."

"What happened to your brother?"

Knowing him, I'd never hear the end of it if he found Atla sleeping with me. That was not something I wanted to deal with.

"Brother is out cold. So . . . I'd like someone to talk with while falling asleep. Please, Mr. Naofumi."

Out cold? That spaz? Don't tell me she had actually physically knocked him out . . . No, surely not. She seemed far too innocent to do something like that. It was nice that she seemed to like me, but I wasn't sure I liked the thought of her sleeping in my bed. Having my blanket stolen once was more than enough.

I knew I probably needed to let that go already, but I still didn't feel like sharing my bed, regardless.

"No."

"Fine. I'll sleep in front of your house, then."

"Why would you do that?"

"Because I don't want to sleep anywhere else."

What was with this kid? Was she going to be Sadeena #2? She showed no sign of giving up.

"Okay, fine. You can sleep in Raphtalia's bed."

"Understood."

I decided to take advantage of the fact that Raphtalia wasn't here and motioned for Atla to come in. I couldn't help but wonder if Fohl was alright. I'd go check on him after Atla fell asleep. Once Atla came into the room, I showed her to Raphtalia's bed and helped her get tucked in.

"Are you not going to sleep, Mr. Naofumi?"

"Not yet. I have to make medicines for us to sell."

Our medicine sales had been booming lately. I was using my shield to make the medicines, but production was still falling behind. Pretty soon I'd have to get serious about teaching the slaves how to make medicine. I wanted to get things set up so that the village had a steady flow of income, but we still needed more people to make that happen. I'd arranged for the medicines to be sold in the neighboring town as well, but our supplies couldn't keep up with demand. We could always sell the medicinal herbs themselves, but none of them were worth that much.

I'd managed to unlock most of the herb-related shields, since I'd been purchasing a wide variety of plants from all over the place. They'd enabled me to identify and analyze poisons, increase the effectiveness of those poisons, and increase my resistances to them, but not much else.

"I can see that you're a hard worker, Mr. Naofumi."

"Only because I want money."

"But . . . I can walk now thanks to that."

". . ."

Something didn't feel right about having my selfish motivations spun around and interpreted as good intentions. The room fell silent.

I wasn't quite sure how to interact with this kid. She didn't try to push her ideals off on me like Raphtalia. Instead, it was like she just openly accepted anything and everything I said. It frightened me to think what might happen if I said something like, "Alright! Spread your legs!" I had a feeling she'd happily comply, and probably even try to jump on top of me.

Just like Sadeena. *Just like Sadeena!* Except the scary thing about that woman was that she'd probably try to do the same thing without me even saying anything. She hadn't tried yet, but considering the way she acted, it could happen at any time. Shit . . . I hadn't realized how dangerous being alone with Sadeena was until just now. I felt shivers going down my spine.

"Mr. Naofumi."

"Huh? What?"

"I was talking to Raphtalia. She told me that she serves as your sword to defeat your enemies for you."

"Pretty much."

I couldn't do anything except defend myself and others. That was the shield's limitation, and it had been that way ever since I set foot in this world.

"Raphtalia goes to great lengths for me, and I know I can depend on her."

Raphtalia was working hard to put an end to the waves, for the sake of this world. Seeing how hard she tried made me want to try, too. All else aside, there was no one I trusted more than Raphtalia in this world.

"When I look around the village, I can sense that everyone here is protected under your wing."

"My wing, huh?"

Was that like a baby chick being protected by its mother's wing? That would make the village . . . a bird's nest. Filo suddenly sprung to mind.

"The villagers are all under your protection, waiting for their time to leave the nest."

"Leaving the nest is all well and good, but ultimately the villagers are the ones that need to protect the village. There will be consequences otherwise."

This village was Raphtalia's home. Once we rebuilt it, Raphtalia would have a place in this world even when I was gone. Even if I went back to my own world, she would still have Keel and Sadeena. I planned on leaving Filo in Melty's care. Everyone loved Raph-chan, so she would probably end up sticking around as the village mascot or something. I was confident the village would last for a long time to come. If anyone—organization, country, or otherwise—were reckless enough to try to destroy the village built by the hero that saved the world, they were as good as dead.

"In my time here at the village, I've heard about all of the amazing things you've accomplished. It truly is . . . impressive, what you're doing. You should be proud. Despite all of the hardships you've faced, you've persevered and overcome them all. I admire you, Mr. Naofumi."

"Oh, umm . . . thanks. I'm not one to be modest, but I guess I have come a long way."

"That said, who is it that protects you, Mr. Naofumi?"

"Huh?"

What was she talking about? Protect me? Why? Why would she be talking about protecting me, of all things? Didn't she realize she was talking to the Shield Hero? How dense could someone be? Although, it was true I wouldn't be here if it weren't for the help of plenty of others. I couldn't forget that.

"Plenty of people do."

Raphtalia, Filo, Melty, the queen . . . All of them had given me a hand at times when my position or my life had been in danger.

"Here's what I think. If Raphtalia is your sword, then I want to be the shield that protects you."

"Shield, huh? It's really not as great as it sounds."

Being someone's shield and always defending that person really didn't feel all that great. *Why do I have to defend this person?* The thought had crossed my mind time and again. It was painful at times, too. But if I worried about that, I'd only end up losing and creating friction. Even so . . . Knowing that I was protecting Raphtalia, Filo, and all the people I cared about outweighed the unpleasantness of it all.

But still . . . *Be my* shield? She'd sure come up with a lofty goal. I guess it was because she had spent her whole life being the one protected by someone else. She'd probably idealized the role of protector. It was like saying if Raphtalia was my right arm then she would be my left. Still . . . I did appreciate the thought.

"How about you save that line for when you're actually strong enough to pull it off."

"Understood. I will become strong enough, no matter what. I will begin tomorrow. I'll do my best!"

"Good. I'm counting on it."

Before I knew it, Atla had begun snoring. Sheesh . . . So

that was what she wanted to talk about?

"Now then . . ."

I picked Atla up and carried her to the house where Fohl was sleeping. And he really was sleeping.

"Hey!"

"Zzz . . ."

"Seriously? Zzz? This isn't a manga! Wake up!"

"Wha?!"

I laid Atla on the bed and took the freshly woken Fohl outside to talk.

"You need to look after your sister better. She showed up at my place saying she wanted to sleep with me."

"She . . . she what?! That means . . . Atla already . . . Noo!"

Fohl was glaring at me like I'd murdered his parents or something. I activated his slave curse and scolded him.

"You think I'd do that?!"

"You bastard! Are you trying to say that Atla isn't attractive?!"

"Oh, hell! Stop being difficult! I have no interest in that kind of thing!"

"Liar! Nadia was hanging all over you, and you're surrounded by women!"

Ugh . . . I couldn't deny either of those things! I'd given up on any fantasies that included surrounding myself with women long ago! I was getting the feeling it was time to start being more careful about whom I ran around with. But then I remembered I'd never cared whether my companions were male or female.

"They could all be men for all I care. Gender makes no difference to me."

"Wh . . . what?! Are you saying that you're . . ."

Fohl turned pale and started backing away. He had obviously misunderstood. I'm sure he probably thought I was gay, now.

"I'm not into that kind of thing! Stay away from me!" he shouted.

"Neither am I!"

These siblings sure were a pain in the neck! Still . . . be *my* shield? She was a strange one, for sure.

Chapter Five: Trash and the Hakuko

The next morning, I ended up making breakfast, since the village slaves practically insisted on it. The cooking division slaves took care of all of the prep work, so all I had to do was cook the food.

"Alright, I made exactly what you asked for."

"Yay!"

They all cheered. Sheesh . . . This must have been what people meant when they talked about kids only looking grown-up. Raphtalia had been a lot more mature by the time she was their size.

"Oh, little Naofumi! It all looks so yummy!"

"Yeah, whatever. You better not start drinking this early."

"I won't!"

Hmm? Sadeena and I weren't the only ones causing a ruckus. Those voices . . . Ah, it was Fohl and Atla.

"It's Mr. Naofumi's cooking! I'm going to lick the plate clean!"

"Atla! No! You have better manners than that!"

I wasn't even going to go there. I went about putting the food on the slaves' plates, which they put on their trays and carried back to their seats. It reminded me of lunch back in elementary school. There were quite a few slaves now. That meant more helping hands, of course, but to think that three massive pots of food would disappear in a single meal . . .

"Huh? Who are you?"

There was a girl was standing next in line, waiting for me to serve her. She sure acted like she was right where she belonged, but I didn't recognize her at all. She looked . . . 15 years old, maybe? She was a human, as far as I could tell. She looked sleepy, like she was only half awake. Her eyes were silver, and her hair was a silverish color, too. She had pale white skin, and something about her made her seem delicate. Being a human surrounded by all of the demi-human slaves made her even more conspicuous. There were soldiers from the castle here, too, but she wasn't dressed like a soldier.

"Yeah, who is that girl?"

The slaves were looking at the unfamiliar girl and whispering.

"Raphtalia, do you know who this is?" I asked.

"No. She doesn't appear to be a soldier," she replied.

"Oh?" said Sadeena quizzically.

"Rafu?"

Filo came running up just then.

"Master! I'm back!"

"Hey, Filo. Are you going to eat, too?"

"Yup! I ate over at Mel-chan's place, but I'll eat again!"

What a pig.

"Huh? It's the clown girl," Filo said.

"Yes," replied the unfamiliar girl.

Clown girl? Did I know any clown girls? Or was it a friend of Filo's? Filo had been going out more on her own to help with peddling and other stuff. She must have met the girl that way.

"Did something happen? What are you doing heeere?" Filo asked the girl.

"Is she a friend of yours, Filo?"

"You've met her before, toooo, Master."

I tried to think of someone that Filo knew, that I had met, and that looked like this sleepy-eyed girl waiting for me to feed her.

"I ha————breakfast . . ." said the girl.

Huh? All I could hear was static in the middle of her sentence. Wait. Hadn't there been someone like that before? I could feel myself breaking out into a cold sweat.

"Who are you? Filo seems to know you, but I don't. Answer me."

"Huh?" she replied, confused.

The unfamiliar girl pulled a pair of scissors out and showed them to me. Umm, nope. That didn't ring any bells. Then, right in front of my eyes, she transformed the pair of scissors into a ball of thread. Then she pulled out a familiar mask and showed it to me.

"Surely this————remember."

"You?!"

That's right. She was showing me the same equipment that had been used by Murder Pierrot—the freak that we had fought with Sadeena several days earlier in the underground coliseum! The Murder Pierrot in the coliseum had been wearing a mask and a weird outfit, so I didn't recognize her at first. But there was only one person in the world that sounded like a sandstorm when they spoke!

"Murder Pierrot?! What are you doing in my village?!"

"I walked?"

"I'm not asking how you got here! And why did you say that like it was a question?!"

Was she trying to be funny? I wished she would stop it with the static already, too.

"Umm . . ."

Murder Pierrot put away the mask and ball of thread she'd used to identify herself and held her tray out to me, as if asking for food.

"Despite what it may look like, I'm not just handing out food for free."

"Oh . . ."

She stuck her hand in her pocket, pulled something out, and . . . placed it in my hand. It was two silver pieces. Umm, I wasn't trying to ask for money. But two silver was more than I would have expected. Thirty copper was enough to get a pretty good meal in this world. Two silver would have bought a really nice set meal—something like fancy broiled eel served over hot rice at a posh restaurant if we had been in Japan. I was going to play along with her joke and say something clever, but she just stood there staring at me, completely serious.

"Oh, fine. Whatever."

We weren't getting anywhere like this. I decided to just feed her and then we could talk later. I put some food on a dish and handed it to Murder Pierrot. She sat down and began eating like everything was completely normal.

"Well, well, well . . ."

Sadeena sat down next to Murder Pierrot excitedly and struck up a conversation, although Murder Pierrot was hardly even responding. It was really more like Sadeena just talking to herself.

"Just who is she, anyway?" asked Raphtalia.

"Who knows? I'll ask her later, but we need to get the slaves fed right now."

It didn't look like she was going to cause any trouble, and I could tell that Sadeena was on her guard just in case she did. The slaves did seem curious, but with all of the new slaves and everything else going on, they didn't really seem bothered by her presence. But why in the world had she come to the village?

I finished serving the food to the slaves and sat down to eat my own breakfast.

"Little Naofumi, the girl told me that her previous contract was terminated, so she's not tied to any employer at the moment. She said she came to find out if she could work for you."

Fighting us at the coliseum had been purely business, I guess. Running off in the middle of a fight didn't seem like it would be good for business, but I guess that kind of thing was probably common in the mercenary business.

"I don't need any mercenaries."

I was already working on training the slaves to fight, and I had no desire to hire a weirdo like her.

"Really? Then let's be friends," the girl responded.

"You realize it seems like you're not actually listening to anything I say, right?"

"Umm, why do you want to associate with Mr. Naofumi?" asked Raphtalia, choosing her words carefully.

". . ."

Murder Pierrot fell silent.

"At the coliseum, you told me, 'You have to work harder, or you'll die.' What did that mean, anyway?" I asked.

"——trying to help."

I was hearing static again. What was that? It felt like talking to someone on a cell phone with really bad reception.

"What's going on, Mr. Naofumi?"

Atla came walking over with Fohl tagging along behind. If they were done eating, they should've already hurried home and started getting ready to head out. We were going to the castle today to reset her brother's level.

"It's nothing. This girl . . . We fought against her in a tournament at the Zeltoble coliseum and now she's here asking to be friends."

"Oh really?"

Atla turned to face Murder Pierrot.

"I sense a transient power that is on the verge of disappearing, together with a separate, untainted power. She doesn't seem to be a bad person, Mr. Naofumi."

"Still . . ."

I'd felt the same when she'd shared her impression of me. Atla's "senses" were just a bit too out there for me. I wasn't quite sure what to make of them.

"Are you refusing to tell us why?" I asked.

Murder Pierrot shook her head emphatically.

"I want to stay——the village until——the waves. I want to help you do that."

I hadn't realized how frustrating it would be to try to have a conversation when you could only just barely get the gist of what the other person was saying. This was beyond annoying.

"Let me ask you this, too, while we're at it. Who are you, really? And what's with your weapons?"

Murder Pierrot stood there thinking for a moment and then started opening and closing her mouth, but . . .

"——and——at——"

Aside from the simplest of words, all I could hear was static. I had no idea what she was saying. What was with this girl?

"Also, about our fight at the coliseum . . . Judging from what I can make out of what you've said, you're . . . the holder of a vassal weapon or a seven star weapon, right?"

I wasn't dumb. It wasn't like I just thought her weapon was odd. It had changed shape repeatedly, and it seemed to have mysterious powers that could restrict an opponent. That kind of performance meant it almost certainly had to be a vassal weapon. The only thing was, none of the seven star heroes had a weapon like hers, according to the queen.

"I'm guessing you were trying to warn us that we could end up getting killed by invading vassal weapon holders if we didn't get stronger—"

When I said that, Murder Pierrot started nodding her head emphatically. So I was right. Also, that meant she could understand what I was saying. I bet that was it—she'd probably snuck into this world to try to kill the holy heroes like Glass and the others had done, but now she couldn't get back home because of the Spirit Tortoise's barrier. Something like that.

"You seem to be under the impression that we're weak, but I've used the power-up methods of all four holy heroes. I'm just in a weakened state because of a curse right now."

Murder Pierrot shook her head. The little brat obviously wasn't satisfied with my explanation.

"——not enough. You——more——"

"Yeah, okay. Whatever. I may not be able to explain it very well, but I know what the waves are. I know that other vassal weapon holders are trying to save their worlds by killing holy heroes."

Murder Pierrot shook her head again.

"——destroy other worlds——even——won't——"

The sandstorm was getting worse. It was almost pure static now. What was with her? Had she unlocked a curse series that made it impossible for her to carry on a conversation or something?

"I'm sorry, but I can't hear what you're saying."

Murder Pierrot fell silent.

"What should we do, Mr. Naofumi?" asked Raphtalia.

"We can't trust her. She could just be pretending to be an ally and end up betraying us when we least expect it."

For all I knew, she was pretending to be a drifter to get close and wait for a chance to try to kill me. Even if she had exposed her own identity, I still couldn't trust her.

". . ."

Murder Pierrot just kept staring at me silently. What was this feeling? Something about her eyes reminded me of Raphtalia or Filo. It was true I didn't detect any hostility. She showed no sign of ulterior motives. Even so, I still couldn't trust her, and if she had no intention of fighting then there was no reason for her to come to me. She could just wait until the next wave and then go back through the rifts.

"If it's money———accommodations———I'll pay."

Hmm . . . So she was offering to fight for me and even pay for her own room and board. Those were certainly favorable conditions. I knew that when something sounded too good to be true, it usually was. But the offer was still hard to refuse. But yeah, she was probably going to try to kill me in my sleep or something.

"I'm smart enough to know there's no such thing as a free lunch. If you understand my words, then you understand I'm telling you to get out of my village."

"Okay."

Murder Pierrot looked down dejectedly. She finished eating and then stood up. Something about her reminded me of Glass, after we had settled our differences.

Another possibility I could think of was that she just wanted to get stronger and had come to this world looking for materials to power up her weapon like L'Arc and Therese had done. It wasn't like going to another world meant she was trying to kill heroes. L'Arc had mentioned that the abilities and stat increases gained in another world could be shared between worlds, after all. And in fact, I'd retained my stat increases despite ending up back at level 1 when I first arrived in Kizuna's world.

Murder Pierrot probably didn't intend to kill any of the holy heroes. She had probably just gotten stuck in this world and didn't know what to do. Still, the power on the verge of disappearing that Atla mentioned did have me a bit curious.

". . ."

Murder Pierrot started walking away at a ridiculously slow pace while stopping to look back at me every few steps, like she was trying to stall or something. Was she hoping I would stop her? I just stood there silently, glaring at her, and she just kept doing the same thing over and over. She would turn around and start walking again, and then stop and look back again.

"Umm . . . Mr. Naofumi . . ."

"Ignore her. She's just hoping that I'll stop her."

"If you can tell that's what she wants, then why not stop her, little Naofumi? You do realize how strong she is, right?"

"Strong enough that she might actually be able to kill me in my sleep. I can't trust her."

"Aww . . . That's too bad."

Murder Pierrot stopped and looked back again.

"I'm not going to stop you, so just give up already."

This was getting a bit awkward. Considering what was coming, it might have been a good idea to keep her around. We could always just kill her if she tried anything. But that wasn't a chance I could take in my current state. Murder Pierrot continued walking slowly while glancing back at me every now and then, all the way to the edge of the village.

"Get out already!"

Once she had finally left the village, I started cleaning up the dining hall. Apparently something had been bothering Raphtalia.

"Umm . . . How did Murder Pierrot get here?"

"She said she walked, but she probably used some kind of portal."

"Wouldn't that mean she'd been here before?"

That was a good question. I should have asked her. Actually . . . I had been so focused on kicking her out that I didn't even think to find out what she knew about fighting against other heroes. Now I was regretting not asking her more while she had still been interested in being friends.

"Should we go after her?" asked Raphtalia.

"That would be like falling for the enemy's trap. We're letting her go unharmed because she doesn't seem to be interested in fighting. But I'm not prepared to let my guard down."

It may not have seemed like it, but I was being plenty lax already. It wouldn't have been a surprise if she had wanted to kill me. Honestly, I was a bit worried about what might happen if she ran across any of the other three heroes. We needed to find them and get them somewhere safe as soon as possible. They might very well end up dead if they were forced to fight against someone like Murder Pierrot.

We had finished eating, so it was time to take care of the day's business.

"I guess we'll start by heading to the Melromarc castle. It's been a while. Raphtalia, Fohl, and Sadeena . . . You're coming with me. We're going to do the level resets we talked about yesterday."

"I would like to go, too, Mr. Naofumi."

"Okay, you're coming, too, Atla."

It was probably a good idea to take Atla along with us. Fohl would probably start causing trouble if I tried to leave her behind. Filo had gone back to hang out with Melty again after she finished eating. Raph-chan had taken it upon herself to help Rishia and the villagers with whatever they were doing. I would have been more than happy to take Raph-chan along, but whatever.

"Portal Shield!"

I used my portal skill to teleport us to the Melromarc castle. When we arrived, Sadeena looked over and commented on the mountains on top of the Spirit Tortoise's back, which were visible from the castle.

"Wow . . . It's been a long time since I came this way. Things seem pretty crazy outside the castle town gates."

"So you've been here before?"

"I *am* a citizen of Melromarc, you know."

Sadeena was still looking at the Spirit Tortoise mountains

as she replied. As for the rest of the Spirit Tortoise . . . Oh? Looking closely, I could see that many of the trees had been cleared away. The reclamation of the land was coming along nicely. Humans sure were a hardy bunch. Disaster had struck, but everyone was working hard to bounce back.

"Where to now?" asked Sadeena.

"We'll go talk to the queen first. We didn't tell anyone we were coming, so they'll probably need some time to make preparations."

It made sense to go see the queen. Unlike class-ups, level resets were probably relatively uncommon, after all.

"Into the castle, then? I've seen the Melromarc castle from the outside like this plenty of times, but I've never actually stepped foot inside."

I guess it would be rare for demi-humans or therianthropes to see the inside of a castle in a human-supremacist country.

"Yeah, that doesn't surprise me. Although, we are in the courtyard right now."

"I've been here many times, now, but the size of the castle never fails to amaze me," Raphtalia remarked.

"It's about the same size as L'Arc's castle. But this isn't a very good place for demi-humans to be."

"You're right. I'm on friendly terms with some of the people here, but it's still uncomfortable."

"I can imagine," replied Sadeena.

Several of the castle soldiers noticed us and saluted, but they looked slightly disconcerted when they saw Sadeena. She was in her therianthrope form, which was normal for her, but I guess it only made sense that we would get some confused looks. But then again, they had invited all the adventures to the celebrations after we defeated the last wave. Hmm . . . Actually, I hadn't really seen many demi-humans there. I guess being a demi-human in this country was hard in more ways than one. I'd started to forget that. It was only the queen that didn't discriminate. The racism was deeply ingrained in the citizens themselves.

"Alright, then. I wonder where the queen is right now."

She was probably staring at paperwork in that office of hers, like always. I asked a castle servant where the queen was. Apparently she had already been informed of our arrival and was headed out to meet us. We could just wait for her to come to us, then. Relaxing in the castle courtyard didn't sound bad to me.

"We're going to wait here," I announced.

"Okay. Atla, aren't you getting exhausted from standing? Do you want to sit down?"

"I'm fine, Brother."

Crash! It sounded like something had fallen over behind us. I turned around to see Trash staring at us with his mouth hanging open like a fool.

"The . . ."

So he was still around, huh? More importantly . . . why was he half-naked? He was wearing nothing but underpants and a cloak. I guess he was going for the emperor's . . . king's new clothes look.

"What's with the new look? Some kind of punishment? Or you lose a bet?"

A smile crept across my face. Why hadn't they invited me to join in the fun? He even had a note stuck to his back that said, "I'm doing a lap around the castle grounds as punishment. Do not assist me in any way, no matter what I say." The note was signed by the queen at the bottom. What had he done this time?

"The Shield finally shows his true colors!"

He pointed at me and started shouting.

"Come! Everyone! After the Shield! We must wipe the Shield Demon off the face of the earth!"

Trash grabbed the note and started running toward us. Several nearby castle guards blocked his path despite being clearly dumbfounded, and then restrained him.

"Let go! The Shield! The Shield has infiltrated the castle along with those hakuko! Bastards! Out of my way! Or else I can't kill the Shield!"

I'd heard that there was bad blood between Trash and the hakuko, but this was an impressive show of rage even for him. And that last line of his was almost identical to a quote famous with otaku back in Japan.

"Huh?"

Atla turned around.

"Err . . ."

Trash had been stomping his feet violently, but he began to lose steam and then stopped completely. And then . . . What was going on? He was just standing there with a really strange look on his face. I couldn't tell whether he wanted to smile or cry.

"Huh? Brother? Why are there two of you?"

Atla looked back and forth between Fohl and Trash.

"What are you talking about, Atla?"

How in the world had Atla managed to mistake Trash for Fohl, of all people? And when they were both right there in front of her? I guess they did share a tendency to be rather annoying, but otherwise they could hardly be more different. I mean, their ages and physical builds . . . umm, were irrelevant since Atla was blind, I guess.

". . ."

Trash regained his composure, turned around, and hobbled back in the direction from which he had come, as if he'd lost any desire to confront us.

"Hey!" I shouted.

It was as if Trash couldn't hear me at all. What in the world was going on?

"What happened? He looked like the empty shell of a person," said Raphtalia.

"He looked really surprised when he saw little Atla," Sadeena commented.

"Yeah."

Had he seen something ominous in Atla's face or something?

"What was all the commotion about?" asked the queen.

Having heard all of the shouting, she'd finally showed up several minutes later. I told her about how Trash had started raving when he saw Fohl, only to up and leave as soon as he saw Atla's face.

"I see . . . So that's what the noise was."

"Any idea what that was about? I've never seen Trash act like that before."

"Miss Atla, was it? Let me take a look at your face."

"Of course."

Atla stepped forward so that the queen could see her better.

"Ah, now I understand."

"You do?"

"It's a long story, but I'd be happy to explain if you have the time."

"Hmm . . . I do have better things to do, but I'm curious after seeing Trash like that."

"Don't worry. I'll skip the finer details."

The queen began to explain why Trash had calmed down when he saw Atla.

"Lüge—the Staff Hero—had a sister much younger than

himself who was blind. Her name was Lucia."

Why was she making a point of not calling him Trash? I guess it didn't matter. But . . . little sister?

"There were a number of issues that made Lüge's birth rather complicated."

"Oh yeah?"

"Yes. His full name is Lüge Lansarz Faubrey. He was born as the thirtieth heir to the throne of Faubrey."

"Faubrey is this world's most powerful country, right? And he was the prince?"

"The youngest prince, but yes. However, there was an incident that prompted him to relinquish his right to the throne. That incident was the murder of his parents and everyone he loved by the hakuko."

It sounded like Trash's life had been one hell of a roller coaster. But now I understood why he seemed to detest Fohl—a hakuko—so much.

"Fortunately, Lüge and his younger sister had been away at the time, which is why they weren't killed in the incident. However, for political reasons, Faubrey made no attempt to hold Siltvelt accountable. As a result, Lüge developed an intense hatred for both Faubrey and Siltvelt. He changed his last name and moved to Melromarc, a country hostile toward the demi-humans."

The queen shifted the subject for a moment before delving into the bloody details of Trash's personal feud.

"Lüge concealed the fact that he was royalty and established an impressive track record for himself as both a soldier and officer of Melromarc's military at a time when the country was constantly at war. He was eventually chosen to wield the seven star staff and went on to make a name for himself as a hero."

It was a picture-perfect story of self-made success. I started to feel a bit jealous. But then . . . a slight look of distress came across the queen's face.

"When I was still young, it was that very cleverness and strength of his that stole my heart."

"I'm not interested in that lovey-dovey stuff. Get back to the explanation."

"Just as things had begun to go his way, Lüge's blind young sister, who he loved dearly, was attacked by a hakuko and . . . presumed dead due to the bloody scene of carnage left behind. But her body was never found. More than ever, Lüge was consumed by a desire for revenge, pushing him to finally confront and overthrow the king of Siltvelt, who was a hakuko."

"And? What does that have to do with his reaction earlier?"

I already had a good idea of what the answer was going to be. More than likely—

"Just as you suspect, Atla is the spitting image of Lüge's beloved younger sister, Lucia."

"I knew it."

"Yes."

This was just conjecture, but the following possibility came to mind. Trash's beloved younger sister didn't actually die. Instead, she was taken back to Siltvelt as a plaything and raped by the hakuko, which is how Fohl and Atla were conceived. But there were several problems with that theory. For example, why wouldn't they have used her as a hostage? Maybe the younger sister and the hakuko were secretly in love, like some kind of soap opera or something.

I had no idea what had actually happened, but the fact that Atla mistook Trash for Fohl probably meant that there was some kind of blood ties that she had sensed. Now that I thought about it, I remembered Fohl mentioning having had a sizable amount of money devoted to Atla's treatment.

"It all seems a little . . . too convenient to be true," said Raphtalia.

"Oh? What about how you and little Naofumi met? Does that not seem too convenient to be true? It sure does to me," Sadeena interjected.

"Well . . . I guess it does, but still . . ."

Oh, come on. Surely Raphtalia and I meeting had nothing to do with fate or anything like that. Sadeena just associated me with destiny because I couldn't get drunk on this world's alcohol.

"Fohl. Atla. Are you two half human?" I asked.

"Who knows? I was too young at the time to remember anything before our parents died. Brother would know more, I think."

"All I know is that our grandfather was supposedly really impressive. We were told to never mention our last name, and our parents died in some war when I was still young, so I don't really remember much. I'm pretty sure they had been well-off, though. We had servants and other helpers, too."

"Did one of the servants run off with all of the money or something?"

This world was full of worthless people. They must have fell victim to one of those people and that's how they ended up as slaves.

"Nothing like that. Once we couldn't afford to pay for Atla's treatment anymore, we divided up the family assets among the servants and said our goodbyes."

So they were bankrupted by Atla's medical fees. And they even had loyal servants. They had gotten lucky with that one.

"Your grandfather, you say?"

The queen looked at Fohl long and hard.

"Fate sure works in mysterious ways," she finally said.

"What does that mean?" asked Fohl.

"Your last name . . . is Fayon, I assume."

"Yeah . . . We were told to never mention it, but that's it. How did you know?"

The queen nodded as if it all finally made sense.

"You should definitely remain by the Shield Hero's side. Your late grandfather would be thrilled."

"Whatever!"

Yeah . . . Fohl was a rebellious little brat. There was no way he would want to stick around with me longer than he had to.

"How do you know about my grandfather?"

"I know because that man who was causing a commotion earlier is the one who killed him."

"Wh . . . what?!"

Ah, now it made sense. Fohl and Atla were the grandchildren of Trash's most despised enemy, and on top of that, he had realized that Atla was the orphaned child of his precious younger sister. No wonder he had left looking like that.

"Do you know much about your grandfather?"

"All my parents told me was that he was a really impressive man. Was he the king of Siltvelt, then?"

"That's all they told you? Perhaps I've said too much, then."

". . ."

Fohl looked like he wasn't sure what to think. I could see how it might bother him to find out about things his parents refused to tell him in a place like this. Still, the queen was being overly dramatic. Surely he would want to know more about his roots. That's what I thought, anyway, but it didn't seem like either Fohl or Atla had any intention of asking the queen for more details.

"..."

Fohl seemed to be lost in thought.

"None of that matters! My loyalty lies with Mr. Naofumi!"

Atla obviously wasn't interested.

"My apologies for the trouble, Mr. Iwatani. How are things going?"

The queen changed the subject.

"Things are progressing well, I guess."

"You're referring to the territory, I assume. I've heard as much. You came at just the right time."

"Did something happen?"

"Let us address your business first. What brings you here today?"

"Oh yeah. I want to reset the levels of a couple of my slaves so that I can level them up from scratch."

I told the queen why we had come and she happily obliged.

"Understood. I will see to it that preparations begin at once. They should be complete by the time you and your companions reach the dragon hourglass."

"Thanks. Now, what was the news that you mentioned earlier?"

The queen opened her folding fan and covered her mouth before speaking.

"There have been sightings of the holy heroes near Melromarc recently and we've been able to determine where one of the heroes is likely to appear sometime in the next few days."

"What? Seriously?"

The queen nodded.

"Yes. We think that the Spear Hero—Mr. Kitamura—will be making an appearance."

Motoyasu, huh? Motoyasu was the last of the three that I wanted to see, but this wasn't the time to be picky.

"We managed to locate one of the Spear Hero's companions."

They found one of Motoyasu's companions? Judging from the queen's wording, she wasn't talking about Bitch. That meant it was one of the other two girls that ran around with him. I'd just call them Girl 1 and Girl 2. I guess that might not make it clear which I was referring to, but I didn't know their names and I'd hardly ever talked to either one. Trying to recall anything about them was a hassle. All I remembered was that they both seemed really annoying.

"You mean a corpse?"

"No. A member of Melromarc's nobility, who is also a father, had expressed concern about his missing daughter. But then he returned home one day to find her helping her mother run the family business, as if nothing had happened."

What the hell?! His missing daughter had just shown up and acted as if nothing had happened? It sounded like some kind of joke.

"And that daughter is one of the other two girls in the Spear Hero's party?" asked Raphtalia.

"If she was one of Motoyasu's companions and it's not Bitch, then she must be," I replied.

"Oh? Is that a friend of yours?" quipped Sadeena.

"Hell no," I snapped.

"Bitch sure is one heck of a name," said Fohl.

"Heh heh heh . . ."

Fohl's comment brought a smile to my face. That was one of my greatest achievements.

"That's nothing to be proud of, Mr. Naofumi," chided Raphtalia.

"It's a glorious achievement, Mr. Naofumi. I am certain she deserved the name."

"Atla . . . I'm not saying that you're wrong, but your way of looking at it is questionable . . ."

Raphtalia was always so serious. I continued my conversation with the queen.

"Did you not take her into custody?"

"We did question her. I was hoping that you would meet her and try to convince her to help lure the Spear Hero out of hiding."

Now it made sense. The queen believed that Motoyasu might try to see the girl. It was a bit of a gamble, but if it meant possibly capturing Motoyasu, then it was worth a try.

"And you think she'll cooperate? She could betray us and leak the details to Motoyasu."

"I already have a shadow keeping an eye on her. She seems fully compliant so far."

"Hmm . . ."

So she was basically trying to protect herself in a plea bargain. It made sense. The girls that ran around with Motoyasu had all seemed like scum.

"Fine. After we finish the level resets, we'll return to the village and then head out to meet her."

"I'll show you her location."

The queen unfolded a map and showed us where to find Motoyasu's companion.

"Alright, let's get these level resets over with and get back to the village. We have an important mission now," I announced.

"Hopefully it all works out," said Raphtalia.

"Sounds like wishful thinking to me, but whatever."

I couldn't help but be skeptical.

Chapter Six: The Fruits of Training

After that, we quickly headed to the dragon hourglass and exchanged greetings with the soldiers at the entrance. They must have already received the queen's orders, because preparations for the ceremonies had already been completed.

"Okay, you go first, Sadeena."

"Okay! I won't let you down!"

Hmm? There were people there to assist with the ceremonies just like when we had classed up, but this time they had a stretcher with them. It seemed strange, so I asked a nearby soldier about it.

"Resets often have repercussions. It will probably take several days to fully recuperate."

I guess that made sense. I'd felt sluggish when the stats I had taken for granted suddenly dropped, too. But my level hadn't changed. I could only imagine how restricted I might feel if I was suddenly back at level 1.

"There is individual variance, of course."

The soldiers began the ceremony. The dragon hourglass began to glow as power flooded into the magic circle on the floor. It looked a lot like when we had done our class-ups.

"The woman standing here before us has chosen to

relinquish her own powers in order to walk a new path. Powers of the world! Grant her the chance to find that path!"

Sadeena was standing in the middle of the magic circle and waving to me.

"Look, little Naofumi! It's the moment of my rebirth!"

She seemed just a bit too relaxed. Moments later, something came rushing out of Sadeena and then scattered in all directions.

"The ceremony is complete. How do you feel?" asked one of the soldiers.

"My body feels pretty heavy, but I can still move."

Sadeena trudged over to where I was standing. I guess that meant she was pretty tough.

"You're next, Fohl."

"Off you go, Brother! Do as Mr. Naofumi says!"

"A . . . Atla! Fine! I'm going!"

I was starting to feel a little bit sorry for Fohl. Regardless, he completed the level reset ceremony and seemed to have no trouble walking, just like Sadeena.

"You guys just reset your levels, but you seem to be moving surprisingly well. Do you not need to use the stretcher?" I asked.

"Would you carry me if I couldn't move, little Naofumi?"

"I'm no wimp!" shouted Fohl.

"You two aren't normal," I said.

I thought about giving Fohl a quick jab to the arm to see if he was really okay . . . but Atla beat me to it.

"Ow!"

Yeah, he was definitely feeling weaker.

"Hahaha! That tickles!"

I tried it on Sadeena, too, but she reacted the same as always. She seemed to be just fine. Maybe the repercussions would be minimized if the person was in good physical shape. Both of them were physically fit. Exercising and getting in shape certainly seemed to fall into a different category than leveling up. I guess staying in shape would make it easier to deal with not feeling so great, unlike some kind of stat boost that the person barely even had to work for. These two had that kind of self-discipline. Raphtalia made sure to keep herself in shape, too. A person's stats would be reduced with a level reset, but the results of their physical training would stay. Other than that . . . the boosts from my shield might have been helping a bit.

So in other words, the people that needed the stretchers were probably people who mostly used magic, or people that had been power-leveled by someone stronger. For example, some spoiled kid from a noble family could pay an adventurer to level him up. That kind of thing was effective up to a certain point. It's basically what I was doing with the slaves back at the village, so it wasn't necessarily a bad thing. The problem was that once someone hit the level cap like that, the only way to further improve would be to get in better shape or train with someone like the old lady.

Heroes had no level cap, apparently, but even I probably should have been doing some kind of training. Things like levels and stats were the norm in this world, so it wasn't unthinkable that training and honing your magic skills on a daily basis could raise some kind of limit, too. That would mean people like Fohl and Sadeena, who had been training hard since they were little, might be able to become that much stronger. I didn't know how it actually worked and I wasn't planning on sticking around in this world forever, so I'd just do my training until the waves were defeated and not worry about it. After all, my levels and stats would mean nothing when I returned to my own world.

The same went for this shield. This stupid shield that I couldn't remove no matter what. Changing it to the Book Shield was the best I could even do to try to hide it. If this stupid thing followed me back to my own world, there's no way it could be considered anything but a curse. A grown man walking around carrying some strange book all the time would be the laughing stock of the world.

It'd be better to just not think about that. There was no point in worrying about something that might not even happen. Even if the shield did happen to follow me back, that's just something I'd have to deal with when the time came.

"Alright, let's hurry back to the village and get ready to head out."

We used my portal skill to return to the village.

"Sadeena, Fohl, and Atla, I want you three to get out there and level up. I'll take the others and head out. Somebody go fetch Filo for me."

"Will do! I won't let you down, little Naofumi!"

Sadeena went walking off toward the ocean by herself, for whatever reason. Seriously? Was she going to be okay by herself?

"You don't have to tell me! Come on, Atla. Let's go. You can just watch."

"No way! Mr. Naofumi! I want to go with you!"

"Sorry, but you need to stay and level up. Where we're going, you'd need to be able to protect yourself at the very least."

We were going to try to lure out Motoyasu. If things went wrong and he struggled, Atla might not make it out with just a scratch or two. I couldn't take her with us.

"If I level up and surpass my brother, then I can have Mr. Naofumi all to myself. I'll do my best!"

"What the hell are you talking about?" I asked.

"Come on! Stop being ridiculous!" Raphtalia snapped.

Right? Although . . . Raphtalia was mostly addressing me when she said that. But Atla sure was mentally tough. What happened to playing the part of the sickly young girl? Anyway, I got Fohl, Atla, and the other slaves loaded up in Filo Underling #1's carriage and sent them off just as Filo came running up.

"Master! You called?"

"Yeah. There's somewhere I need to go. Can you come with us right now?"

"Yup!"

I would take . . . Raphtalia and Filo should be plenty, I guess. Rishia was busy training under the old lady with Eclair. Nothing bad could come from having her master the Hengen Muso style. Besides, Rishia made Motoyasu uncomfortable. Taking her along would probably only make things more complicated, so I'd just leave her behind.

"Alright, it's just going to be the three of us. It's not like we're going to be selling anything, so maybe we should just ride on Filo's back."

"Caaaarriage!" squawked Filo.

"Okay, yeah. Fine."

"I finally get to pull my own carriage! My own caaaarriage!"

Ever since I started using my portal skill more often, most of the carriages we'd been riding in were rentals. Filo hadn't had many chances to pull her own carriage lately. Peddling was about the only time she got to use it. Going by carriage would be fine, I guess. It didn't really matter either way.

"On the way back . . . maybe we'll see if we can't sell a thing or two."

Alright, we needed to hurry up and get to Motoyasu's companion. Raphtalia and I loaded up into Filo's carriage and we headed off in that direction.

Chapter Seven: The Plan to Capture the Spear Hero

"Elena! Thank goodness! You're alive!"

After receiving the queen's report, we rushed to the location of Motoyasu's companion. But when we got there, the one and only Motoyasu was right in the middle of chatting up Girl 1 at the counter of a big shop where she was working. We were looking on from an alleyway a short distance away, by the way.

Damn it! Our prey had shown up before we even had time to talk strategy! With Motoyasu already here, we could forget about making any preparations.

"Well, well, well. If it isn't the Spear Hero," Girl 1 responded coldly.

Hmm . . . If I wasn't mistaken, she had been more of the loud and annoying, ditzy type, but that wasn't how she was acting now. Even assuming she had decided to cut ties with Motoyasu, I would have expected her to be acting like much more of a bitch. Even so, Motoyasu still seemed surprised by the way she responded.

"Wh . . . what's the matter?"

"Are you really asking me what's the matter?"

"I was really worried about you!"

"You don't need to worry about me. What's more surprising is that you're still alive."

"Of course I am! There's no way I could die with you and the other girls on my team!"

Motoyasu seemed to be enjoying the conversation now. Girl 1, on the other hand, remained icy cold. She looked at Motoyasu with a stony gaze. This must have been what people meant when they talked about looking at someone like they were trash.

"Mr. Naofumi? Are we not going to go talk with him?"

"I was hoping to enjoy their conversation a bit more, but I guess you're right. We should probably go have a talk with him."

"Umm?"

Filo was looking at Motoyasu and . . . making a kicking motion. I'd ordered her to kick him whenever she saw him a while back.

"What do you say? Let's get back to saving the world!" Motoyasu went on.

"Sorry, but I'm being forced to take over the family business. I can't run around with you anymore."

She remained emotionless as she responded. It was clear she had absolutely no interest in accepting his offer.

"N . . . no way!"

Motoyasu seemed to realize that and had no idea how to respond. I'm sure everything had always gone his way up until now. But to be honest, I envied him. I'd been given the title of count and even had my own territory now, and yet here I was cooking meals for the slaves every day. Frankly, I felt like I was playing mommy to them. I'd even overheard the soldiers quietly referring to me as the Cooking Hero, recently. The conversation had gone like this:

"Man, the Cooking Hero really does make some delicious food!"

"You better be careful about what you say. That's the Shield Hero you're talking about."

"Oh yeah, you're right! It's just that his shield reminds me of a pot lid . . ."

"You might want to go to the clinic and get your head checked out."

"Hahaha!"

What the hell? Pot lid? I wasn't going to forget those soldiers. I'd work them to the bone while I had them helping with the reconstruction. But whatever, that didn't matter right now. I needed to focus on Motoyasu.

"Seriously, what's the matter? You're not acting like the Elena I know."

"If you say so. It's just that I know an opportunity when I see one."

"Huh?"

"Listen, Mr. Moto . . . or rather, Spear Hero. I was already at my limit. I can't stomach the thought of running around with you anymore."

"Wh . . . what are—"

that affected the surrounding terrain could cause interference.

I had initially planned on setting a trap before Motoyasu arrived, so that we could interfere with his teleportation skill before I even tried to persuade him. But the prey had arrived before the trap was set. So we'd need to either knock him out clean in a single blow or sap his SP.

We started creeping forward toward Motoyasu, and he thrust his spear up high into the air.

"Portal Spear!"

Damn it! Motoyasu's appearance started to waver and distort, and an instant later he had disappeared.

"I guess he got away," I said.

Things had gone pretty much exactly like I'd expected, but still . . . Catching a hero sure was a pain in the neck.

"I wonder where he went," said Raphtalia.

"Who knows," Girl 1 replied.

"Well then . . . long time no see. Or should I say nice to meet you?" I asked her.

"Either way."

It was time to have a talk with Girl 1 . . . Elena, was it?

"I'm sure you've probably already explained everything to the people from the castle, but I'd like to ask you about what happened."

"Yeah, okay. Fine."

Elena let out a long, drawn-out sigh and then began to talk.

According to Elena, this was what had happened.

Just like Ren and Itsuki, Motoyasu had headed for the country where the Spirit Tortoise had been sealed away in an attempt to get the jump on me.

"This should be a breeze for anyone around level 60 or higher. That monster over there drops super nice weapons and materials."

That's what Motoyasu told Bitch and his other groupies while pointing at the Spirit Tortoise off in the distance. Of course, the beast was heading in their direction, so all of the locals were running away in the opposite direction Motoyasu and his party were headed.

"Ha, ha, ha! Commoners! You need not run! For I, the Spear Hero, shall make quick work of the Spirit Tortoise!"

Motoyasu's declaration echoed out loudly as he held his spear up for everyone to see.

"Wha . . . the Spear . . . Hero?!"

"Sorry for showing up unannounced, but there just happens to be a little world event here that I plan to clear. I'll show you all just how much stronger I am than the Shield Hero!"

And then the fool took off running toward the Spirit Tortoise, like Don Quixote charging at windmills. Torn between wanting to believe in Motoyasu and wanting to ensure their own safety, the people looked back over their shoulders from time to time as they continued to run about haphazardly, trying to escape.

"It may be huge, but don't worry! It only looks scary! Let's do this!"

"Okay!"

"Let's go!"

Elena and the others took off toward the Spirit Tortoise along with Motoyasu. Everything went downhill from there. The Spirit Tortoise summoned its familiars and began to harvest the lives of any and every living thing in its vicinity. Motoyasu, Elena, and the rest of the party fought the familiars off as they continued running. Before long, they arrived at the foot of the Spirit Tortoise.

"Here I go! Thunder Spear!"

Motoyasu launched straight into his finishing move, but . . . it simply made the Spirit Tortoise screech and left nothing more than a scratch on its face. On top of that, the scratch regenerated and healed instantly.

"Wh . . . what?! Shooting Star Spear!"

The Spirit Tortoise familiars began to crowd around Motoyasu. He fought the familiars off but showed absolutely no sign of being able to defeat the Spirit Tortoise.

"Umm . . ."

"Don't tell me . . ."

"No way . . ."

Bitch, Elena, and Girl 2 started whispering to each other. The last straw was when the Spirit Tortoise just ignored

Motoyasu and continued walking. In other words, he wasn't a threat. He was nothing.

When I'd fought the Spirit Tortoise . . . it'd been firing off finishing moves and casting gravity-altering magic like crazy. With Motoyasu, it must have just figured that the familiars would be able to take care of him on their own. Of course, going up against the Spirit Tortoise was kind of like telling someone to defeat a man with a toothpick. Even with the help of Raphtalia, Filo, Eclair, and the old lady, it's a miracle we were able to damage it as much as we did. And even when we did manage to defeat it on the outside, it just regenerated. Kyo wasn't wrong when he said it was our loss.

"A . . . alright! Everyone! I'm going to take this thing down, so back me up with your magic! Here I go!"

Motoyasu let out a battle cry and went charging at the Spirit Tortoise, but Elena turned her back on him and ran without hesitation. She had been completely focused on escaping and ended up getting separated from Bitch and Girl 2. Later, after she had gotten clear of the Spirit Tortoise and waited for all of the commotion to die down, she returned home.

Elena's mother was just glad that her daughter was alive. She told her that the life of an adventurer was just too dangerous and demanded that she carry on the family business instead. She said that they could talk it over when her father came home, but for the time being all that mattered was keeping her daughter alive. If they had gone to the authorities, there was always the chance that she could be charged with a serious offense and end up being executed. And so they eventually came up with the plan to use her father's connections to work out some kind of plea bargain that would involve luring Motoyasu out if he tried to get in contact with her.

And that was Elena's story.

"I figured there was no way he could have survived fighting against that monster. Unbelievable."

"You realize you're saying that to the guy that defeated it, right?"

"Oh yeah. So that was you guys that downed it, huh? That's pretty amazing. I really messed up. I never imagined you'd drag yourself out of the mud and actually make something of yourself . . . I sure picked the wrong hero to suck up to."

Elena let out a deep sigh. Honestly, the level of bitchiness she was displaying made me want to punch her in the face, but there was something strangely refreshing about it, too.

"But whatever. Mr. Motoyasu did give me a bunch of gifts and leveled me up, so I guess it's fine. Now I just have to put up with helping out with the family business."

"Seriously?"

"You're not a very enthusiastic person, are you? You seemed a lot more excitable when we met before," said Raphtalia.

"Oh, that's right. We got into an argument at the castle before going to the Cal Mira islands, didn't we? That was a real hassle, to be honest."

So it was just an act? I couldn't even imagine putting up with pretending to agree with Bitch all the time. Having to kiss the ass of a bitch like that would give me a stomach ulcer.

"Hmm?"

Filo had been responding that way a lot lately. Where did she pick that up?

"Anyway, if he shows up again I'll let you know, but it doesn't look like that's going to happen."

"Probably not. I guess you don't happen to know where Bitch went, do you?"

"No idea. She's not the type to die easily, though, so I'm guessing she's still alive."

Capturing Motoyasu was a real hassle and Bitch was nowhere to be found. Elena had cooperated with the queen and us in luring out Motoyasu, so I guess it wouldn't be right to punish her now. Then again, it wouldn't have been hard for her to get off the hook anyway. She could just say, "We were just doing what the hero told us to! We didn't know any better!" Well, I guess we could still punish her even if she said that, but the queen probably wouldn't go that far.

Motoyasu was the real problem. To put it in game terms, it'd be tough to capture him without inflicting some kind of silence-type status effect on him, to keep him from casting anything. Plus, we'd have to keep it active nonstop or he'd run the moment it wore off. I couldn't persuade the bastard if he wasn't willing to listen. Was there no way to stop him from teleporting? The Scroll of Return skill in Kizuna's world could be disabled using the dragon hourglasses, but that wouldn't work with our portal skills here.

Motoyasu didn't want to listen. If we didn't set a trap and ensure that he couldn't escape before trying to talk with him, there was no doubt that he would run. We would be screwed if he ended up getting himself killed somewhere out there.

"Anyway, thanks for the help," I said.

"No problem. Oh, by the way, I heard you started doing a lot of buying and selling. That's the rumor."

"I guess you could say that. Can't do much without money, after all."

"I might be heading that way to sell some of our goods before long. What a hassle."

"I might be interested, depending on what you've got. You know, you sure don't seem to want to do much of anything."

"I just want to have an easy life."

I had to wonder just what Motoyasu had seen in this woman. The same went for Bitch, of course. I couldn't understand that guy.

"You sure are something," Raphtalia told Elena after we'd wrapped up our conversation.

"You better not end up like that, Raphtalia."

"I won't!"

"I wanna run!" Filo shouted.

Well that came out of nowhere. It was like Filo hadn't even noticed Elena or anything that happened. She must have been bored.

"Later, then," I said.

"Yeah. Goodbye."

Elena let out another deep sigh and then sat back down behind the counter with her chin in her hands, like she had nothing to do. What a lazy bum.

And so, just like that, our plan to capture Motoyasu had failed.

Chapter Eight: The Day the Game Ended

"Huh?"

We were making our way back to the village after failing to talk some sense into Motoyasu. I had Filo pulling her carriage since I'd figured we might as well sell some stuff while we were on the road. But when we came to the next town, someone was causing a commotion in front of the town's vigilante corps guard station. I was about to ignore it and keep going, but . . .

"Why are you treating me like a suspect while this trash gets off scot-free?!"

I heard a familiar voice, so I stopped the carriage and went to have a look. I couldn't see what was going on because of the crowd that had gathered, so I asked someone standing nearby.

"What's going on?"

"Apparently one of the heroes captured some bandits and brought them here, but something about it doesn't add up."

That scenario rang a bell. Although, in my case, I'd taken the bandits' money and set them free.

"A . . . aren't you the Shield Hero?!"

I'd been recognized. Of course, there *was* a huge carriage behind me with Filo pulling it, after all. The crowd parted in front of me and I saw who had been causing the commotion.

The bandits were standing there grinning while Ren was arguing with some members of the vigilante corps. I had a pretty good idea of what had happened. These bandits had tried to pull the same stunt when I captured them before. I figured I should probably step in, so I made my way toward Ren through the opening in the crowd.

"Yo."

Things might've gotten dangerous if he got any more worked up, so I tried to be nonchalant.

"Is that you, Naofumi?"

"Long time no see."

Ren beckoned me over like he was glad to see me. I'd actually been talking to the bandits and not Ren, but . . . whatever. Running into Ren had been lucky for us, too. I couldn't let him escape like Motoyasu had. I needed to be careful not to get him excited.

The bandits went pale the moment they saw me. Of course, I'd run into them twice already. This made three times. They couldn't pretend like they didn't know who I was. Besides, now I had enough authority to force the vigilante corps to take them in if I felt like it.

"You guys never learn, do you? Did you really think you could get off playing the victim just because your captor is a has-been?"

"Sh . . . shut up!" one of them shouted.

This could be a good little experiment. While it was true that I'd instigated Filo at the time, it was these idiots that had been the original source of her little human-eating act.

"Filo!"

"Whaaat?"

Filo leapt over the crowd and came to my side. The bandits grew even paler.

"Eat up," I said.

"Huh?"

"What kind of order is that?!" snapped Raphtalia.

I ignored her. Filo had been pulling her carriage, so she was currently in her filolial queen form. She looked plenty intimidating, although she didn't seem to realize that herself. Filo took one menacing step forward and the bandits all clung to the vigilante corps members.

"We're the true criminals! Please, save us!"

They had confessed quickly! Was Filo really that scary? Now I just needed to get them to give up their hideout and go collect the stolen goods. These idiots always bounced back surprisingly fast. I guess it was because they weren't actually that weak. And they were really good at building up their stash. Maybe I should let them go this time, too, and cash in again later. Nah, that probably wasn't going to work this time.

"We're bandits! We'll tell you anything you want to know! We'll give all the money back! Just don't let the bird eat us!"

"Umm, Master? I'm getting a bad feeling about this. Is it just me?"

"Don't worry about it. Just bite his head or something."

"Umm . . ."

The crowd started whispering.

"Does the bird god really eat people?"

"Nah, I heard the Shield Hero is just really good at intimidating people."

"Really? I knew it! I heard people from several villages mention seeing the bird god having fun playing with the village children."

Filo should have been happy. Apparently people didn't really believe that she was the filolial embodiment of hunger itself. It would be up to her now whether people treated her as a monster or a person in the future.

"So there you have it. Those guys tried to do the same thing and frame me back when I had a bad reputation. Make sure you tie them up nice and tight."

"U . . . understood."

The vigilante corps members had a bewildered look on their faces as they nodded to me.

"There's a bounty for these guys, right?"

"Umm, yes. But you'll need to turn over their leader first."

"Hideout, guys . . ."

"Of course! Here's a map right here!"

Their obedience sure made things easy.

"Alright. Filo, take Raphtalia to this location and you two take care of any bandits there."

"Okay!"

"Understood. But what about the Sword Hero?"

"He's less likely to get excited if I talk to him alone."

Ren had his own portal skill, so we had to be careful or he'd just flee like Motoyasu had. If he was going to run, at least I could try my best to talk some sense into him first.

"Understood. We'll be back soon."

I gave the map to Filo and Raphtalia and sent them on their mission. I told the vigilante corps that the rest of the bandits would be arriving soon and asked them to give the bounty to Raphtalia.

"The Shield Hero sorted everything out."

"Getting those lying bandits to confess like that sure was impressive."

"I guess that shows they know there are things worse than being arrested."

"I guess so."

I couldn't have agreed more. Just because you do the right thing doesn't mean that the bad guys will get the punishment they deserve.

"Long time no see, Ren."

"Y . . . yeah . . ."

Ren tensed up and started to back away slowly.

"Hold up, it's not like I'm here to capture you or anything.

I just want to talk. I'm no threat to you alone, right?"

Part of the reason I'd sent Raphtalia and Filo away was to show Ren that I had no intention of fighting. I figured it was the only way to get him to loosen his guard.

"I . . . guess so. It's just that everyone seems to be treating me suspiciously lately."

Ren replied sulkily. I'd say he had it pretty good if that's all he had to deal with. I'd been cursed and called a demon for reasons I didn't even understand. It was mostly because of Trash, Bitch, and the Church of the Three Heroes, of course.

"Why don't we go to the tavern and talk?"

I sure hoped I could get through to him. Why did these idiots always seem to show up when we were unprepared?

I took Ren to the tavern. We sat at the bar and ordered some drinks. Hmm? The barkeep handed me a rucolu fruit along with the drinks and looked at me with a twinkle of anticipation in his eye. Oh, whatever. I tossed it in my mouth.

"He's the real deal!"

"Crazy!"

I guess eating a rucolu fruit had become the gold standard for proving my identity. I wasn't really sure how to feel about that. Sadeena got oddly excited whenever she saw me eat one.

"Sounds like you've been having a tough time."

I decided to start the conversation with something neutral that wouldn't upset Ren. The guy was a lone wolf who had been pushed into a corner, so it was hard to know how he'd react. And actually, revenge was all I thought about before I had Raphtalia and Filo with me, too.

"Yeah. The guild is constantly harping on me to return to Melromarc. So I go clear out monsters or hunt bounties on my own, and then someone takes a cut of my reward money. Then, to top it all off, something like this happens!"

The self-professed imperturbable Ren was visibly angry as he aired his complaints. Of course, it's not like I couldn't understand how he felt. I'd experienced the same thing.

"So I've been selling monster drops and whatever else, basically living hand to mouth. I've had enough. Everyone is treating me completely different than before. Why should I have to protect this world?"

I wanted to roll my eyes. All he was worried about was being praised. He was still treating this all like a game, as usual.

"That's just the way people are. I had it at least that bad, if not worse, when I was still the Shield Demon to them."

I mentioned my own experience and pretended like I sympathized with him. That must have earned me a bit of trust, because he nodded.

"I . . . I guess so."

It was tempting to let him experience a little bit more of what I'd gone through, but if he lost all hope and ended up dying on us, that'd just be more trouble for me. But what a little weakling. Everything about him was just weak.

"So what should we talk about?" I asked.

I tried to think of something to talk to Ren about, but nothing came to mind, honestly. I mean, I could have told him to get serious about the waves or asked him what happened with the Spirit Tortoise, but I didn't want to get him worked up.

". . ."

Ren and I sat there in silence. With the state he was currently in, Ren would only think I was boasting if I tried making small talk, like mentioning what I'd been up to lately. I didn't have any other ideas, so I decided to bring up what happened with Motoyasu, who was in a similar situation. Then I could appeal to how Ren *surely* wouldn't want to be so childish.

"I ran into Motoyasu a few hours ago. I tried to explain that neither I nor Melromarc was interested in punishing him or anything like that, but he just ran away. He showed basically no interest in listening to me, or even to one of his party members that survived."

More accurately, Elena had completely rejected Motoyasu. But I left that part out.

"Oh yeah? So his party members survived, huh?"

Ren seemed to grow even more despondent as he replied in a near-whisper.

"By the way . . ."

Had Ren's party members been killed? I seemed to

remember Kyo saying something like that, but . . . maybe they had survived. I know Kyo said they had charged at the Spirit Tortoise like a pack of wild boars.

". . ."

When I didn't say anything, Ren slowly opened his mouth and began to talk.

"I wanted to get the jump on you, so I went to defeat the Spirit Tortoise."

Apparently in the game that Ren was familiar with, the whole surrounding region ended up damaged beyond repair by the Spirit Tortoise. It was so bad that the country established an inquiry commission to look into the incident. I had to resist the urge to insert a jab about how they'd made it even worse in real life. Ren explained that level 60-ish was appropriate for the encounter, and that defeating the boss—the Spirit Tortoise—at level 80 should have been a breeze.

Motoyasu had said pretty much the same thing. They wanted to get the jump on me by getting their hands on the powerful Spirit Tortoise weapons. I couldn't deny that the weapons were ridiculously strong. But when you took into account our basic stats and abilities, even with those weapons the other heroes still wouldn't have even come close to the level of strength I'd reached at the Cal Mira islands.

According to Ren, he had pointed at the Spirit Tortoise

when it appeared in the distance and then darted off into its direction, accompanied by his party members.

"Alright! Let's do this!"

Surprised by the overwhelming size of the Spirit Tortoise, Ren's party members questioned him.

"It's huge . . . Can we really defeat that thing?"

"We can beat it! We're plenty strong now!"

Ren shouted back confidently as they continued running toward the Spirit Tortoise, drawing closer and closer. While running, Ren noticed someone firing off skills near the beast, but assumed it was simply adventurers fighting and paid no attention. Ren leapt at the Spirit Tortoise and swung his blade, smug in his conviction that no hero other than himself—much less an ordinary adventurer—would be able to defeat the beast.

"Hundred Swords!"

Ren's Thunder Sword skill took longer to cast than Hundred Swords, so he timed the activation to ensure that the skills flowed together smoothly.

"Thunder Sword!"

But . . . the skills failed to inflict any significant damage on the Spirit Tortoise. This part of Ren's story was basically the same as Motoyasu's, so I'll leave out the details. Confused, Ren swung his sword again. He wasn't going to give up. He was going to defeat the Spirit Tortoise and save the people. And so he continued to fight, his impassioned battle cries ringing out through the air.

Before he realized it, Ren was surrounded by . . . the corpses of his party members. And not just that . . . The corpses were so badly mangled that it would have been near impossible to determine their identities. Still, what did remain of them was just enough for Ren to realize that his companions had all died.

"Wha . . . No way . . . I'm sure they were all at least level 80 . . ."

Overcome with disbelief, Ren's mind went blank. He just stood there in a stupor for a while. He found himself grasping at the vague possibility they might be revived like in a game. But even Ren understood that wasn't going to happen.

As he stood there in utter despair, something or someone took him by surprise and knocked him out cold. It was probably a Spirit Tortoise familiar controlled by Kyo. When Ren finally woke up, he found himself in a bed at the hospital.

"I lost because my party members were weak. And they died because they were weak . . . If we'd coordinated better, we would have won."

Ren whispered in a matter-of-fact tone, as if to say none of it had been his fault. He was . . . beyond saving. His companions had trusted him and fought until the bitter end. They must have been turning in their graves.

"It's not my fault. It's because they were weaker than I expected. It's not my fault. It's not my fault!"

He knew what he had done, and he was trying to run away from the reality of it. There was no need for me to show sympathy here. But I had to make sure he didn't get worked up or he might end up running away.

"In that case . . . there's nothing you could have done."

I forced out an insincere response. To be honest, it was obvious that Ren's negligence was to blame. He'd charged at the beast based solely on his knowledge of a game, and now he was trying to run away from his guilt by rationalizing the death of his companions.

It made me wonder . . . How strong had Raphtalia and Filo been back when all of this was happening? At the very least, they'd held their own against the Spirit Tortoise. I wanted to believe that there's no way they would have ended up dead. They'd had at least that much strength hidden within. Even Rishia could have survived the encounter if she played her cards right. I wanted to tell Ren to try reflecting on his own actions before blaming everyone else. But I restrained myself.

"Ren. Now is your chance to use what I told you guys and get even stronger. Then you can find new companions to help you fight the waves. We have two months and three weeks before the seal is broken on the Phoenix."

There was still time. If Ren used what I had told them and made an effort, he should be able to bounce back by then. To be frank, I wanted to just completely denounce Ren. But it wouldn't have been any good for me or this world if he ended up dead.

If the holy heroes didn't cooperate with each other, this world was going to be destroyed by the waves, or the Phoenix. Of course, if what Ost had said was true, it was also possible to bring peace to this world by sacrificing its inhabitants. Still, there was no guarantee that something wouldn't go wrong like it had with the Spirit Tortoise.

"Yeah."

"If you want to keep a low profile, you could always come stay at the village I'm overseeing. You know Raphtalia, right? It's the village she's from. It's where the first wave happened, so we're working on rebuilding it now. You can borrow some of my companions to group with for the time being if you want. As long as you treat them well, of course."

"You wouldn't mind?"

Ren responded to my suggestion favorably. Things were going in a good direction. I'd reel him in with kind words, and then once I'd tamed him, I'd hammer the power-up methods into his dense head. If I could do that, I wouldn't have to worry so much about him dying anymore. Then he could feel free to leave the village anytime. What Ren needed right now was a way to become truly strong. If I told him some of the things that only we knew, I was sure it would broaden his horizons, too.

"Okay, I'll go."

"Great! In that case . . ."

While still in mid-sentence, I caught a glimpse of a familiar figure outside of the tavern.

"Wait here for a few minutes, will you?"

"What is it?"

Taking Ren right now would be dangerous. But depending on how I replied, he might start to suspect something. Ren seemed to have a sharp intuition, so if I didn't word my response carefully, then our whole talk might end up being for nothing.

"Oh, nothing. I was just thinking we should probably wait for Raphtalia and Filo to get back before heading back to the village. But I remembered I left something important in the carriage. I'm going to run and get it real quick."

"Oh, okay."

"I'll bring back something good to eat. That'll give you something to look forward to."

I had some smoked meat in the carriage that I'd been saving for a special occasion. Filo had gone on about wanting to eat it, and she was picky about flavor. I was sure Ren would like it, too, if he gave it a try.

"Just relax for a bit here in the tavern."

I'd have Ren wait in the tavern.

"Okay."

Ren gave a dispirited nod from his seat at the counter. I stood up and exited the tavern before rushing off in pursuit of the figure I'd just caught a glimpse of.

Chapter Nine: I Dub Thee Witch

I started the tail solo. It would have been nice if Raphtalia were there, but I'd sent her to hunt bandits. I'd just have to make do. I would have liked to have Raph-chan with me at the very least, though . . . Now I wished I'd brought her along.

My mark was apparently tailing someone, too. Or more accurately, he seemed to be waiting for the right time to approach the person. We were walking through an area with hardly any other people around. Just how far did he plan on going?

Damn it . . . Without Raphtalia around, I had to stay hidden in the shadows of the buildings. It was super annoying, but if I tried just talking to him, he was sure to run. If it turned out he was staying somewhere nearby, it would be best to wait for Raphtalia to get back and then come up with some kind of plan to ambush and capture him.

"What should I do? I sure hope it doesn't turn out like it did with Elena."

I guess my mark still hadn't noticed me following him, because he was still looking straight ahead and walking around nervously. What in the world was he so worried about? I followed his line of sight to see what he was looking at when the idiot came to a sudden standstill. When I saw what he'd seen, I found myself dumbstruck as well.

It was Bitch and Girl 2 . . . and for whatever reason, they were in the tavern talking to Ren. What were they talking about? I decided to ignore the idiot, a.k.a. Motoyasu, and approached Bitch. That is to say, I intended to capture her. I couldn't capture Motoyasu since he would just use his portal skill to flee, but things were different with Bitch. What was that bitch whispering to Ren in the first place?!

"The Spear isn't worthy of being called a hero. From the very first time I met you, I was certain that you would be the hero that saved the world, Mr. Ren."

The shit that came out of her mouth was unbelievable. I wanted to leap over there and smash my fist right into her face. I ignored Motoyasu and proceeded over to the tavern.

"Plus . . . the Spear tried to force us to do things with him just like the Shield did to me. I wanted to refuse, but I couldn't. Now that I'm finally free, I've been searching for you, Mr. Ren."

What an utterly ridiculous line. And to think she would try to regurgitate it this late in the game. Had she forgotten just how many months she'd spent running around with Motoyasu? I found myself looking over at Motoyasu, who was so flabbergasted that he hadn't even noticed I was standing next to him.

"Grr . . ."

Wow. He was literally making the gununu face while peeking into the tavern.

"I have to say I do seem to recall the queen mentioning you having some long-standing issues."

Even Ren wasn't thick enough to take the bait without suspicion. Bitch had put on a real show, after all.

"You don't know how mother really is. That woman used to be known as the fox of Melromarc. She set things up so that she could benefit from humiliating me. So that she could gain the trust of the fiendish Shield. And now the Spear has fallen for her deception as well."

Bitch continued to press Ren. Her words left me completely speechless and shaking with anger.

"And I know who was controlling the Spirit Tortoise from the shadows. The Spirit Tortoise that killed your companions. It's the same person that has snatched up the trust of the people of this world with his vile tactics. That's right, it's the Shield Demon!"

What the hell was this bitch saying? So everything was my fault now? She hadn't changed one single bit. I was going to have her executed for sure this time.

"A . . . are you serious?! So that's why it was so tough!"

Hey! Don't tell me he actually believed her! Her whole spiel was riddled with holes! And then finally, Bitch embraced Ren and began to run her hand through his hair.

"Mr. Ren . . . I'm sure you've felt just terrible this whole time after losing your companions. It's okay to cry now. Don't worry. Even if the whole world insists you're a criminal, I still believe in you, Mr. Ren. I believe you were fighting for the sake of the world."

Bitch sure knew how to take advantage of someone in a weakened state. Wait a second . . . Was she stealing Raphtalia's line? Oh, hell no! She was tainting a precious memory that belonged to me and Raphtalia! That was unforgivable! I was about to scream at Bitch, but just a split second before the words came out of my mouth . . .

"Hold on!"

Motoyasu yelled as he dashed toward them. His eyes were filled with anger and resentment. Could this have been an elaborate ploy to satisfy a cuckolding fetish? No, no, no . . .

"Well, well, well, if it isn't the Spear."

Bitch flipped her hair back and made an incredibly nasty face while slowly turning to glare at Motoyasu.

"What happened to you?" she asked.

"That's what I want to ask! What in the world happened to you?! Why are you trying to win Ren over?! I've been searching for you!"

"Ha! I'm not so stupid as to rush into such a reckless attack. Listen to this, Mr. Ren."

Bitch clung to Ren while pretending to sob.

"When things started looking bad, the Spear turned to us and demanded that we attract the Spirit Tortoise's attention to give him time to run away. He tried to use us as a shield! But we were scared, so we ran. And then he tried to chase us down, saying that desertion in the face of the enemy was unforgivable."

"Lies!"

My head was starting to hurt. Motoyasu's expression reminded me of something. Well, duh. It was the exact same expression that had been on my face back then!

It was just more of the same from Bitch. She was trying to sink her fangs into a third hero now. Bitch had transcended the realm of bitchiness. Henceforth she would be known as Witch. She was the bitchiest of bitches, and on top of that she was as wicked as a witch.

Maybe I would just kill her and say she struggled. It would be the perfect way to get Motoyasu on my side! It didn't matter how weak I was at the moment. I was sure I'd still be able to make quick work of Witch.

"Look, Mr. Ren! The Spear brought the Shield Demon with him! They're conspiring together to capture you, Mr. Ren!"

Yeah, I'd made up my mind. I couldn't imagine doing anything but killing her. But damn it! If only Raphtalia and Filo were here, I could choke the life out of that shitty woman without relying on Motoyasu!

"So that was your plan, Motoyasu? You're as bad as Naofumi, if not worse. Anyone willing to betray the trust of another is a disgrace to humankind."

"Ren! Whore is lying to you! You have to believe me!" Motoyasu pleaded.

"Why would anyone believe you?!" snapped Ren.

"Exactly! You forced yourself on us every single night . . . threatening to kill daddy if we didn't comply! Continuing to call me 'Whore' is a testimonial to that fact!"

"Stop lying! I . . . I was really worried about you!"

"If you really cared about me, you would call me by my proper name!"

"I only called you that because I would be punished otherwise!"

I was tempted to continue enjoying Motoyasu's misfortune, but I couldn't take it anymore.

"Your ability to continue spouting off such blatant lies really is impressive, Witch."

Witch raised her eyebrows. Her expression was clearly an attempt to appear unperturbed despite being faced with someone she despised. I knew because that's exactly what I was doing, too.

"Sorry, but I've decided to kill you. Consider it punishment for trying to create discord among the heroes."

She had gone this far. Surely even the queen would

recognize that execution was the only choice. She could have just gone back to the castle without causing any more problems . . . Was causing discord among the heroes the only thing this woman knew how to do?! Upon hearing my words, Ren was the first to act.

"You stay away from Myne!"

Ren swung his sword. A clanging sound rang out and sparks flew as the sword struck my arm. Screams echoed throughout the tavern. A fight had just broken out between heroes, after all. The other patrons began to scatter and run for their lives.

"Come on, Ren. Think about it. Between me and Witch, which one of us can you actually trust?"

I had never told Ren a single lie as far as I could remember. I wasn't trying to say that I was an honest person, but I'd pretty much never really tried to deceive him.

"Shut up! You stay away from Myne! Shooting Star Sword!"

Whoa, now! I wasn't sure how strong Ren's attacks were now, but Motoyasu was standing behind me. I couldn't have him getting killed by a stray bullet. I held my shield out and stopped the attack. It looked like Motoyasu had readied himself to fight, too. This wasn't how I'd hoped things would go, but I guess there was no other choice.

"Ren, you're better off not trusting Witch. She's exactly the kind of person the queen said she was."

She was the kind of person who could falsely accuse

someone without a second thought and then enjoy watching them suffer. I had no doubt that she would deceive Ren and toss him aside before long, too. Just like she had done with Motoyasu!

"Take a good look at Motoyasu. Is that not a pathetic face? Do you honestly believe that's the face of someone who did the things she's accusing him of?"

"Stop it! I heard about how he's being deceived by the queen! You and the queen are the root of all of this evil, Naofumi!"

"You realize the source of that information is a single person, right?"

"I don't care! I'm going to fight for the person that believes in me!"

"Calm down. The Ren I know would understand if he stopped to think for just a moment. Besides, I believed in you, too."

I refrained from saying what I actually wanted to tell Ren. It may not have seemed like it, but I was trying to compromise here.

"Shut up!"

Yeah . . . This wasn't going to work. He seriously believed he was doing the right thing. It's not that I had no idea how he felt. In the very beginning, even if something seemed strange, I just ignored it and kept telling myself to have faith. And right now, Ren was much more emotionally unstable than I was back then. Witch had told him what he wanted to hear, so he wanted to believe her.

All said and done, he'd just chosen to believe the attractive woman instead of the guy.

"It was you, after all! You caused all of this! The death of my companions and my being persecuted now . . . It's all your fault, Naofumi!"

What the . . . And then I heard it. *Pop!* I literally heard myself snap. It's just too bad that Raphtalia hadn't been there. If she had, I might have been able to retain some sense of composure.

"Oh, is that right? If that's how you want to play it, then let me tell you how it really is. Blaming it all on someone else sure makes things easier, right? So your companions died, huh? Well yeah, that's what you get for continuing to treat all of this like a game. Your attack on the Spirit Tortoise was reckless. If you want to resent somebody, then resent yourself for murdering your own companions."

"What?!"

Ren shouted back at me with a fierce look of anger on his face. I couldn't take it anymore. I couldn't bring myself to have any compassion for a fool that only believed what was convenient for himself, especially when it was this outrageous.

"What? If that's all you can say to your friends that believed in you . . . You're not worthy of being called a hero. You're not even worthy of being called a human!"

At least he could have tried to make it sound good by saying it had been for the sake of his companions or something. But no, all he could say was that it wasn't his fault. This bastard . . . I bet selfishly bossing around lower-ranking players was the only way he knew how to play a game, just like I'd imagined. He'd gone on a suicide mission and challenged a boss that was too strong for him, and when all of his companions ended up getting wiped out he blamed it on them being too weak. Just like I thought, it'd all been nothing but a game to him.

"This is not a game world that we're living in. Continuing to think like that is only going to cause more problems."

"Sh . . . shut up!"

"Regardless of how much you or I may regret it, we're stuck here until the waves have ended. It's true that the people of this world basically kidnapped us with their selfish hero-summoning ceremony, and yeah, maybe we're not to blame for that. But whining about it isn't going to change the fact that we have to fight if we want to survive."

"You—"

"You once said to me, 'Things don't go your way, so you decide to turn tail and run away? How weak.' So let me ask you, are you going to fall to the level of 'weak'?"

He'd gotten what he deserved. Could he not have figured out if things were too dangerous before his companions ended up dead? Even I made a point of testing the waters to make sure we had a fighting chance before proceeding into battle, but

this idiot based all of his judgments on his knowledge of some game. He was the type who went around attempting encounters based on what others had learned and posted online rather than trying to figure anything out on his own. It was cowardice, in a way. I doubt he'd ever actually discovered anything on his own.

"The game is over. Your game knowledge isn't going to help you anymore."

"You're wrong! It's . . . It's not my fault!"

"Don't let the Shield's words deceive you, Mr. Ren!"

Witch jumped between us, interrupting our exchange. The woman was irritating to no end.

"Shut the hell up, Witch! If you speak again, I will end you without hesitation!"

Witch must have sensed my murderous intent, because she let out a small scream. Even so, I could tell she was still about to try to say something.

"Oh, so you do want to die? Shield Prison!"

A cage of shields appeared and trapped Witch instantly. Good. Now all I had to do was switch to the Shield of Wrath and slaughter her with Iron Maiden. But in a brief moment of sound judgment, I stopped myself. Would things really be okay if I used the Shield of Wrath right now? Without Raphtalia or Filo here? I'd be in a real mess if I ended up being consumed by anger and incinerating Ren with dark curse burning S.

"It's not my fault! Release Myne!"

"Why would I release her? The bitch causes at least as much trouble as Motoyasu."

These idiots were so annoying. It was always "release me, release me!" with them. If they wanted to be released so bad, I'd be happy to just release them from this life.

"Besides, weren't you the one that told me my actions were unforgivable once? If you refuse to admit it, then I'll be the one to say it. What you did was unforgivable. You're a bona fide murderer in every sense of the word."

"Silence! Shut up! Shut your mouth!"

Ren was shaking violently as if he had finally begun to blame himself. It reminded me of the time I'd told him about how he'd driven a bunch of people to their death in the village with the epidemic. He'd admitted that what he'd done was wrong and immediately tried to head back to the village. Deep down inside, he knew it was his fault. But he couldn't admit it. Or rather, he couldn't allow himself to admit it, I suppose. But the truth was, he knew.

"I know it wasn't on purpose. Regardless, you're still alive. And it's exactly because you're still alive that there are other things you need to be doing, right?"

"Shut up! Shut your mouth!"

"I'll say it as many times as you need to hear it. The truth is you already understand, right? You already know what you need to be doing right now. And I can say for a fact that believing that shitty woman is not it."

"Sileeeennceeeee! I believe in Myne!"

Ren drew his sword back and swung it down hard. I parried the attack with my shield, and it made a light clanking sound. Hmm?

"Eat this!"

Ren followed through and swung his sword at my face. I . . . didn't even attempt to dodge. I heard a metallic clanging sound come from near my ear and Ren grinned. But then immediately after, his eyes grew wide with disbelief.

"Wha . . . Impossible . . ."

"That sword that you're using now seems to be made from the Spirit Tortoise materials you wanted so badly, but . . . don't you think it's a bit weak?"

That's right. I'd withstood Ren's attack without even needing to lift a finger. Of course, my shield had been fully powered up, but even so, he was just too weak. If it had been Raphtalia that just attacked me, I'm certain I would have sustained some kind of injury. That was true even despite the fact that powering up vassal weapons was less effective than powering up legendary weapons, and even with her stats currently being one-third of their usual values due to the effects of a curse.

"Mr. Ren, we should retreat for now!"

Damn it . . . Shield Prison had worn off while we were going back and forth. I had to make my next move before Ren could use his portal skill. Normally I would have used Raphtalia or Filo, but right now there was only one person here I could rely on.

"Motoyasu! You know what to do, don't you? Take that bitch out immediately!"

"O . . . okay!"

"No way! You cheater! Stop hogging all of the power!"

How many times had he called me a cheater now? I was pretty sure it was him that actually wanted to cheat. I was tempted to use that as a comeback, but this wasn't really the time for that.

"Take a good look at the reality of the situation! The reason you were defeated—"

The air was filled with clanging sounds as Ren struck me with his sword repeatedly, but not a single one of his attacks left a mark. He bellowed out a long, drawn-out battle cry. He'd gone completely mad at this point. The Ren I knew would have been able to analyze the situation more calmly. Damn it . . . All he could do was keep calling me a cheater. The situation he was in now was so bad that thinking rationally was probably no longer even possible for him.

I'd just ignore Ren for now. We needed to hurry up and kill Witch. It was obvious she was up to no good again.

"Motoyasu! What are you waiting for?! Hurry up and do it!"

"A . . . alright!"

Motoyasu finally seemed to understand. He readied his spear and began to approach them. Just like Ren, he appeared to be in a pretty serious state of confusion. Regardless, he seemed willing to follow orders, so I'd have him kill Witch.

"Mr. Ren!"

Witch called out loudly to Ren, and he snapped back to himself. Maybe it was because he realized that if he didn't do something Witch was about to die. Damn it! If only he had just gone on attacking me endlessly . . .

"Flashing Sword!"

He must have finally realized they were at a disadvantage, because Ren nodded at Witch and shot off a skill. His sword flashed, blinding me momentarily.

"Ugh . . ."

Motoyasu had been blinded too and couldn't make a move.

"Damn it . . . You bitch!"

I was seeing stars. I reached out to try to grab Witch to keep her from getting away, but it was already too late. Ren grabbed Witch and Girl 2 and raised his sword up high into the air.

"Transport Sword!"

Just like Motoyasu had before, Ren began to disappear. Witch too.

"Witch, it looks like you've managed to get away this time, but mark my words, I will chase you to the fiery depths of hell. You fear for your life and wait for me, damn you."

"Pfft!"

Witch snorted at me before disappearing completely. These portal skills sure were a pain in the neck. I turned and looked at the other remaining hero, Motoyasu. He was sighing with his head hung low, as if he had lost every last ounce of motivation. He looked like the empty shell of a man.

"What's wrong? You're not going to run?"

"I don't care anymore . . . I believed in my companions and spent all this time searching for them, and this is how it turns out . . . The people in the towns and villages treat me coldly. I'm exhausted."

His eyes were blurry. They were the eyes of someone who had lost every last shred of hope. I was worried that he might be consumed by a curse.

"First, I'm going to take you back to the castle, Motoyasu. Then I want you to listen to what I have to say, now that you've finally seen how things really are."

Surely this had been enough for Motoyasu to finally understand just how much of a bitch the woman he had wanted to believe in was. Sharing a common enemy would create solidarity between us, and then we could share our power-up methods. It worked out for both of us. Then, with our newly deepened bonds, we could go out together and kill Witch.

"Yeah, yeah. Whatever. Take me wherever you want. Kill me if you want to."

Motoyasu gave a perfunctory reply and nodded.

"No one said anything about killing you."

I guess after what had just happened his response was understandable, though.

"Everyone expects me to come and save them like it's their God-given right, but when I make one small mistake they're all suddenly casting stones . . . I believed in Whore and Elena, but it turns out they're actually nothing like I thought they were . . . I don't care what happens anymore . . ."

In other words, he'd believed in his companions and was finally on his way out of a tough situation, only to come face to face with the true nature of those companions, which drove him to despair.

The sun was starting to set. I started to think maybe we should just head back to the village, but I was still waiting on Raphtalia and Filo.

"Feel free to blame the disaster on me . . . Would that make you feel better?"

"Come on, I already know it wasn't your fault . . . Why do you think I crossed over to another world?"

The cause of the disaster had been Kyo, right? It certainly wasn't Motoyasu.

"Just leave me alone . . ."

It was probably best not to take him back to the village like this. The place was in a constant state of commotion, and there was a good chance Motoyasu would get worked up. Seeing Atla and Sadeena hanging all over me would probably just make him feel even more lonely and depressed. I guess there was no other choice . . . We'd just get a room at an inn in this village for today and wait for Motoyasu to sort himself out emotionally.

"We're back, Mr. . . . Naofumi?"

Raphtalia and Filo had returned with the tied-up bandits in tow.

"What happened heeeere?" asked Filo.

"Well . . ."

I explained to Raphtalia and Filo what had just happened.

"I wonder why she feels the need to take it that far . . ."

Raphtalia was in utter disbelief when I told her about Witch stealing her line.

"I'll never forgive that bitch," I said.

Filo poked the dispirited Motoyasu with her finger. Sheesh, was he really this depressed just because he'd discovered the true nature of a few women? Actually, he might have just been completely worn out from everything he'd been through. I didn't really care either way and I was enjoying seeing the suffering on his face. I had a feeling Raphtalia was giving me a bad look.

"Mr. Naofumi? Is something wrong?"

"Nah, it's nothing. Let's hurry up and get a room at the inn."

"We're not going back to the village?"

"Motoyasu is . . . in a fragile state right now. If he sees how successful I've been and compares it to his own current state, he could end up attempting suicide or something. That's the last thing I need."

"U . . . understood."

"I'll go back to the village and let them know later. This is a good chance for us to relax a bit, anyway."

There were plenty of problems waiting for us back at the village, after all. Like Atla and Sadeena, for example. It wouldn't hurt to take a night off and recuperate a bit.

And so we took Motoyasu with us and got a room for the night.

Chapter Ten: New Awakening

They didn't serve meals at the inn we were staying at, so we took Motoyasu and went to the tavern to get something to eat. As soon as we entered the tavern, Motoyasu sat down at the bar and ordered a drink. He sipped away at the drink and stared at the counter. I guess that was what happened when someone who only thought about women ended up losing those women.

A slutty-looking girl approached Motoyasu.

"Care to join me for a drink?"

"Sorry, but I'd prefer to drink alone. Please leave me be."

Yeah, he was broken. Didn't he realize Witch had been that way from the start? Had he really believed in her that much?

Raphtalia, Filo, and I ordered a few meals and ate dinner. The portions were generous, and it was pretty good food for the cheap price. From the looks of it, a lot of the dishes used that red tomato-looking fruit from that village to the southwest. Filo was in good spirits after having a reasonably tasty meal, and she started singing along with the tavern bard.

"Sing one more for us, little miss!" someone called out.

"Sure! Nooo problem!"

Filo started really getting into it and was putting on a real performance. She did have a nice voice. Filo and the bard really hit it off and started singing some strange song that sounded like the theme song from an anime or something. I wondered if maybe it was a song she'd learned in Kizuna's world.

Maybe I was just imagining it, but . . . something seemed strange about the expressions on the faces of the people in front of the stage. Actually . . .

"Mr. Naofumi, I once heard of a type of monster that sings songs that deceive sailors, causing them to wreck their ships."

"What a coincidence. I was just thinking about that same monster. Maybe this is some kind of strange magical song that she learned while she was a humming fairy."

She'd given us a glimpse of something similar during our fight at the coliseum in Zeltoble. Filo knew all kinds of different songs, and she seemed to be able to combine them with the bard's songs to create something new altogether. Anyway, harpies, sirens, and other similar monsters used their beautiful voices to deceive others. The way everyone seemed lost in her singing with dreamy eyes reminded me of those monsters.

Before long, Filo finished singing and the air filled with cheers. The audience called out for an encore, but Filo must have had enough because she yelled out "nooo!" and ran off the stage. People were giving her bouquets of flowers in appreciation of her performance. Someone gave her some kind of vegetable that looked like a carrot, too. When Filo reacted more favorably to the edible item, everyone started to give her

THE RISING OF THE SHIELD HERO 11

food. With her hands full of gifts, Filo went and sat down next to Motoyasu for whatever insane reason.

"What's wrong? You're usually a lot more energetic. This isn't like yooou."

That reminded me. Appearance-wise, Filo was Motoyasu's type, apparently. He'd been throwing himself at her all the time, before he'd disappeared. I remembered him saying something about having a thing for angels, too. I'm sure it had to do with some character in a game that he fantasized about or something. Although, he was the kind of guy who already tended to think of women as angels in the first place.

". . ."

He seemed incredibly annoyed as he glanced over at Filo before returning his gaze to the counter. So he was going to ignore Filo, too . . . despite having a thing for the way she looked? Yeah, he was broken, alright.

"It happens to me when I'm hungry. I start feeling tired. I'll sing you a song that will make you feel better."

Filo got back up on the stage and started singing. What happened to her not wanting to sing anymore? The song had a nice rhythm. But that made me think . . .

"Filo sure knows a lot of songs. Is it just me, or has her repertoire not expanded since the time she was a humming fairy?"

"It's because we've traveled to so many towns all over

Melromarc. She's always liked singing, I think. Whenever we went to taverns, she was always listening attentively to the bards and learning their songs."

Now that I thought about it, Filo always sang when she was in a good mood.

"The children in the village enjoy her singing, too. She was singing them lullabies recently."

"Oh yeah. She was, wasn't she? I remember her singing back at the village when she wasn't staying the night with Melty."

Filo faced Motoyasu and danced while she sang. Watching her even made me start to feel better. But why did something about it remind me of a sci-fi anime about shapeshifting aircraft? Huh? Who taught Filo this song? Was it Kizuna? Kizuna was a gamer, and she seemed like the type who would watch anime, too, despite being obsessed with fishing.

When she finished singing, Filo went back over to Motoyasu.

"Come on, just leave me alone, okay? I hate women right now."

"Okaaay!"

Filo started digging around through the vegetables and flowers she'd been given.

"Eat this! It'll help you be true to your usual desires!"

It almost seemed like she was toying with Motoyasu as she offered him one of the carrot-looking vegetables and a flower.

I guess she was just being true to her own curiosity, though. Motoyasu was almost never downcast like this, so seeing him like that probably sparked her interest. The village children had shown a similar lack of ambition in the beginning, too. I'd just assumed Filo had overheard me complaining about having to get Motoyasu on board with things, so now she was trying to help out in her own way.

At least, that's what I was thinking when Motoyasu looked over at Filo and started quivering.

"Waaahhhhhhhh!"

Motoyasu suddenly embraced Filo and started crying.

"Ahhhhh!"

Filo let out an ear-piercing shriek. She started trying to wriggle her way out of Motoyasu's embrace, but he must have been stronger than expected because she couldn't escape.

"Wahhh! Waaahhhhh!"

Motoyasu was bawling his eyes out.

"Maaaster! Heeeelp!"

Filo looked like she was about to cry, too, as she reached out to me and called for help. How had things ended up like this?

"What were you thinking . . ." I asked her.

I started to make my way over to help Filo, who was struggling as Motoyasu pressed his face up against her chest while sobbing. I guess if Witch was no longer an option he'd just settle for Filo. But then again, he *had* openly admitted that he had a thing for the way Filo looked in her human form a long time ago.

"If you switch back to your filolial form, maybe it will surprise him and he'll let go," I suggested.

"O . . . okay!"

Motoyasu had been traumatized by her filolial form, after all. He wouldn't come anywhere near Filo when she was in her monster form. Just like I suggested, Filo switched back to her monster form. But . . .

Sniff! Sniff!

"It's Filo-chan's scent!"

Motoyasu was still holding on to Filo in her filolial form and now he was sniffing at her. Whoa! Talk about creepy!

"He won't let go! Maaaster! He won't let goooo!"

This was Motoyasu we were talking about here. He wasn't letting go of Filo in her filolial form?! What was going on?! Then again, I had a pretty good idea of why. I figured I might as well say it.

"You whispered sweet nothings into his ear when he was depressed, so what do you expect? Now accept the consequences and take care of him!"

"Wait just a minute. By that logic, wouldn't you be treating me the same way, Mr. Naofumi?"

"What in the world are you talking about, Raphtalia?!"

Raphtalia was obviously pretty mixed up, too. But then again, I'd basically indirectly ordered Filo to cheer Motoyasu up, so pushing the responsibility off on her wasn't really fair. Actually, I'd tried flattering Ren, too, but it didn't work. The fact that Witch succeeded pissed me off. I guess I was mixed up, too.

"Stooop!"

"Filo-tan! Filo-tan!"

Motoyasu started rubbing his cheek up against Filo's face. Filo tried to use her superhuman strength to pull herself away from Motoyasu, but he was hugging her with all his might and remained stuck to her like an octopus. Her feathers looked like they were about to be ripped right off of her body. The pain must have been preventing her from using her full strength. Filo had a surprisingly low pain tolerance, after all.

"Heeelp!"

Now Filo was bawling and crying out for help. I wasn't really sure what to do.

"Umm . . . Motoyasu . . ."

"Filo-tan!"

It was no good. He wasn't listening. He obviously wasn't hearing Filo, either. Motoyasu had finally cracked. Or maybe he had just discovered a new fetish. I guess he was fine with Filo in her filolial form now. What happened to the trauma from being kicked in the nuts?

"Maaasteeer!"

We were supposed to be taking Motoyasu with us, but it looked like that was no longer an option.

"If you can't take responsibility for him then give him a mouthful and go get rid of him somewhere."

"Okay!"

"That's terrible! He's not some pet monster that you can just throw away," Raphtalia snapped.

"Motoyasu, if you're feeling better, then that's good enough for now. Have faith in the power-up methods that I told you about and do your best to power up your weapon!"

"Got it! Filo-tan!"

Filo dashed out of the tavern with Motoyasu still glued to her.

"Wha . . ."

Raphtalia's voice conveyed a sense of dull bewilderment.

"So yeah . . . we'll just save taking Motoyasu in for another time. He sure did recover from his suffering fast, though."

Motoyasu the man-whore. He'd gotten ditched by Witch and the others, but got right back in the saddle and went after Filo . . . Filo was kind of like a horse . . . so that saddle bit was pretty witty, right? Right? Yeah, that was terrible.

"I have a feeling he went right past suffering into a whole new level of despair," Raphtalia replied.

"I'll just have Filo act like a bitch and I'm sure he'll go back to normal. Once he's being a little more rational she can just tell him she only approached him because she thought she might get a meal out of it or something."

"Do you really think Filo can pull off a performance like that?"

Who knows? I figured it should be possible if I told her exactly what to say, but . . . I did still have my doubts. I sat there in silence for a moment, thinking, before finally coming to a conclusion.

"I'm sure it will work out one way or the other," I said.

"I wonder . . ."

"It will . . . probably."

I couldn't help but have a bad feeling about it all, but I'd feel guilty if I didn't tell myself it'd be alright. Motoyasu was in good spirits now. He'd be fine. I was sure he'd be back out chasing some tail by this time tomorrow.

Filo took Motoyasu and threw him off the side of some cliff before coming back, by the way. She was unforgiving. She had several patches of feathers missing, too. I guess she'd literally risked her own life to get rid of him. I figured that was the end of that . . . until the next morning.

"Alright, we're putting Motoyasu on hold for now. Let's go give the queen an update and then head back to the village."

It was a glorious morning without the usual onslaught of

the sexual harassment corps back at the village. My stress levels were down, and I felt like I'd slept really well. But we had a lot to do today, so we needed to get to work.

"That sounds good," Raphtalia replied.

"Master, I want to hurry up and go home . . ."

Filo begged me with a terrified look in her eyes. I guess she'd been traumatized by Motoyasu. Well, she'd hated him in the first place, so I guess it was just an extension of that. If she hated him so much, why had she gotten involved, anyway?

"Why did you even try to cheer him up? I mean, I have a feeling you were trying to help out, but still . . ."

"He seemed down, so I tried to cheer him up like I did with the village children."

Sheesh . . . It had worked all too well in Motoyasu's case. He was going to be a real hassle.

"Next time we see him, you say exactly what I told you and then give him the cold shoulder."

"Okaaay!"

"Alright, I still have to make breakfast so let's hurry back. Filo, we're going to use my portal to go back. You take the carriage and meet us there."

"Noooo! That spear guy is gonna show uuuup!"

"Don't be ridiculous. Not even Motoyasu—"

I opened the door to the room.

"Good morning, Father."

I immediately slammed the door shut. Why was Motoyasu standing guard in front of our room? And he was talking nonsense on top of that. Why was he calling me father all of a sudden? I was pretty sure I didn't have a son that was older than me. Besides, this was Motoyasu. There was just no way I could possibly be his father. I looked down and held my hand to my forehead.

"What just happened?" I asked.

"What's wrong?" replied Raphtalia.

"Umm . . ."

I'd just woken up and my brain was still half asleep. I didn't feel like explaining it to Raphtalia, so I stepped aside and motioned for her to open the door. Raphtalia cocked her head to the side in confusion and opened the door.

"What's a tanuki pig doing in Filo-tan's room?! Unacceptable!"

Jab!

"Ugh!"

Raphtalia rapidly thrust the hilt of her katana into Motoyasu's stomach and closed the door. Tanuki pig? That certainly wasn't a word I was expecting to hear first thing in the morning. That was just plain verbal abuse.

"Umm . . ."

Raphtalia mimicked my pose and nodded.

"Now I understand. What should we do?"

"How long has he been out there, anyway?" I wondered out loud.

"I thought I heard someone making noises outside earlier, but I never imagined it would be him out there waiting this whole time," she replied.

"I heard some noises, too, but I just figured it was adventurers walking down the hallway. So that was Motoyasu . . ."

He seemed to be doing well for someone that had been thrown off a cliff.

"Filo."

"Noooo!"

"If you don't tell him what I told you to, he's going to chase after you forever. Go tell him to power up his weapon properly and prepare for the waves."

"Boo . . ."

Filo wrinkled her eyebrows discontentedly and opened the door.

"Oh! Filo-tan!"

Motoyasu tried to leap at Filo, but Raphtalia grabbed him by the ear and held him back.

"Let go of me, tanuki pig! I need to give Filo-tan a loving embrace!"

". . ."

Raphtalia had a smile on her face, but she was emitting a dark and menacing aura. She signaled Filo with her eyes. What the hell was Motoyasu saying, anyway?

"Umm . . . I just approached you because I thought I could get a meal out of it. I think you misunderstood."

"Love begins with misunderstandings, Filo-tan! Don't worry, I'm willing to accept your selfish motives!"

"Noooo!"

He wasn't going to budge. Our plan had been a failure. As I was standing there unsure of how to respond to the absurdity of the situation, Motoyasu turned in my direction and stared at me with a look of complete seriousness on his face.

"Father, I would like to ask for your blessing to be with your daughter."

"I'm not anyone's father!"

While it might have been true that I'd raised Filo, I sure didn't remember fathering a daughter that transformed into big bird.

"Father, your daughter rescued me. She opened my eyes to true love. I promise to make her happy, no matter what. Please! Give me her hand!"

"I'm telling you I'm not her father! I may have raised her, but why should I have to give you her hand?!"

"Noooo! Master! Heeelp! Mel-chaaan!"

Now Filo was getting mixed up, too! Unfortunately for her, Melty wasn't here with us.

"Don't be ridiculous! She's your daughter! What you're implying is a crime, Father!"

"Were you even listening to me?!"

"You can try to gloss over it however you want, but that kind of relationship between a father and daughter is unclean, Father!"

"Oh, shut up!"

Raphtalia threw Motoyasu out of the room and closed the door. He was in worse shape than I'd imagined. He'd already cracked, but I had a feeling we'd gone and shattered him beyond all repair.

"Let me in, you tanuki pig! Release Father and Filo-tan!"

"Get ahold of yourself!" I yelled.

Motoyasu was banging on the door. My head was killing me . . . It'd been practically impossible to have a civilized conversation with Motoyasu before, but now it was like something in his brain had snapped. Motoyasu had switched into full-on stalker mode. Now what were we supposed to do?

As for the cause . . . it was undoubtedly because Filo had been kind to him. When people are driven into a corner, it's easier than you would imagine for them to become obsessed with something or someone. It had been the same for me and Ren, too. I had no idea why the incident from yesterday affected

Motoyasu like it did, but the end result was that Filo had saved him from a broken heart.

Now that I thought about it, Motoyasu had always been the type to get fired up about love and romance. But wait, judging from the way he was acting now, did that mean he was the kind of guy that liked to chase after girls instead of being chased? Actually . . . I couldn't have cared less. Thinking about that would be a serious waste of time.

"You sure are being loud!"

I heard the voice of some female adventurer who had probably been trying to get some rest next door.

"Quit your squealing, pig! Get lost!"

"P . . . pig?! What's your problem?!"

Motoyasu, the ladies' man, was telling off a woman. She must have been pretty damned ugly. I was curious, so I cracked the door and peeked outside.

Motoyasu was standing there arguing with a fairly good-looking woman. I was pretty sure she was a dancer from the tavern. I could never have imagined the Motoyasu I knew doing something like this. Just what was going on up there in that head of his? I wondered what he saw now when he looked at Raphtalia or that woman. My curiosity had been piqued. Maybe he had been affected by some kind of curse.

"What should we do? We can't leave with him out there like that," said Raphtalia.

"Filo. Take responsibility and go drag Motoyasu—"

"Noooo!"

I wondered what we should do. Motoyasu didn't seem like he was going to give up easily.

"Let's just go out the window for now. We'll explain the situation to the innkeeper and then run. As for the carriage . . ."

"U . . . understood."

If we tried to go to the shed where the carriage was parked, I had a feeling Motoyasu would be expecting it and get there before us.

"My carriaaaage . . ."

Filo must have understood that, because her eyes were darting around worriedly. Motoyasu must have seriously had some kind of mental deficiency. Why had things ended up like this? It didn't make any sense. Why the hell were we running from Motoyasu? Hadn't it been the other way around yesterday?

"Motoyasu will notice if we make too much noise, so just forget about the carriage for now. We'll come back for it when it seems safe!"

"Okay . . ."

Filo's disappointment was apparent, but she nodded hesitantly. So she actually chose getting away from Motoyasu over her carriage? She must have seriously disliked him.

And so, just like that, we made our escape from the inn.

We used my portal and made our way to the castle. I wanted to give the queen an update on Witch. Filo was still looking around suspiciously.

"I'm sure you'd know if Motoyasu were here. You're overreacting."

"I knooow, but still . . . it's like I can feel him nearby! Yuck!"

I don't think she could have disliked him any more than she did now. Motoyasu going all gaga over her had only made things worse.

Still, even Motoyasu wouldn't show up at the castle . . . probably. People would recognize him in the castle town, so it would be impossible to hide. He'd always relied on crystal balls and never actually studied magic, so I was pretty sure he didn't have any new tricks up his sleeve. I doubt he could use magic to hide himself like Raphtalia could. Even if he could, Raphtalia would be able to sense him.

If he had a skill that allowed him to hide himself, then we wouldn't be able to do anything about that. But judging from how he'd been acting so far, I had no doubt he'd just come charging at Filo like a naïve fool. Besides, he was probably still standing guard back at the carriage.

"Don't worry about it."

"Boo . . ."

We headed to the throne room, where the queen was taking care of some official business. I told the queen about what had happened yesterday.

"Can you not do something about that witch daughter of yours? I wanted to kill her as soon as I ran into her."

I was sure Witch was up to no good, so it was probably best to just put a bounty on her head and have her killed.

"Even so . . . I would like to recommend that she be brought in alive, if at all possible," replied the queen.

Brought in alive after all of this? That didn't seem fitting for someone with a bounty on her head.

"I wonder how that child made it across the border. The Spear Hero's other companions were accompanied by their parents, so I can understand how they made it across, but her . . ."

"Considering what Elena and Motoyasu told us, there's no doubt she crossed over from another country."

I was sure someone would recognize Witch if she tried to cross at a border checkpoint. She was a former princess of Melromarc, after all. To get around that, she would have to . . . cross over the mountains, I guess. But Witch? She wasn't the type to do anything that made her suffer. I couldn't imagine her returning to Melromarc by such a crude method. Maybe she smuggled herself in. She could have hidden among some cargo. That one seemed possible, at least.

"Can you not use the slave curse to smoke her out?"

"I'm not sure how she's managed to interfere with the curse, but . . . I haven't been able to. There is another problem, as well."

"What now?"

"The controlled area that was functioning as a prison for the country was damaged by the Spirit Tortoise attacks. I've been informed that the vast majority of the criminals were killed by the attacks, but . . ."

"But what?"

"It is possible that there were survivors."

"Hmm . . ."

That meant the country's criminals could be alive and on the run. I guess that did sound like a problem.

"This is just my intuition, but I have a feeling there's a connection with that child's shenanigans. Many of the government officials that had ties with the Church of the Three Heroes were sent there after being dismissed following the incident with you."

Hold on. That meant that those people were on the run, right? That was a major problem. And now that scum was hiding out in Melromarc, huh? I guess finding out about it before anything major happened counted for something, though. It seemed like I was always suddenly getting caught up in some nonsense without any warning, which made it hard for me to keep up. It was nice to hear about something ahead of time for once.

But yeah, there was almost certainly a connection between that and Witch. The Church of the Three Heroes was probably involved in getting her across the border.

"Can we just kill that woman already, no questions asked?"

"I'd like to avoid that, if at all possible . . ."

The queen must have made the same connection I did.

"If we take her alive, we can force her to expose her connections with the remnants of the church," she suggested.

"I see . . . Then get as much information as you can so that we can capture her."

"Of course."

"Are criminals not given slave curses?"

"They are, but the guard that had ownership died in the Spirit Tortoise attacks."

Ah, that made sense. The person that had the authority to punish them was no longer alive. What a mess.

"There was another reason I wanted that child captured alive, originally."

"What's that?"

"Specifically, I intended to use her as a means to avoid war. Let's just say it involves choking back my tears and offering her as a sacrifice."

A sacrifice, huh? I guess that was why Witch didn't show up at the castle. But no . . . the queen wasn't evil. If Witch hadn't caused so much trouble, I'm sure things could have been settled more amicably. That much was clear from the way the queen was always humoring me.

"But succumbing to such a fate is something that child

hates the idea of from the bottom of her heart. Indeed, to avoid it, she would thrash around in refusal, plead with me, and even run away without looking back. Grouping with one of the heroes exempted her from that punishment."

"Oh? In other words, she voided the exemption herself."

What an idiot. She should have just stayed quiet and kept her fangs sunk into Motoyasu.

"The details would make any noble female want to commit suicide. In other words, it's a punishment worse than death."

Hmm . . . I kind of wanted to know what the punishment was, but at the same time I felt like it was probably better not to know.

"This was the most effective threat I had to use against that child. It looks like it will no longer simply be a threat now, though."

"Whatever. Fine, let's make the bounty for 'dead or alive,' but you can specify 'alive if possible' and make the bounty bigger if they bring her in alive."

"I suppose there is no other choice. As you wish, Mr. Iwatani. It's the least I can do as a mother, as well. We shall stop her before she causes any more trouble."

The queen nodded and then gave the order to one of her subordinates. And so Witch became a criminal, wanted dead or alive. The problem was that she was with Ren now. I just had to hope he didn't go on a rampage and end up being made the leader of some opposing power or something.

Chapter Eleven: Loincloth Pup

After finishing my talk with the queen and heading back to the village . . .

"Welcome back, bubba!"

I could hardly believe my eyes when a puppy in a loincloth with Keel's voice ran up and welcomed me back. It looked like a Siberian Husky. The puppy had a fluffy coat of fur and stood at maybe a bit over two and a half feet tall from head to toe. The reason I say it was a puppy is because its face and several other features seemed too puppy-like for it to be an adult. The puppy was wearing a loincloth and looked really proud of itself as it walked around on its hind legs.

"K . . . Keel?" Raphtalia muttered.

"You . . ."

"Heh, pretty awesome, huh? Sadeena taught me how."

Keel puffed her chest out proudly, but . . . the other villagers looked like they weren't quite sure what to make of it. Awesome? She'd turned into a cute little pet. It was just too bad it had to be a puppy. I guess technically it was a therianthrope form, but dog form was a more fitting description of the way Keel looked now. Sadeena looked a little bit proud, too. She annoyed me. She seriously annoyed me.

"I could tell little Keel had potential, so I showed her how to do it," she said.

"Potential, huh?" I mumbled.

"Isn't Keel so cute?!"

Rishia, who had been really lackluster lately, must have been taking a break from her training. She came over, picked Keel up, and started petting her.

Rishia seemed to be training with the old lady quite frequently lately. She had kept up her training while we were fighting in the coliseum tournament whenever she wasn't busy gathering information. The old lady mentioned that our fights in the other world had hastened the development of her abilities. She'd only been able to use her awakened state against Kyo so far, but if she could learn to use it at will, that would be something worth getting excited about.

"Hey! Let go of me, Rishia!"

Keel complained, but Rishia didn't stop petting him. I could totally understand. In short, I'd wanted to pet puppy Keel when I saw her, too.

"And? Is there anyone else in the village that can use a therianthrope form like this? How does it affect her stats, anyway?" I asked.

"It depends on race, but stats get boosted in most cases, like with me," Sadeena replied.

"Hmm . . ."

"It's extremely rare for someone to have potential, so I wouldn't get your hopes up about the other villagers," she said.

"I see. What about Raphtalia?"

"Little Raphtalia is an exception."

So Raphtalia could use a therianthrope form . . . or maybe a Raph-chan form? If not that, those stoneware tanuki statues came to mind. I stood there staring at Raphtalia for a few moments, and then she got upset.

"You're thinking about something rude, aren't you? That I would look like Raph-chan if I used a therianthrope form or something, right?"

"Is that really what you were thinking, buddy?"

Keel seemed genuinely curious. I turned away and acted like I had no idea what they were talking about.

"Oh my, does she really look that lovely?" asked Atla.

"Yes. Keel is so cute!" Rishia squealed.

Atla walked over to us with Fohl and was listening to Rishia with a confused look on her face. Even if Atla could sense someone's presence, I guess it only made sense that she couldn't judge appearances since she was blind.

"Stop saying cute! You mean I look cool, right?"

"Cute definitely describes it better. You could give Raph-chan a run for her money," I muttered.

Keel dropped her head in disappointment.

"Rafu raful!"

Raph-chan noticed the commotion and came over and stood next to Keel. It was perfect. We had our village mascots taken care of now. Filo? Nah.

"No way . . . I thought I finally looked cool . . ."

"If anything, you've gotten further from it," I said.

Keel's usual girly looks would've still classified her as cute, though. Sadeena was looking at Keel and cackling before she dropped a real bomb.

"By the way, little Fohl has potential, too."

"Alps sure is talented."

"What in the world is 'Alps'?! Is that supposed to be referring to Fohl?" snapped Raphtalia.

"Yeah. It's a little nickname I've been secretly using for him after something he said made me think of it. You think we should make it stick?"

"I'm sure the reasoning for it is something horrible," Raphtalia retorted.

"I can't argue with that."

"No . . . way . . ." moaned Atla.

Huh? What was Atla upset about?

"A . . . Atla?"

"You've been given a nickname by Mr. Naofumi, Brother. And on top of that, you can learn how to transform into something cute. You intend to try to steal Mr. Naofumi's heart, don't you? I'm jealous. Envious!"

"Y . . . you're wrong! I intend to do no such thing!"

I wasn't even going to go there. I decided to ignore those two and check up on the levels of the village slaves. Oh? They had all leveled up a pretty respectable amount.

Rishia was . . . Hmm? She was level 69, which meant she'd hardly progressed at all. Back when we fought the Spirit Tortoise . . . Itsuki had already gotten her to level 68, and then we went to Kizuna's world after that. Once we returned to this world, she started helping out with the slaves, but still . . . her progress was ridiculously slow.

Her progress had been similarly slow in Kizuna's world, too. She'd been stuck right at the point where it seemed like she might turn 70 at any time. It was like she had gotten to level 69 abnormally fast and then she hit a wall right before 70. It was as if she were being forced to pay for getting to 69 so quickly. Was this a sign that she was about to finally fulfill her potential? I'd have to keep an eye on her.

I guess things were going as expected. In any case, the village slaves that had shown an interest in fighting had all reached around level 40. That meant it was almost time for their class-ups. I figured we should probably just go take care of the ceremonies all at once sometime soon.

"Well, it looks like all of you are about ready for your class-ups."

"Ooh! Class-ups?!"

Keel perked back up and responded excitedly.

"Yeah. From the looks of it, you and several of the other slaves need to class up soon. You do want to class up, right?"

"I do!"

The other slaves started getting excited, too.

"Alright, let's take you all to class up then. Filo, you know what that means."

"Yup! But the spear guy . . ."

"You don't have to worry. I'm sure he's not going to show up at the dragon hourglass."

We'd used my portal to leave, so I wanted to believe that Motoyasu was still back at the inn waiting for us to come out.

That reminded me. I'd talked with the old guy at the weapon shop about having him take one of the slaves under his wing. It would have to be someone good with his hands.

"Are the lumos around?"

"What is it?"

The lumos all gathered near me. They were good with their hands, and they really took the initiative to handle most of the odd jobs around the village. The whole bunch had settled in rather quickly at the village since we already had Imiya there. Right now, they were working on digging a hole at the edge of the village to function as their living quarters.

"Have you all been leveling up, too?"

"Yes. Those of us who had already leveled a bit previously have already reached level 30."

Imiya's uncle answered for the group. Imiya was working hard to make accessories, clothes, and other daily necessities, so I was just letting her do her own thing.

"I see. I want one of you that's willing to learn blacksmithing to come with me. I'm going to have someone I know take you in and teach you the trade."

"Blacksmithing? In that case, I'll go."

Imiya's uncle raised his hand. Huh? Did he have experience or something?

"I did some blacksmithing back at our village, so that should help."

"I see. Alright, you come with me."

"Understood."

"I'll probably be looking for someone to work in the coal mines before long. Is there anyone that can do that?"

"All of us excel at mining."

What a handy bunch. Little by little, I'd have the slaves learn to handle new types of work to get this operation running smoothly. That was my job. Just like Kizuna and the others.

"Got it. The rest of you just keep at your tasks and leveling and don't slack off."

"We will!"

What an energetic bunch.

"Alright, Raphtalia, use your Scroll of Return, will you?"

"Sure. Your portal is still on cool down, isn't it?"

"Yeah. Besides, your skill will get us to the dragon hourglass quicker."

"Okay, once everyone has gathered we'll head out."

And so, after waiting for a while, we teleported out.

Chapter Twelve: The Decision

We teleported to the dragon hourglass using Raphtalia's skill.

"Whoa! Shield Hero?!"

The soldier standing guard yelped in surprise when we suddenly appeared. The soldiers over at the castle seemed to have gotten used to it already, since we showed up there fairly frequently.

"We're here to class up a few of my companions."

"U . . . understood!"

They began preparing for the ceremonies just like when Raphtalia and Filo had classed up.

"Filo."

"Whaaat?"

"I may have you leave the building, just so you know."

"Whhhyyy?"

"Otherwise, the same thing that happened to you and Raphtalia might happen to the slaves."

Ultimately it wasn't a bad thing, since it resulted in an overall increase in stats, but not all of the slaves might be happy with it. With that in mind, we would have to pay attention to where Filo was during class-ups, since her presence could interfere with the outcomes.

"Boo . . . Fine. The spear guy isn't outside, is he?"

Alright, Filo had agreed!

"If he is, call for me," I said.

"But you didn't protect me before, Master."

Ugh . . . What did she think I could have done in that situation?

"Filo, I promise I'll take care of it somehow if he is, so please don't argue."

Raphtalia assured Filo, who then nodded hesitantly.

"Okaaay."

This trauma that bastard Motoyasu had inflicted on Filo sure was a hassle . . . Anyway, it was time for the class-ups.

"Hold up, everyone," I said.

"What's up, Bubba Shield?"

"I might as well ask you all. What we're about to perform here is the class-up ceremony. Do you know what that entails?"

"I've known about it for ages!" shouted Keel.

The slaves all looked at each other and nodded.

"Okay then. It's my policy to have you all decide your own future. Of course, I'm talking about something different than the reconstruction effort to prepare for the waves that you're all working on."

"What do you mean, bubba?"

"Those of you interested in participating in the fight against the waves have been focusing on leveling so far. But at the same time, you need to think about what comes after the waves have ended."

". . ."

Raphtalia stood there silently, staring at me. That's right. The whole idea of rebuilding the village had been for her sake. But regardless of that, it was still important that the slaves decided their own future for themselves.

"The class-up that you're about to undergo will open up new possibilities for you, but it may close others off at the same time. You realize that, right?"

The slaves nodded. After I made sure they understood that, I moved on to my next question.

"There's a possibility that something you weren't expecting might happen. The class-up path that results in the greatest increase in your stats might be automatically chosen for you before you have a chance to make your own decision."

"Can that really happen?"

I nodded emphatically.

"Raphtalia and Filo both fell victim to the phenomenon."

The two of them each gave a quick raise of the hand.

"That cowlick . . . crest feather of Filo's is special. It will choose your class-up path without your permission. But the path that it chooses will result in a huge increase in your stats."

"Are you serious?!"

"Yeah, but you all have long lives ahead of you and combat

prowess isn't everything. If there's something in particular you want to do with your life, then I believe, without a doubt, that it's worth it to choose for yourself and specialize in that thing."

I didn't want them getting stronger at the expense of having any control over their lives. That's why I wanted them to decide if they were okay with having an irregular class-up.

"Of course, I'm pretty sure that both Raphtalia and Filo would be able to do anything they wanted to without a problem now. But there's no guarantee it will be the same for you."

It wasn't like their class-ups had made them impeccable superhumans. I was sure there was no such thing as perfect in this world. That's exactly why the decision was important.

"Make sure you choose a path you won't regret."

The slaves began whispering amongst themselves.

"I understand, bubba. I . . . I want to be the strongest I can be. If there's a chance it will make me stronger, then that's the only option for me."

Keel spoke up first and nodded. Keel was in charge of teaching the slaves discipline. Suffering a major injury from being attacked by a Spirit Tortoise familiar had turned out to be a good experience for her. She didn't act recklessly during battle anymore. I was looking forward to seeing how things would change now that she could use a therianthrope form.

A boy standing next to Keel stepped forward.

"I . . . would like to choose my own path."

"Got it. Okay, everyone split up into two groups. Those who want to choose and those who don't."

The slaves followed my orders and split up.

"Okay, Filo. We'll start with those who are fine with not choosing. Once we move on to the ones who want to choose, I want you to go outside."

"Okaaay."

"Me first!"

Keel raised his hand and then reached out and touched the hourglass. She must have been excited, because her tail was wagging. The magic circle appeared below Keel and an icon popped up in my field of vision.

"Whoa!"

Filo's cowlick popped out and leapt at the icon, interfering with Keel's class-up. The area filled with smoke, and just like what had happened with Raphtalia, Keel's stats all skyrocketed. But . . . I had a feeling the difference wasn't quite as drastic as it had been for Raphtalia. Then again, Raphtalia was always doing push-ups and exercising in her spare time, so it was probably just a matter of her being more physically fit.

"Awesome! My body is overflowing with power. I feel like I could do anything!" Keel exclaimed.

We continued on with the class-ups for the slaves who didn't care about choosing and just wanted to be as strong as possible. Once we had finished those . . .

"Okay then, Filo, you go wait outside."

"Yup, I knooow."

It was time to perform the class-ups for the slaves who wanted to choose their own path, so I had Filo leave the building. That would probably be enough to prevent the interference. Just as I thought, the class-ups went normally.

"Bubba! Bubba, let's see how strong I am now! Let's go hunting and you can see for yourself!" shouted Keel.

"I guess we could do that . . . I probably should see how strong you've become with my own eyes."

Raphtalia, Filo, Rishia, and Eclair were acting as sparring partners to the slaves under the guidance of the old lady, but the reality was that there were certain things only I'd be able to see.

"Alright, let's borrow one of the castle carriages and have Filo take us somewhere where there's likely to be some monsters."

"Buuut . . . I'm scared . . ."

She was so worried about Motoyasu that she didn't even want to go outdoors now . . . She was in critical condition.

"Don't worry about it. If he shows up again, just give him a good kick and you'll be fine."

Motoyasu did have a few screws loose, but he wasn't a threat.

"It's not like the Spear Hero is a bad person, you know . . .

You were the one that kicked him every time you saw him, in the first place, Filo. I'm pretty sure that makes you the bad one . . ."

"You're standing up for him after he called you a tanuki pig? I guess you turned out to be a good kid, after all, Raphtalia."

Did the fact that I was getting a little bit sentimental mean that I'd softened up? Nah. It was probably more like my interpretation of Raphtalia's response as well-meaning was a result of me being twisted. It made me happy that Raphtalia had turned out to be such an honest, straightforward girl.

"What are you getting emotional about? I've never seen you make that face before . . ."

"Boo . . ."

Filo's cheeks were puffed out like she was upset.

"In any case, Filo, if we do run across Motoyasu, all you need to do is give him a good kick, just like you always have. I'm sure he'll like that."

"Okaaay."

"I have a feeling this whole conversation is really messed up, bubba."

"You're not wrong about that, Keel. If the Spear Hero does show up, you help me control him, too, okay?" said Raphtalia.

"S . . . sure! I don't really know what's going on, but you can count on me!"

I got the feeling that Raphtalia didn't completely agree with my plan.

"It's not that I don't understand how you feel, but . . . I'm not sure that kicking him is the answer," she said.

"Oh? You do realize that it will only make things worse if I have her stop kicking him, right? Are you prepared to sacrifice an opportunity to hunt monsters?"

Raphtalia gave up when I put it that way.

"Okay, Filo. Just pull the carriage like you always do. I'll order a new carriage for you later, so cheer up."

"Really?!"

Filo's eyes sparkled. Well, a carriage that hadn't been used much, at least. Besides, I hadn't said that I'd buy a carriage that was any nicer than her previous one.

"Yeah, absolutely."

"Okay, I'll do my beeeest! And if the spear guy shows up, I'll kick him!"

Filo excitedly dashed off toward the castle to get a carriage.

"Umm . . ."

Imiya's uncle raised his hand meekly.

"Don't worry. I plan on stopping on the way," I told him.

"U . . . understood."

Shortly after, Filo returned with a carriage and we all climbed inside.

"Filo, stop by the weapon shop before heading out."

"Okaaay!"

Once we were all loaded up into the carriage Filo was pulling, we made our way to the weapon shop. When we arrived, I jumped out quickly and popped into the old guy's shop.

"Oh! It's you, kid!"

When I entered the weapon shop, the old guy was standing behind the counter like always. There was always something comforting about seeing the old guy. I guess I really did trust him.

"How are things? Have you made progress with the armor and shield?" I asked.

"Not even a tiny bit. That ore from the Spirit Tortoise has some real peculiarities."

"Oh?"

"It's really difficult to work with, so it's a hot topic of research in several places right now. Take a look for yourself."

Hmm . . . I guess that meant it was difficult to process for use in weapons and equipment.

"It's easy to add enchantments and other options, and since the material is so tough, all you have to do to make a weapon is carve it into the proper shape."

I'd seen several in Zeltoble. I remember they were super expensive and looked really crude. The sword and spear blades looked like tortoiseshell. I guess those blades had just been carved into that shape, then.

"That said, I don't feel right about calling something like

that a weapon. The skill of the craftsman never even comes into play. Worse comes to worst, we'll end up seeing crude hammers on the market."

"So it's just a matter of principle?"

"Well, I guess you could say that about the weapons, since we're talking about the skill of the craftsman. But that's not the only problem when it comes to armor."

"Oh really?"

"Really. The material doesn't respond to air wake processing, apparently. It has no effect at all."

Air wake processing? I was pretty sure that was supposed to make heavy armor lighter. That reminded me of the gravity field equip effect on several of my shields. The effect seemed to be able to generate a gravitational field meant to alter gravity and it showed up on a lot of the Spirit Tortoise series shields. Even if such a property only affected the Spirit Tortoise materials a slight amount, it would make sense that they might not respond to air wake processing. It was a nice feature to have on a shield, but it wasn't doing us any favors in the armor department.

"The material itself tends to be heavy, too."

The Spirit Tortoise's shell had to be pliant enough to be able to rebound attacks. But it would still need to be heavy.

"I considered trying to make it lighter, but . . . then you lose precious defense."

"I see."

It was clearly a difficult material to work with. I figured the old guy still hadn't managed to finish any pieces, but . . .

"I've made two prototypes so far. Have a look."

The old guy took me to the back of the shop and showed me the prototypes. The first was straightforward. It was a simple, no-frills shield made from the Spirit Tortoise's shell. The problem was that it was huge and thick.

"This?" I asked.

"Yeah."

"Mind if I pick it up?"

"Go ahead."

I went to give it a try, but it was really heavy. I could lift it, but using it in battle would be tough. I couldn't really swing it around. It made a huge thud when I sat it down. But there was an even bigger problem. Weapon copy hadn't activated. In other words, it wasn't even being recognized as a shield. I wasn't really sure what the criteria were, but it was probably more accurate to consider this . . . a wall, maybe. But I had felt something like a little tingle, so it probably just barely fell short.

"What do you think?"

"Apparently it's not a shield."

"Yeah, it's definitely a failure."

"And the second?"

"This one here."

The old guy handed me an ultra-thin, semi-transparent

shield made out of tortoiseshell. It looked absolutely gorgeous. I held it in my hand. It was light enough to carry comfortably. Swinging it around shouldn't be a problem, either. But . . . hmm? This one seemed more like a shield, but nothing was happening.

"Heh. I figured you'd notice something was wrong, kid."

"What's the problem?"

"I went all out to make that shield as light as possible. The tradeoff is that it has zero defense. A single hit would shatter it."

A single-use shield? Or more like . . .

"Isn't this just a dinner plate?"

"I can't really argue with you there. Just after I finished making it, I saw practically the same thing for sale at a souvenir shop. I felt like crying."

"It's heavier than it looks, though."

"Yeah, it is. That material sure is difficult . . ."

"Aren't these prototypes both a bit extreme? Is there no middle ground?"

"I understand where you're coming from, but the stuff is hard to work with. Everything ends up being really mediocre."

Could we not do something with it? The materials were a parting gift from Ost. I wanted to make good use of them. It would be nice if my shield could modify the materials in some way, but that didn't seem likely. Was there nothing I could say to help?

"That reminds me. When I was in Zeltoble—"

I told the old guy about the Spirit Tortoise Sword that I'd seen in Zeltoble. I mentioned that one glance was enough to tell that it was a one-of-a-kind sword made by a real master craftsman.

"It must have really been something for you to say so, kid. I have a feeling I'd know who made it and how, if I could get a look at it."

"Are you trying to tell me to go buy it? Give me a break. There's no way I could buy a weapon that expensive."

I might be able to get the money by selling the weapons that the old guy had made for us, but that would be defeating the purpose. That made me think . . . Selling rare and unique weapons dropped by monsters was an option, too. They would probably sell for a good price since they were so uncommon. I'd have to give that one some more thought.

"By the way, I brought one of my slaves that I'd like you to take on as an apprentice."

"Which one?"

I pointed Imiya's uncle out of the slaves I had with me.

"It's been a while, hasn't it? I see you actually completed your apprenticeship with Master and opened your own weapon shop."

"Oh! It's you, Tollynemiya!"

His name was longer than I expected.

"You know each other?"

"Yes."

"From a long time ago."

It turned out that Imiya's uncle and the old guy were both apprentices of the same master when they were younger.

"That said . . . I ended up having to quit halfway through due to various circumstances. Things were difficult at home, and I had to help raise several nieces and nephews, including Imiya."

"Master's business wasn't doing too well back then, either," added the old guy.

"Despite being a master craftsman?" I asked.

That seemed a bit strange.

"It had to do with some big business deals and women. Our master was a real sucker for women."

Their master sounded like Motoyasu. I'd picture Motoyasu in my head any time I thought of the old guy's master now. Although, the Motoyasu I knew had turned into a Filo fanatic now.

I wondered just what kind of life Imiya's uncle had led. He and Imiya had both become slaves, so I couldn't really imagine how things had turned out the way they had. I was sure he would tell me if I asked, but forcing people to talk about their own painful memories was something not even I was interested in doing.

"Alright, then. You already know each other. That makes things easier."

"I guess that's true, but . . . I certainly never imagined my new blacksmithing master would be you," said Imiya's uncle.

"I'm surprised, too! But I did tell the kid I'd take on an apprentice, so at least this will make things easier on me."

"It's just like old times. The memories are coming flooding back."

"Including lodging expenses. How much should I pay you to take him on?" I asked.

"As a live-in apprentice, right? I don't need you to pay me anything as long as I can work him like a horse."

"Your generosity is appreciated," I said.

"Hey now . . . I hope we're not talking about hard labor for life here," Imiya's uncle retorted.

"What are you saying? You're the kid's slave! With you around, I should be able to save money on mining, too."

It wasn't much, but with my shield adjustments he should be tougher than your average demi-human or therianthrope. I wondered if that meant the old guy would be a hard-ass teacher. Speaking of images, Imiya's uncle seemed like the kind of character that would always be puffing on a pipe or cigar. But he didn't. He just wore overalls like some country bumpkin.

"I'll just have you doing the same kind of work we used to do way back when."

"That'll kill me for sure."

"Hahaha! It's surprisingly not that bad."

The old guy and Imiya's uncle went about chatting as they got to work. It seemed like things were going to work out just fine.

"Alright, we have some other stuff to take care of," I said.

"Gotcha. I'll make sure he learns everything there is to know about running the shop."

"I'm hoping you'll either come set up shop at my territory or teach him the skills he needs to run his own."

I wanted to have Imiya's uncle make weapons and equipment back at the village, but that would depend on whether he was only skilled enough to work the counter or if he could actually give the old guy a run for his money.

"I haven't really given it that much thought. Either way, I need to see what he can do now, before anything else."

"I've continued to work with ironware a bit, but that's about it."

"You're just being modest. I need to see you actually swing the hammer to judge your true skill."

"You're in for a real treat, then."

Imiya's uncle was always really polite when talking to me, but that wasn't the case with the old guy. They acted just like you would expect two reunited old friends to. It was kind of nice. Imiya's uncle . . . . Tollynemiya, was it? I'd call him Tolly.

"Alright, if I need anything else I'll drop back by again. If you need to get in touch with me, just send word to the village or the castle."

"Will do, kid."

"Despite having lost both of her parents, Imiya seems to be really enjoying herself. I want to do what I can to help you out, too, Shield Hero. I'll do my best to master the trade."

"I'm counting on you."

I sure hoped the two of them could put their heads together and figure out a way to make good use of the problematic Spirit Tortoise materials.

And so we left the weapon shop and continued on our way.

Chapter Thirteen: Oodles of Ambushes

So we had departed, which was all well and good, but . . . that certain someone showed up, after all.

"Nooooo!"

"Filo-taaaaa—"

I sighed as I watched Motoyasu fly off into space for the third time today. He must have been using his teleportation skill to get ahead of us somehow, but it was still pretty impressive. Raphtalia and all of the slaves had shrieked in unison the first time it happened. But I guess witnessing a person being kicked off into space *would* get a shriek out of most.

"That guy with the spear was smiling as she kicked him. That's pretty freaky."

"I'm probably going to have nightmares about that."

"That's scary. Just scary."

Great, now Motoyasu was traumatizing all of my slaves, too. Maybe it was my fault for ordering Filo to kick him, though.

"Just what in the world is he thinking?" asked Raphtalia.

"Who knows?"

I had been wondering how we should try to take the broken Motoyasu into custody, but if he was going to keep showing up this frequently then we could just try to talk some sense into him somewhere along the way. As we made our way further away from human habitation and deeper into the mountains, I suddenly noticed someone standing in our path.

"Is that Motoyasu?" I asked.

"Nooope!"

Oh? Filo sure had good vision. She seemed to be confident, even though the person was quite far away.

"Then I guess you should try not to hit them."

"Okaaay!"

Filo continued running at her normal speed. I had planned on just passing by, but the person spread their arms out and blocked the way.

"What does that mean? Do they want us to stop?" I wondered out loud.

It could have been an emergency or something. Filo must have read my thoughts, because she came to a stop in front of the person.

"What is it?" I asked the person.

There were people that stopped our carriage like this every now and then when we were out peddling our wares. It was usually someone who had been injured or who had run into some monsters and needed help.

The person looked like a man. I wasn't sure how old. He was rather small, but he looked older than his size let on. Maybe he was in his twenties. It was hard to tell. His hair was brown. His face reminded me of one of those comedians who are impossible to hate, despite being a bit of a scoundrel and always telling dirty jokes. I guess he was a human, but it seemed more appropriate to describe him as a mousy fellow. He was wearing a cloak that hid his clothes underneath, and it looked like there was some kind of red liquid spattered on it. Maybe he had been injured.

"Eeehehe . . . Stop the carriage, will ya?" said the man.

"We're already stopped."

He sure was an arrogant little bastard. Did he not realize that standing in front of a carriage and trying to stop it might be a little dangerous?

"Just making sure, but the Shield Hero is in that carriage, right?" he asked.

The queen had been nice enough to hang the Shield Hero sign on the carriage. That was supposed to be a sign that I was on board.

"Yeah, I'm Naofumi Iwatani, the Shield Hero. What do you need?"

Judging by the way things were going, this is where he would ask for my help. But the man's response was completely unexpected. Suddenly, standing before us was . . . a new enemy.

"Oh really? Eeehehehehe! In that case . . . die!"

The man threw his cloak open and hurled a small ball of magic at me. What the hell? "Die"? Was he a member of the Church of the Three Heroes?

"Shooting Star Shield!"

I cast a defensive barrier centered on me and prepared to defend against the attack. It wasn't that I was being careless. There was only a handful of people in this world that could injure me, since the curse hadn't affected my defense. That was my only consolation. But for someone to even try to ambush me was just ludicrous.

At least that's what I wanted to think, but then Murder Pierrot popped up somewhere in the back of my mind. It was always possible that there might still be someone out there unlike anyone else I'd encountered before. Just in case, I jumped on Filo's back and readied my shield. But I never thought that this would actually turn out to be one of those cases.

Just before the ball of magic reached my Shooting Star Shield, it began to swell up and then exploded with a loud pop.

"What?!"

"Whoa!"

The explosion was centered on my shield and blew the roof of the carriage behind me right off. Hold on! Just how high was this guy's attack power?!

"You're full of openings!" he shouted.

The man swung a sword that looked like a shamshir at me and Filo.

"Zweite Aura!"

I quickly cast a spell to raise Filo's stats.

"Here I goooo!"

With me still on her back, Filo did a flip and kicked at the man. But the man used his sword to block her kick.

"What's the idea, all of a sudden?!"

Raphtalia unsheathed her katana and swung at the man.

"Oh! I heard the hero with the holy weapon drags pretty little girls around with him, and it looks like the rumors are true! Eeehehehe! You are the harem type, after all!"

This bastard seriously pissed me off with his annoying laugh. The man appeared completely unpressured as he drew another sword with his free hand and blocked Raphtalia's katana. No way! Her stats may have been lower than usual, but I was pretty sure Raphtalia still had a huge amount of attack power. Her strike would have sliced right through most blades with ease.

"—?!"

Raphtalia seemed to have noticed a weakness or something, because she readied herself to use a skill.

"Brave Blade! Crossing Mists!"

It was her finishing move that used dual katanas to produce a cross-shaped strike. It would be really something if he could block that.

"Oh!"

Apparently blocking Filo's kick and Raphtalia's finishing move at the same time was pushing his limits, because the man took a step back. Not on my watch!

"Air Strike Shield!"

I produced a shield behind him to stop his retreat backward.

"Oh! Safeguard! Earthen Wall!"

A wall shot up out of the ground right in front of Raphtalia while she was still in mid-attack. She swung her katana down, striking right through the wall at the enemy, but the man crouched down and dodged the attack. I didn't even think a dodge like that was possible! Producing shields haphazardly was obviously pointless. The exchange had only lasted a few moments so far, but I could already tell that the man knew how to handle himself in combat.

"Magic Shot! Meteorite Mobilization!"

The man rapidly formed a hand seal and cast something that seemed like magic. He was fast! Then again, that wasn't really anything to get worked up about as there were people out there like Trash #2, who had been so proud of his ability to cast magic without an incantation.

"Bubba!"

Keel called out to me when she and the others finally recovered from their state of shock, but this was no time for chatting. A massive meteorite appeared above in the sky and was headed straight for us. And it was crazy fast! What kind of magic was this?! I'd never seen anything like it. This was just a guess, but I had a feeling this guy was from another world, just like Murder Pierrot. But I didn't have time to think about that at the moment. I had Keel and the other slaves with me, and this guy was casting magical area of effect attacks on us.

"Filo! Raphtalia! Restrain him!"

"Okay!"

"Understood!"

"Second Shield! Dritte Shield! Shield Prison! And Zweite Aura!"

I used my Second Shield as a platform to suspend me in the air and then cast my Dritte Shield up above me. I used E Float Shield for extra protection above and readied my shield. I had cast Zweite Aura on Raphtalia to try to buy us a little time, but . . .

"Disarming Shot! Earth Evasion!"

Raphtalia blocked the man's magic, but . . .

"My . . . strength?!"

There was a visible decrease in Raphtalia's speed.

"Eeehehehe! Is this the first time you've had support magic nullified? Have you never been in a real fight?"

I had a feeling the man still wasn't struggling. Damn it . . . We'd found ourselves hurled into the very predicament that I'd feared was a possibility.

"Huh?"

Raphtalia cocked her head to the side in confusion. But at that moment I had to figure out what to do about this meteorite barreling toward us! The meteorite had smashed through my

Dritte Shield and Shield Prison up above, destroying them. E Float Shield finally reached its limit and shattered, too. Now the meteorite was coming straight for me.

"Ughhh . . ."

I felt the massive impact hit my shield and reverberate throughout my body. I'd just barely been able to withstand it.

"What are you doing to bubba?!"

Keel and the others drew their weapons and began running toward the man.

"Wait! You all stay back!"

Keel and the others ignored me and kept running.

"Too late! I was hoping this might be more of a challenge. Eeehehehehe!"

"Keel!"

Raphtalia called out to Keel. At the same time, the man must have determined Keel to be a weak link, because he turned in her direction and raised his shamshir. Raphtalia was doing everything in her power to come between Keel and the attack, but it was questionable whether she would be able to make it in time. It might have just been my imagination, but it seemed like Raphtalia was moving quicker than just a moment ago . . . but it still didn't look like she was going to make it.

Shit! Keel and the others still couldn't keep up, even with their newly increased stats. They were nothing but a hindrance right now. I began to see everything in slow motion, and just as the man's shamshir was about to pierce Keel's chest, that's when it happened! A loud clashing sound rang out as a large pair of scissors appeared in front of Keel and guarded her from the attack.

"Huh?!"

I couldn't believe my eyes. Murder Pierrot was standing before the man with her scissors in hand.

"Spider Web!"

"Bah!"

Murder Pierrot wrapped the man's shamshir in thread and attempted to restrict his movements, but the man cut the thread and leapt away.

"You ok—?"

Murder Pierrot spoke to Keel, but her words were mixed with static like usual.

"Y . . . yeah!"

Just as Murder Pierrot appeared in front of Keel to protect her, the meteorite that had been looming overhead as it pressed against my shield exploded outward. Ugh . . . I'd been able to withstand the impact, but it hurt pretty bad. My armor was damaged in several places. I jumped down off of Second Shield, landing firmly on the ground, and turned toward the man with my shield readied.

"Well if it isn't the vassal weapon holder from the destroyed world. I guess you're still alive, huh? Eeehehehe!"

I guess they knew each other. Murder Pierrot glared at the man belligerently. Destroyed world?

"But yikes, the holy heroes in this world sure are weak. I get to take it easy and enjoy myself this time. Eeehehe!"

What was with this creep? The way he spoke implied that he was from another world. But . . . the impression he gave was unlike Kyo's arrogance, Trash #2's selfishness, or even L'Arc and Glass's sense of purpose.

"Are you a vassal weapon holder?" I asked him.

"Me? That would be nice, but I didn't make the cut. Eeehehe!"

"This jerk————friend of the chosen heroes———— another world————"

Murder Pierrot tried to explain. I guess that meant that the enemy was in a position kind of like Keel or Filo. Kind of like Therese, maybe. Taking a better look at the man, I noticed he was wearing a strange pendant that hung down over his chest. Maybe it was an accessory that was translating for him or something.

"What a disappointment. I was hoping to enjoy this a little bit more. Eeehehe!"

"Are you saying . . . we're weak?"

Raphtalia pointed her katana at the man as she replied.

"Honestly, you're weaker than I expected. This is easysauce."

"We'll see about that!"

Raphtalia moved at an incredible speed as she slipped into the enemy's guard and prepared to strike with her katana.

"Oh my! What's this? You sure sped up all of a sudden!"

The man's eyes were wide with surprise. I was surprised, too. Why was Raphtalia able to move that fast?

"You made a big mistake when you used that spell to nullify Mr. Naofumi's support magic."

Mistake? I hadn't noticed any miscalculations in the man's attacks so far, but . . . Wait. If he had nullified my support magic, that meant he had erased a beneficial buff. In other words, it was highly possible that his spell could have similarly removed any lingering detrimental effects.

"Your spell seems to have removed a curse that I was stuck with."

"Bah!"

Raphtalia unleashed attack after attack, and the enemy could no longer do anything but defend.

"Eeehe! Impressive! But now it's my turn!"

Raphtalia swung her katana at the enemy as he brought his hands forward to prepare to cast a spell. He launched his magical attack with an incantation that bordered on nonexistent, but it failed to hit Raphtalia. She continued to swing and dodge, driving him further and further into a corner. I guess he hadn't actually been that strong, after all. But something about the fact that he wasn't even a vassal weapon holder didn't seem right.

"Damn . . . It looks like I should probably retreat for now. Eeehehe."

"You think we're going to let you do that?" I asked.

"Indeed, you're not going anywhere!"

Raphtalia snapped at him as she continued to attack. Clearly not wanting to pass up a good chance, Murder Pierrot set her sights on the man, too.

"Nah, escaping is a breeze! I'll be back, so prepare yourselves!"

The man brushed his hand against his pendant before forming a ball of magic and thrusting it into the ground. A bright flash of light filled the air and blinded us for a brief moment. With abilities like this, despite not being a hero . . . I guess he was kind of like a powered-up version of Therese or something. Damn it! They always managed to escape like this! Just as I was about to get pissed off—

"Gah!"

Huh? I blinked a few times and looked over at where the man had been standing to see Murder Pierrot holding her scissors buried into his chest.

"I thought you might———so . . ."

"Ee . . . eehe. You got me! That won't work next time!"

Murder Pierrot jerked the scissors from his chest. Blood spattered out and the man crumbled to the ground. He was dead . . . or was he? Murder Pierrot snipped her scissors shut loudly, turned to face me, and stepped off to the side, implying that I should inspect the man.

I took a close look at the man that Murder Pierrot had killed. It was just a hunch, but I figured I might learn something by inspecting the corpse, since he had been from a different world. Just then, I noticed that there was a faint light seeping out of the man's body. What was that? Don't tell me it still hadn't ended! And then, all of a sudden, the man's corpse faded away as if it had been a mirage.

"Huh? What the hell?"

"Those guys————"

Murder Pierrot tried to explain, but the static was terrible and I had no idea what she was saying. After a brief moment, Murder Pierrot seemed to give up on explaining and asked a simpler question.

"You ok————?"

"Yeah, but . . . wasn't your timing just a little bit too good? Are you sure you're not in cahoots with that guy?"

"Oh, come on, Mr. Naofumi. Aren't you being a bit overly suspicious?"

"She's right, bubba!"

Raphtalia and Keel spoke up in defense of Murder Pierrot. I understood what they were trying to say, and I wanted to trust her myself, too. But her timing had been just too good. I couldn't ignore the possibility that they had planned the encounter in order to win my trust. I realized I was being overly skeptical, but there was just too much at stake that I needed to protect. Allowing myself to trust others easily just wasn't an option.

"That's not——"

Murder Pierrot reached her hand out to my shoulder and plucked something from my armor. It looked like one of those marking pins used when sewing.

"I used this to keep an eye——use it——come to you at any time."

"Is it like a portal skill, then?" I asked.

My skill could only teleport to bound locations, but I guess Murder Pierrot's skill could teleport her to wherever she had placed the pin.

"When did you even . . ."

"——the coliseum."

"Aha, so you put it on me during our fight? Wait, that means you've been observing me!"

Murder Pierrot looked away, but I could see beads of sweat forming on her forehead.

"I don't want to see——of the holy weapons get killed. I want to help——"

It seemed like Murder Pierrot was trying to say she wanted to help me out, but . . .

"I see——curse had lowered your stats."

"Yes. Although, that's been taken care of now."

Raphtalia sheathed her katana as she responded.

"It sure was lucky that the spell the enemy used to nullify my support magic removed the adverse effects of the curse, too," I said.

I doubted we'd get that lucky the next time. If there had been one enemy like this, there were bound to be others, too. I couldn't afford to be running around with my stats lowered by a curse when there were people out there looking to kill the holy heroes. Also, I needed to find Ren, Motoyasu, and Itsuki fast or they were likely to get killed by these creeps. I wouldn't have had to worry quite so much if those jerks would've just used the power-up methods I'd told them about.

"Mr. Naofumi, it's a fact that Murder Pierrot saved Keel and the others. Don't you think we should at least let her tag along?"

"Hmm . . ."

I wasn't quite sure how I felt about the fact that Murder Pierrot had been observing us, but it might not be a bad idea to keep her close, even if she was planning on setting a trap.

"Hey bubba. Is this girl strong?"

"Well, her speech is always cutting out. But yeah, she seems to be on the strong side."

Something the enemy said had me curious: vassal weapon from a destroyed world?

"What was the enemy talking about when he mentioned a vassal weapon from a destroyed world?"

Murder Pierrot cast her gaze downward. Then she glanced at her scissors.

"In my world———were killed, and the world———"

An expression of deep regret came across her face as she mumbled quietly. I suddenly remembered the legends we'd learned about in Kizuna's world. Glass and the others had been trying to kill the holy heroes of other worlds to protect their own world. That meant . . . Murder Pierrot must have been the survivor of a world that had been destroyed by that kind of fighting.

Maybe the reason Murder Pierrot's speech cut out is because her vassal weapon was beginning to malfunction, since her world had been destroyed. Perhaps she had snuck into another world and her own world had been destroyed while she was away. And then in order to stay alive, she had been traveling to different worlds using the waves ever since. It made sense. When she showed up at the village, she'd asked me to let her stay there until the next wave.

I sighed.

"Fine. But this doesn't mean that I trust you. I'm going to keep a close eye on you."

"Okay . . ."

"Even so, you really saved us there. Thanks."

"Sure . . ."

Murder Pierrot nodded. I shifted my gaze from her to Keel and the others.

"Alright then. I wanted to see how strong you all have become after your class-up, but it looks like that will have to wait until another time."

"That really sucks, but I totally understand, bubba."

"Alright. Murder Pierrot, what's your real name?"

I couldn't imagine her ring name being her real name. Murder Pierrot was a mouthful, so I figured it would be best to find out her real name.

"S'yne Lokk."

Hmm . . . Her first name was only one letter off from Witch's adventurer alias. It was getting harder and harder to trust her. Witch's adventurer alias was originally Myne Suphia, by the way. It had been changed to Whore now.

"Alright then. Nice to meet you."

"You too . . ."

And so it turned out that S'yne would end up staying at the village after all.

Chapter Fourteen: Official Request

After we got back to the village, S'yne wandered off to a little nook and started sewing. It was probably best to just think of her vassal weapon as a sewing set. From the looks of it, she seemed to be making a stuffed doll. What was she up to?

It had become apparent that it was about time to really focus on finding Motoyasu, Ren, and Itsuki. I couldn't imagine those three winning a fight against an enemy like the one we'd faced earlier. Motoyasu had been ambushing Filo repeatedly, but even he hadn't shown up for close to a week now. I'd been on high alert watching out for new attackers from other worlds ever since our encounter with that man. S'yne always seemed to be keeping an eye out at the village, too. The whole . . . not knowing when they might show up thing was just creepy. I didn't like it.

Other than that . . . bandits running wild within my territory had become an issue, too. It wasn't like I hadn't been doing anything for the past week. I'd been busy with everything from training Keel and the other slaves to traveling around selling our wares to make some money. I couldn't just sit around on the lookout all the time.

"Hmm?"

I was walking around mulling over how to deal with all of these problems when I came across two familiar characters. One was a nervous girl that gave off an aura of misfortune, and the other was a stubborn woman in a plain set of armor. In other words, it was Rishia and Eclair.

"We're back," said Rishia.

"Greetings, Mr. Iwatani."

I'd heard that they had gone off somewhere recently to do some more serious training with the old lady.

"Hey. Did you two finish your training?"

"Not yet. I was told to come back and give you a hand for now," Rishia replied.

"Me too."

Give me a hand? What was that all about?

"Have you noticed any results from your training?"

"I think Rishia and I are supposed to be back to get some experience in actual battle. Our training is probably going to continue after that."

So the old lady sent them to me to have them experience real combat before continuing. That made sense, but that old lady sure wasn't making things any easier on me. The real problem was Eclair, though. What did she think her job was, anyway? She was supposed to be deputy governor, but whenever she had a spare moment, she'd run off to train with the old lady. It was so bad that even Melty had been complaining. I guess she just intended to let me and Melty take care of all of her duties.

"But I've only really learned the Hengen Muso style on a superficial level," said Eclair.

"I'm in the middle of learning the style in its entirety."

"Superficial level?" I asked.

"Anyone can learn the style on a superficial level, but only those with a special aptitude for the art can master it at a deeper level."

"Hmm . . ."

I stared at Eclair.

"What is it, Mr. Iwatani?"

"Is that really okay? I'm afraid if you only learn the style halfway, you're just going to end up being the underdog that gets bitten."

"Ha! Who do you think I am? I was the one who continued sparring with the teacher when Rishia here ran out of energy and collapsed!"

"You're comparing yourself to Rishia, though . . ."

"Fehhh . . ."

Rishia had probably gotten stronger to a certain degree, but I was sure she still had no stamina—from a rudimentary stats perspective, anyway.

"The style emphasizes fundamental movement patterns and the flow of magic and life force over skills or techniques. Getting the hang of it has been difficult," Eclair explained.

The old lady was crazy strong, so I trusted her skill, but I didn't really understand the style very well. You could apparently cheat by using life force water to help you get the hang of it more easily, though.

"I've gotten the hang of it for the most part," said Rishia.

"Oh? Does that mean you've unlocked that mode that you could only use against Kyo before?"

"P . . . probably. I'm starting to be able to recreate something that feels similar."

"Now that's something to get excited about, right?"

Rishia had a puzzled look on her face. Was her awakened mode already her new normal or something? Was she one of those characters that keeps powering up to ridiculous levels of strength? Maybe she could take me out in one hit now. I knew a manga where something like that happened. That would suck if that actually happened, though.

"What about you, Raphtalia? You haven't been able to train properly since you're always running around with me, right?"

Raphtalia looked at me with a troubled expression on her face.

"Umm . . . I told you this when we were training with Glass, but I can already use the style to a certain degree. I just can't use the same kind of techniques that Eclair and Rishia can because of the vassal weapon."

"Oh? The old lady did mention being able to enhance skills or something, though."

"That's true. Focusing your power can make them more effective."

So I guess Raphtalia could already do something similar. I remember being just on the verge of managing something similar, too. I think they had mentioned Filo could already do it. That's just what Raphtalia and Glass had told me, anyway.

"I probably should spend some time training seriously, though," she said.

"Right now, we can't be sure when there will be another attack. Of course, we'll never get anything done if we're too busy watching our backs," I replied.

Sending Raphtalia to train might be an option, but it wasn't one I could choose in our current situation. I really needed to spend some time training myself, too, but . . . I just didn't have the time.

"What does the old lady say?" I asked.

"She said that Raphtalia still has a lot to learn since she's your most trusted companion," Rishia replied.

"I see . . ."

Having Raphtalia around was a big help. We'd been together forever, too, which made coordinating with each other easy. Still, spending some time training wasn't a bad idea. For her, and for me, too. We had to be wary of attacks, so I'd have to give the timing some thought.

"What do you plan to do now, Mr. Iwatani?"

"We can't just stay cooped up here watching our backs forever. We have an overgrowth of dangerous monsters and they've started showing up near the villages, so I'm thinking about going to take care of that. Melty asked me to do something about the bandits that have been active in the area, so we can do some bandit hunting, too, while we're at it."

"Ah."

"What's that response? You realize both of those are things you're supposed to be taking care of, right?"

"Ugh . . ."

I'd hit the nail on the head and Eclair fell silent. Oh well . . . I'd been thinking I should do some leveling of my own before long, and a periodic monster cleanup could provide me with a regular source of experience. My stats may have been decreased, but that didn't mean I couldn't raise my level.

"I . . . I'll go with you, then. Rishia will, too, of course."

"Perfect. You can show me how much you've improved."

So . . . me, Raphtalia, Rishia, Eclair, and . . . Filo for transportation. We should be able to face pretty much any enemy with that lineup. If we did end up getting defeated somehow, it'd be safe to assume we had no chance of winning to start out with. Anyway, S'yne would probably come running if anything did happen. She still had one of her marking pins stuck to my armor, after all.

"Also . . . Atla."

"Yes, what is it?"

Atla showed up as soon as I called her name. She'd been so quick that it made me wonder if she had just been hiding somewhere waiting for me to call. To think she'd started out as the token sickly girl . . .

"What?!"

Fohl glared at me with a vexed look on his face. These two were actually pretty active around here. They were still far from being able to class up, but I wanted to see what they could do. But what was up with Fohl's reply, anyway? All I'd done is call Atla's name and that's the response I get.

"We're going to level and I want you two to come help out."

"Understood. I've been looking forward to accompanying you, Mr. Naofumi."

"Atla! You don't have to—"

"Save it, Brother."

Fohl was about to make a fuss, but Atla gave him a sharp jab to the chest with her finger.

"Guh . . ."

That was all it took for Fohl to hug his stomach and fall to the ground. Huh? It seemed like Atla was the stronger of the two.

What was that move, anyway? She must have hit a pressure point or something.

"Mr. Iwatani, according to the master, there is no need to teach Miss Atla here the Hengen Muso style. Apparently, being blind has greatly increased her aptitude for the art," Eclair explained.

I guess that meant the old lady had already taken a look at the new slaves of the village. She was kind of like my combat adviser, so she did stay in the village, after all. Judging whether someone had an aptitude for the style was supposed to be a specialty of hers. This was before I'd bought Atla, but I remembered her mentioning that Filo and Sadeena were particularly adept.

So Atla was adept, too, huh? Even more than her lively big brother, Fohl? But I guess when I thought about it, she had been going about her daily life normally, despite being blind. So she must have had a good sense of life force and all that. She might have actually been a better purchase than her brother.

"Umm . . . I guess she should be fine if that's the case. I'm counting on you, Atla. Alright, let's head out."

"Mr. Iwatani, where have the bandits been showing up?"

"Apparently they've banded together in a certain area of the mountains lately and are building a stronghold there."

I unfolded a map and showed Eclair where the bandits had been active. It was a prime location for ambushes.

"Heh heh . . . Sure was nice of them to gather up all in one spot for us, right?"

"Why do you look so excited, Mr. Iwatani? I've never seen you smiling like that before."

Eclair seemed a bit creeped out. Had my expression really been that odd? Bandits were good about stockpiling all kinds of valuables. They were perfect for robbing. Plus, this was an official request, so there would be a reward. It was killing two birds with one stone.

"Mr. Naofumi seems to enjoy hunting bandits," said Raphtalia.

"It's a lucrative venture, after all. And we get to make the territory a safer place at the same time."

Eclair eyed me suspiciously. Whatever. Someone that prioritized training over running the territory had no room to speak.

"Apparently there's a new bandit chief that's risen to power lately, and we'll be wasting our time unless we capture him."

These new bandits were supposedly well organized, which was going to be a hassle. I'd captured some bandits yesterday while we were out selling some goods and I heard them whispering about it.

"Chief?"

"According to some of the bandits we captured, the guy recently became the boss of a nearby group of bandits. They say he's really combative."

The slaves had been ambushed while out vending but

managed to turn the tables on their attackers. It was comforting knowing that they had gotten a lot stronger.

"And this guy is fleeing despite being combative?" asked Eclair.

"That's the thing. I don't know all the details, but apparently the boss is really distrustful and rarely makes appearances. But he's also supposed to be strong enough to pick off even the toughest of adventurers one by one without a problem."

"It doesn't really make sense . . ."

I couldn't argue with that. It sure didn't sound very boss-like. You could make it sound good by calling him a strategist, but you could also say he was being petty. Either way, the type made for a really annoying enemy, and that's exactly why it'd fallen on us to get serious and go take care of him.

"The bandits do exactly as the boss says. He targets a group and the bandits cause a disturbance. They force the members of the group to separate in the confusion, and then the boss picks them off himself, one by one. That's their strategy."

Still . . . why were they using such troublesome tactics? It was hard to tell what they were really after.

"That's why even if they manage to round up his subordinates, they can't capture the boss. Our job is to catch that chief."

"Hmph. What a troublesome bunch of bandits."

I couldn't argue with that, either. They were definitely

troublesome. As long as the boss was alive, he could always get more subordinates. And if they were using such elaborate tactics, they would probably have more than one hideout, too. But that meant more bandit hunting profits, too.

"Either way, the plan is to head out to where the bandits have been showing up and do our monster hunting there."

"Okay."

"Got it."

"Understood."

Just then, Raph-chan came waddling over.

"Rafu!"

"Oh? Hey, Raph-chan!"

It'd been too long since I'd last given Raph-chan a good petting. She was in charge of keeping stress levels low among the slaves, so she hadn't been spending any time with me lately. Raph-chan kept her distance when Raphtalia was around, probably to try to keep Raphtalia happy. That polite restraint was one of the things that made Raph-chan so cute.

"Rafuu!"

"Yeah, you're a good little girl, aren't you?!"

"Mr. Naofumi? Why do you look like you're enjoying yourself so much?"

"Because I am."

Raph-chan was so cute. She really was the best. I hadn't had much time to play with her lately, so if I had a chance to pet her,

I wasn't going to pass it up.

Raphtalia sighed.

"You want to come bandit hunting with us, Raph-chan?"

"Rafuuu!"

Oh? It looked like she wanted to come, too. I guess I would take her along. I was really starting to look forward to this.

"Mr. Iwatani . . ."

Eclair sighed.

"Don't give up, Raphtalia."

Eclair seemed to be trying to encourage Raphtalia for some reason. Did something happen?

"Rafu?"

"Alright! Filo is over in the next town with Melty, so somebody go fetch her. We're gonna go clean up some monsters and hunt some bandits!"

I gave the order and everyone quickly began making preparations.

"You're moving so much better. I hardly even recognize you."

Rishia took the lead and went straight to stomping out monsters. It must have been a result of the old lady's training. Anyone that knew the old Rishia would probably think they were seeing some kind of illusion. Actually, that's exactly how I felt.

She was using a short sword—the Pekkul Rapier—as her primary weapon along with a whip and a throwing knife with a rope attached to it. She would throw the knife while using the whip to grab a monster at the same time. As soon as the knife hit the target, she'd pull the monster in and skewer it with the Pekkul Rapier. That final stab was a Hengen Muso attack known as Bound Thrust or something. The name of the skill was a bit simplistic. It sounded like something made up by a teenage otaku stuck in their own little fantasy world. Other than that, I was impressed.

Plus, she was fast. Even before, Rishia got really strong when she got overly emotional, but she had surpassed that and become even stronger now, as far as I could tell. She was really good at throwing objects and hitting her targets, too. Add in some defense penetration or something and she'd be hard to beat.

I really needed to start taking my training seriously. I'd put it on the backburner after establishing an amicable relationship with L'Arc and Glass, but . . . considering the kinds of enemies we were going to be facing from now on, it probably wouldn't hurt to be able to pull off some similar moves.

Rishia was level 70 now, by the way. It looked like she would hit the next level quicker than she'd gone from 69 to 70, but she still had a long way to go. I thought she might experience some kind of awakening when she hit level 70, but there hadn't been any big change when it happened. Even so, she was a lot stronger than her stats would have implied. I was really surprised, honestly. This was just a guess, but I bet if Itsuki saw Rishia now, he would ask her to come back. Although, he was an exceptionally proud person, so he probably wouldn't actually say the words.

"Really? I don't really feel much different . . ."

So she hadn't noticed the difference. I guess even if she had gotten stronger, the fundamentals remained the same. As I mulled over the thought, I noticed Eclair cut down a monster. It was a pretty impressive attack, although not quite as impressive as Rishia's. She'd definitely become stronger than before.

"That was amazing, Eclair."

Raphtalia complimented Eclair, clearly impressed.

"I still can't compare with you, Raphtalia, but I am one step ahead when it comes to the Hengen Muso style. You better catch up soon."

"You can be certain I will."

It seemed like Raphtalia and Eclair had become friends. Completely disregarding their exchange, Atla came over and called out to me.

"Watch this, Mr. Naofumi."

"Okay."

Now to find out what Atla could do. I wondered if she was stronger than her brother.

"Atla! This is my mon—"

"You're in my way, Brother."

"Oof!"

Atla jabbed Fohl. He fell forward onto the ground and she climbed up and stood on top of him. A huge wild boar monster called a razorback was barreling toward them, but Atla stopped its charge head-on with just one hand. All she had done is place a single finger on the tip of the razorback's nose. The razorback appeared to be trying to charge forward with all its might, but it didn't budge an inch. Huh? It was like she had superhuman strength or something.

"Forgive me."

Jab!

Atla leapt toward the razorback and poked it in the forehead. That's all she had done and yet . . . the razorback's eyes rolled back into its head as it began foaming at the mouth and fell over. Huh? Was it dead?

Received 70 EXP

I'd gotten experience. It was like some kind of assassination technique or something. For some reason, it seemed like it would do more damage than defeating the monster normally. Had she gouged out its brain or something? It hadn't looked like she'd done anything but poked the thing.

"I did it!"

"N . . . nice . . ."

Genius is a scary thing. Atla appeared light-years stronger than Rishia or the lady knight. And barehanded?! I'd just realized I hadn't given Atla a weapon. No, wait. I was sure I must have given her one along with the rest of the slaves. I guess she just didn't use it.

The monsters here were . . . around level 40, on average. That was child's play with this group. I poked Fohl, who was still lying on the ground with Atla standing on top of him. I felt kind of bad for the pitiful brother.

"Yah!"

Filo was in her filolial queen form jumping around and kicking monsters left and right. Like usual, it was clear she knew how to handle herself in a fight.

Anyway, we were mowing through monsters without any need for me to use my shield. I probably should have been doing something, but I just felt redundant. Everyone had gotten so strong . . . I was starting to feel a bit alienated.

"Mr. Naofumi, is something wrong?" asked Raphtalia.

"Nah."

"Raphtalia, bring us some more monsters so Mr. Iwatani has something to do. Otherwise, Sadeena is likely to steal him away from you!" Eclair quipped.

"Understood!"

"I wasn't asking anyone to worry about me! And why are you nodding so vigorously, Raphtalia?!"

What the hell was Eclair talking about?! And why the hell do I have to end up with that drunkard?!

"Oh, whatever. If it's going to be like that, I might as well use this. Hate Reaction!"

I'd just use Hate Reaction to draw nearby monsters to us as we made our way to a location with monsters that were a bit tougher. We made our way deeper into the mountains, and before long we started to see some monsters with dragon-like characteristics.

Ah, that reminded me . . . Dragons lived in really remote regions. I guess we had left the area the bandits had been active in. But that was fine since it was a chance to see just how far we could go. Besides, I could absorb the materials into my shield to get some nice little stat boosts. Or at least that's what I figured, but for some reason I hadn't been able to unlock any dragon-related shields. The Demon Dragon Shield had been really slow to appear, too.

"Mr. Iwatani!"

"Mr. Naofumi! You're needed!"

"It's finally my turn, huh?"

There was finally a monster that they needed my help with. I held it down, and the others attacked it. The rest of the monsters were weaklings, and everyone went about clearing them out on their own. We'd all leveled up after a while, but one person's growth had been particularly remarkable. The instant her level changed from 70 to 71, all her stats shot through the roof.

Her name: Rishia Ivyred.

Was it because of her training? No, I was pretty sure increasing physical fitness wouldn't affect status magic, so that shouldn't cause a sudden rise in stats. Since we hadn't run into any bandits that day and just ended up fighting monsters the whole time, Rishia made it to level 72 and when she did her stats shot up another thirty percent or so. Her stats had already reached about half of what Raphtalia's were before being chosen by the vassal weapon.

That may not have seemed like much since Rishia's stats had been a measly one-third of that to start out with. But if Rishia kept improving at this pace, she should catch up to where Raphtalia was by the time she hit level 75. Apparently the awakening of Rishia's abilities started when she hit level 71. I guess I could finally really look forward to her making a significant contribution on the combat front.

Chapter Fifteen: The Masked Man

"Alright then, we got some good leveling in, so let's actually focus on finding those bandits now. We can do some more leveling after we steal their loot."

I called everyone together after we had finished cleaning up plenty of the dangerous monsters.

"Hold on! Just what do you plan on doing with the stolen goods?!" Eclair snapped.

"What? Are you going to tell me to return them to their original owners when we have no way of knowing who they are?"

Eclair groaned at my reply. She had said something similar back when we were dealing with the Spirit Tortoise.

"If you can prove they belong to someone, I'll be happy to return them to that person. But do you think you can do that?"

Eclair seemed to have given up and sighed deeply.

"And I guess you'll say governing a territory requires such toughness, Mr. Iwatani?"

"Raphtalia, is stealing the bandits' loot wrong?"

"Huh? Is it wrong? They're the thieves, so aren't they the bad ones?"

"R . . . Raphtalia?"

"Hmm . . . I have a feeling Eclair's response is actually the proper one."

Still, it wasn't like I was going to change my mind now.

"Regardless, the bandit loot belongs to me. It will help cover the funds for reconstruction."

It was always possible that I'd have a sudden need for money, like when I wanted to buy up the Lurolona slaves recently. There was no such thing as having too much money.

"So it's a necessary evil, in other words? I . . . I don't know what I should do . . ."

Eclair was at a loss. What happened? I'd actually expected her to show a little more resistance, but . . . Oh well. That just meant less trouble for me, so I wasn't going to complain.

Eclair sighed.

"Rafu?"

Oh? Raphtalia and Raph-chan had both cocked their heads to the side in unison. It was beautiful! Now I was really getting excited.

"I can't help but feel like the reconstruction is going better in your village than in the town," mumbled Eclair.

"The grass is always greener on the other side. Don't let it bother you."

She had the cooperation of Melty and some of the nobility, so the reconstruction of the town that Eclair was overseeing had progressed a bit, too. There was still a shortage of hands in my village, after all. It was nothing but a few houses and some farm plots right now, so it was a long way from what you would call a town.

"Still . . . if things continue like this, it's only a matter of time until . . ."

"If it bothers you that much then stop training all the time and give Melty a hand!"

Sheesh! She had no place envying me if she was going to be a training-obsessed musclebrain. She needed to decide whether she wanted to be a martial artist or a politician.

"Anyway, we've cleaned up enough monsters. Now it's time for some bandit hunting."

We started making preparations in the mountains near the road that the bandits had infested.

"I'm sure you all know this, but most of the bandits are going to be maybe level 40 at the highest. Just do your usual thing and we'll be fine."

People couldn't class up if they weren't trustworthy, so the levels of the bandits wouldn't be that high. Of course, it was possible that there might be drifters who had classed up in Zeltoble or something. We'd come across one once while out peddling wares a long time ago. Someone would probably need to have a successful fighting record in the coliseums to do that. But it didn't make much sense for someone to become a bandit if they could make money fighting in the coliseums. Whatever, it wasn't like I actually cared.

"For now, we'll split up into groups of two and go look for bandits or their hideouts. We need more intel before we can worry about their boss."

The quickest way to find their hideouts would be to find some bandits and make them talk. We needed to round up several bandits to really get started. As for groups . . . I'd just split everyone into pairs based on who would get along or complement each other well.

"Let's go with Fohl and Atla, Raphtalia and Eclair, and Filo and Rishia. If you'd prefer a different partner, then just split up however you like."

I scooped Raph-chan up into my arms and started walking away.

"Raph-chan's with me. Come on, Raph-chan, it's petting time!"

"Rafu!"

"What is that?!"

Raphtalia started to complain.

"We should avoid moving around in big groups. Based on what we know about the boss, I'm going to pair with Raph-chan so that it looks like I'm on my own and see if our prey doesn't take the bait. If anything happens, Raph-chan will let you know, Raphtalia. Right, Raph-chan?"

"Rafu! Rafu rafu!"

Being a familiar, Raph-chan was able to send Raphtalia a

distress signal if needed. Since Raphtalia was one of the more capable fighters among us, I wanted her to be able to move around freely. Raph-chan seemed eager to help out, too. Sure, if I ran into any monsters I might have trouble killing them, but fleeing would be no problem. It wasn't like there was a rule that said I had to stand my ground and fight any monsters or attackers that appeared. Worse comes to worst, I was sure S'yne would come if I called for her.

"That makes sense. Got it. Let's go, then," said Eclair.

"Understood."

Raphtalia seemed convinced when Eclair agreed.

"Atla, I'm counting on your heightened senses. Go find me a bandit hideout."

"Leave it to me! Come, Brother! Let's go!"

"Ugh . . ."

Fohl was acting bitter toward me like usual, but his sister dragged him off and they began their search.

"We'll be back in a while, then," said Rishia.

"See you laaater, Master!"

Rishia seemed calm as she and Filo left to begin their search.

"Now then . . ."

Raph-chan and I started looking for the bandits and their hideouts, too. It wasn't like the bandits were going to be able to injure me, even if they took me by surprise. This was an easy mission for me. I was just walking down the mountain path enjoying a leisurely stroll, playing with Raph-chan.

"Rafuuuuu!"

Raph-chan shrieked and pointed her finger as if trying to warn me about something. What was it? I turned around, but no one was there. But then, all of a sudden, a dark shadow appeared in front of me, so I instinctively raised my shield.

"Assassinating Sword!"

"What?!"

Sparks flew from my shield. The weight of the impact made it clear that it had been a powerful and determined attack. I wasn't sure if anyone else would have survived such an attack.

"What's the big idea, all of a sudden?!"

I swung my shield and tossed the ambusher off to the side. I took a quick glance at the person who had tried to stab me.

"Fight me fair and square!" he shouted.

"Wha . . ."

Even I couldn't believe my eyes. I stood there looking at the attacker, speechless. The attacker's face was hidden behind a shady-looking black mask made to look like some kind of skull. But based on his build, voice, and the way he held his weapon, I already knew exactly what his face looked like. It was Ren Amaki. The Sword Hero readied himself, with a sinister, jet-black sword gripped tightly in his hands.

"Hmph!"

It might have been my imagination, but his equipment seemed even shabbier than before. From what I could see through the openings in his mask, he had a gloomy expression and something about his eyes just seemed off. No, I may not have been one to talk, but it was well beyond off. His pupils were dilated like his mind had snapped or something.

"R . . . Ren?!"

"Hide . . . Sword!"

Ren began to shimmer like a mirage and then disappeared. What the hell? Had he cast some kind of illusion magic on me that was making me see things? Either way, the fact that he was using a skill with "hide" in the name was plenty suspicious, so I prepared myself for combat.

"Rafu!"

Rafu was telling me where he was. What was that about fighting fair and square, in the first place? He'd attacked me from behind suddenly and then used a skill to make himself disappear. Just what kind of mental state was Ren in? Was "fair and square" supposed to be according to some game's fighting system? Either way, there was something oddly ambitionless about the way he spoke. But whatever, I needed to focus on the enemy right now.

"Hate Reaction!"

This skill attracted monsters, but I'd figured out that it actually had an additional hidden effect while we were at the

Cal Mira islands. That was, it drew out and exposed enemies that were using simple concealment magic or skills to hide themselves. We'd noticed the effect when I'd used Hate Reaction at the same time Raphtalia used her Illusion Blade skill. The concealment effect of her skill was canceled out. So when something or someone was hiding, I could use the skill to find them.

I guess Ren had been trying to circle back around behind me again, because he was right in the middle of moving toward my rear left. His stupidity was really kind of silly, but that only pissed me off more. If he was going to use a skill that lame, he should have taken the chance to withdraw temporarily. That probably wouldn't have worked against Raph-chan or Raphtalia.

"Damn . . ."

"Ren . . . It's you, right? What's going on?"

". . ."

It would have been nice if this were only an illusion, but . . . I never imagined he would be hiding out here. Could it be that Witch was the bandit chief? That would have suited her perfectly. She certainly wasn't the princess type. Something like a pirate or a bandit was definitely a better fit.

"Maneater! Shooting Star Sword!"

Ren swung his sword at me using the same motion he used for Shooting Star Sword. A cloud of black particles that twinkled like stars shot out from the tip of his sword and rushed toward me. I held my shield out and blocked the attack. It hadn't been that strong, so I was able to block it with no problem. Ren was weak, like usual. I wished he would hurry up and use the power-up methods already.

I'd left myself open while thinking about how weak Ren was and he didn't pass up the chance to attack.

"Chain Bind! Chain Needle!"

Ugh . . . My shield withstood the attacks, but I felt a slight dull pain run up my arm. I had Raph-chan to protect, so that was close. Ren continued straight into the next skill.

"*Let this foolish sinner pay for his transgressions with an execution by beheading! With nary the time to scream, let his own head be separated from his torso and then he shall know despair!*"

"Guillotine!"

Chains suddenly shot up from out of the ground and wrapped around my body before transforming into something like barbed wire and piercing my skin. Then an instrument of execution appeared from out of nowhere with a massive blade suspended above my head.

This attack . . . Judging from the look of it, the skill was the same type of attack as the Iron Maiden skill on my Shield of Rage. Damn it! There was no way I was going to eat that!

"Not happening!"

I tore the chains off and stopped the falling blade with my hand. Damn, that hurt! I could see blood. Had Ren finally broken through my defense? It was a bit depressing that he had done it with a skill instead of using the power-up methods I'd shared with him. My SP tanked.

"Ren . . . quit messing around. You better stop this fight before I really get mad."

"Mr. Naofumi!"

Raphtalia had heard Raph-chan's warning and came running. She turned to Ren and swung her katana at him. Good! Keep him occupied!

"Transport Sword!"

"Ah! You bastard! Don't run!"

Before I could grab him, Ren used his teleportation skill as he leapt away and disappeared. What the hell was that? Was it a monster or some other person pretending to be Ren? But the attacker had broken through my defense and that meant he was a real force to be reckoned with. The only other way that might happen is if someone could use defense ignoring or defense rating attacks like the old lady.

The attacker had started off hidden and used a skill called Assassinating Sword. Judging from the name and the skill itself, it must have been a finishing move that had to be used while concealed, in stealth mode, or hiding somehow. There were similar moves in some games. In terms of classes, the skill would be used by something like an assassin, ninja, or scout rather than the more orthodox warrior or knight. That wasn't at all like the Ren I knew. And he'd been using a sinister sword that screamed curse series.

But . . . a sudden ambush . . . Was he trying to be a player killer like in an online game or something? Don't tell me Ren was the bandit chief . . . His behavior matched up exactly with what we already knew about how the chief operated. Well, I guess he had come from playing some weird VRMMO game, after all. And to top it all off, he had used an attack that screamed curse skill. If it had been anyone other than me, not only would they have died instantly, but they'd have been sliced clean in half. If Raph-chan hadn't warned me, I might have been taken out from behind with that first attack. The thought of it made me nauseous.

"Are you okay?" asked Raphtalia.

"Yeah . . . but . . ."

"Unbelievable. I saw it, too."

Eclair came running up, seething with anger.

"What in the world is he thinking?" she snapped.

I cast some healing magic to heal my wounds. Oh, and by the way, that Guillotine skill hurt like a bitch thanks to the curse effects I was suffering from. Plus, my wounds took longer to heal now. It had only been thirty minutes since we started our search for the bandits, and I already had a really bad feeling about how this mission was going to turn out.

We ended up finding the bandits' hideout, but we didn't find Ren. That meant he was using a cowardly strategy of only fighting people when they were alone, just like we'd heard.

"Alright then . . . What should we do now?" I wondered out loud.

"To think that the Sword Hero is the bandit chief . . ." mumbled Eclair.

"It's safe to assume that Witch is behind this."

"The former princess? Just how long does she plan to act so foolishly?"

Witch hadn't been in the hideout, either. She was probably staying low somewhere else. I guess I'd start by getting the bandits to spill . . . hmm?

"Umm . . ."

I approached one of the bandits that had been in charge of the hideout and looked at his face more closely. I'd seen this guy before. And recently, too. Wait, wasn't he one of the bandits that Ren had captured? What was he doing here?

"Hey . . . Didn't you get captured?"

He was one of the bandits that was always there when I used Filo to threaten them. He'd been acting real tough when we first showed up at the hideout, but his legs started shaking and he started looking around nervously as soon as he saw me. So I'd pointed over to Filo.

"Ra! Fu! Fu!"

Raph-chan had an evil grin on her face. I just loved how she always played along so well. Raphtalia could've learned a thing or two from her.

"Alright, Filo, eat—"

"I surrender!"

The bandit had given up immediately, and that's how we'd ended up here. Like always, the other bandits had started calling our bandit friend names like "scaredy-cat." Of course, I swiftly put them in their place.

"Why are you on familiar terms with a bandit, Mr. Iwatani?" Eclair asked.

"We seem to be stuck in an unfortunate relationship. Our first encounter was before I'd cleared my name. I couldn't take his group of bandits to the vigilante corps, so I stole their loot. Then we ran into each other again during the whole Melty abduction mess and I used his hideout as lodging."

"So you couldn't really capture him even if you had wanted to."

"Pretty much. After that, I saw him again around a week ago when he'd been captured by Ren, and now this makes the fourth time."

"And why is he here now?"

"That's what I'm trying to ask him."

My subordinates swiftly took care of any bandits that still had some fight in them. There were more of us this time, so things were going really smoothly.

"Who are these people?! They're monsters!"

"Exactly! These monsters are just as strong . . . no, they're even stronger than the chief!"

"Complimenting us isn't going to get you anything. In fact, pay up."

"What are you charging him for?!"

Raphtalia was really on top of her straight man game. I was starting to feel like this was a comedy sketch.

"Ugh . . ."

"Anyway, we turned you guys in, so what are you doing here being bandits?"

When I thought about it, nothing about this guy made sense. He should've been behind bars in some prison or something by now.

"That's right. What happened?" asked Raphtalia.

"When we were being transported, our carriage was ambushed by a bandit and we got away."

"Hmm . . ."

What a mess. The carriage was ambushed while they were being transported . . . Did that mean a friend had rescued them or something? The security measures in this country were surprisingly lax. I should probably have a word with the queen about that.

"It was the chief."

"Reeeeennnnn!"

I screamed out unintentionally. That idiot! What the hell was he doing rescuing bandits?! Even worse, he'd rescued the very bandits that he had captured! What was he thinking?! Was this like that sockpuppeting thing I'd heard about online? No, I guess that was different.

Raphtalia sighed.

"What in the world is he thinking?"

Her voice was filled with exasperation. I felt the same way. Even Eclair had been thrown off balance by the bandit's reply.

"And when was this?" I asked.

"Umm . . . Around a week ago."

That meant it was only shortly after Ren had fled. Had Witch lured Ren in and then immediately organized the gang of bandits?

"I see. In that case, the mastermind . . . probably isn't Ren. Did the chief have a skanky redhead chick with him?"

Raphtalia sighed.

"I could say a thing or two about your choice of description, Mr. Naofumi, but I can't deny that it does sum her up well."

"Chick? The chief is always by himself."

"Yeah, I guess he is always alone. He even kept his distance from his party members," I said.

In online gaming terms, Ren was what you would call a solo player.

"I don't know why, but I'm starting to feel sorry for him."

Ren was so pathetically alone that even Raphtalia felt bad for him. But Witch was probably still with him for the moment. Anyway, it didn't seem like the bandits were trying to hide Witch or anything. As far as I could tell, they really didn't know anything and hadn't seen her. Did that mean Witch wasn't with Ren anymore?

Actually, I noticed that his equipment seemed really beaten up. I'm sure he had plenty of money since he was robbing adventurers. It wasn't like he'd be selling his better equipment to make ends meet or anything. Maybe he was giving all the money to Witch to fund her extravagant lifestyle or something. Nah . . . That didn't seem too likely, judging by how much loot the bandits had piled up here.

"What in the world are they trying to accomplish, I wonder," mumbled Raphtalia.

Was Witch pulling the strings from behind the curtain, or had she already abandoned Ren? I guess we could wait until we caught him to find that out. Now that he had appeared, we needed to make capturing Ren our top priority.

"Ren was using a sword that I'm guessing is part of a curse series. Confronting him could be dangerous, so we need to be careful."

"I noticed," said Raphtalia.

"But assuming it's cursed, I wonder what the curse is."

Based on the types of skills he was using and how powerful they were, I had no doubt it belonged to a curse series. If figuring out the details could help us predict his behavior, it was worth giving it some thought. The question was: what was the curse?

We already knew there was wrath . . . Assuming there were other curses, they might correspond with the seven deadly sins or something similar. But the skill Ren had used was . . . Guillotine. It was similar to my skill in that it used an instrument of torture or execution, but it still wasn't the same skill. If there were different curse series, then it would make sense that the weapons would have different effects.

"My Shield of Wrath . . . Well, originally it was called the Shield of Rage, but either way I'm guessing the naming comes from the seven deadly sins. Does that concept exist in this world?"

Raphtalia was from a rural area, so it was probably better to ask Eclair about something like this.

"Yes, I've heard about a similar concept of sins existing in records of legends left by previous heroes."

Some previous hero that had been from another world like I was had probably introduced the concept. After all, the heroes that were summoned from other worlds were probably the kind of people who liked that kind of thing.

"Let's make sure we're talking about the same seven deadly sins. There's pride, envy, wrath, sloth, greed, gluttony, and lust, right?"

Eclair nodded in response to my question.

"Those are the ones."

My curse series had been unlocked by the anger, or the wrath, that I had felt toward Witch, Trash, and everyone else in this world. As for Ren . . . We could probably rule lust out. The remaining sins all seemed possible, so there was no way to tell which it might have been.

"Anyway, I wonder why we haven't heard any talk of the bandit chief being the Sword Hero."

"Maybe it's because he's been wearing a mask," suggested Raphtalia.

"I guess that could explain it."

If he changed his sword, they wouldn't know he was a hero. The Sword Hero running a gang of bandits . . . I guess any rumor that sounded that crazy would have been snuffed out before it ever made it to us.

"Did none of the bandits recognize the Sword Hero's voice?" I asked the bandit.

"We were threatened and told we'd be killed if we said anything. We kept quiet because he would have killed us!"

Ah, yeah, Ren was really secretive. That was probably why he was trying to hide his face with a mask, too.

"Honestly, getting captured like this is a relief. I'm just glad it's finally over."

"Oh yeah?"

What in the world was Ren thinking? I mulled it over while we tied up the bandits and proceeded to steal their loot.

"Good grief, are all the heroes like this?"

"Hell if I know. Don't group me with those idiots."

"Mr. Iwatani . . . Is this another necessary part of governing a territory?"

"That again? Once again, hell if I know. And anything you think you know about how your dad ran the territory is hearsay, anyway."

"You think my father had his hands in shady business, too?"

Eclair seemed to be distressed about something. I guess I'd have Raphtalia or Sadeena play therapist for her later.

"Anyway, we need to worry about Ren right now. If we let him keep running wild, not only are more people going to get hurt, but it's possible that he'll run into those people trying to kill the heroes. We have to capture him somehow."

Ren was still acting like this was all a game, and whenever things didn't go his way he wouldn't trust anyone that didn't sugarcoat things in his favor. He needed an attitude adjustment. At least in my case, I was suspicious of even the smooth talkers. On the contrary, those were the most suspicious people of all. We needed to figure out who was pulling the strings. If not, who knew when it would come back to bite us? Right now, that meant capturing Ren and making sure he didn't get killed.

"But . . . capturing someone that's out of control and has a curse series weapon is going to be really difficult," I said.

"That is a tough one. We have to make sure he doesn't die, too. It wouldn't be so bad if all we had to do was defeat him," Raphtalia replied.

"The fact that he considered me some kind of boss or something and attacked me by surprise could mean that he's after experience points."

"It's scary because it seems so likely."

You could gain experience by killing humans in this world.

"In that case, the curse could coincide with gluttony, if you thought of it as devouring experience points," I suggested.

Ren was the type that would enjoy leveling up characters. If we assumed he'd been consumed by that kind of desire, then he probably saw me as a sitting duck, since I was walking alone, even if I did have Raph-chan with me.

"Then there's greed . . . It could be that he wants to own everything and so he's using the bandits to gather up loot. So greed is a possibility, too."

I wanted to say that greed was my specialty, but I hadn't unlocked that series for some reason.

"I have a feeling you're thinking about something self-depreciating."

"Man, you're good."

"Well I've known you for a long time."

I had to give Raphtalia props for her impressive ability to

guess what I was thinking. Were my expressions really that easy to read?

Anyway, if the curse series that were attainable differed with each weapon, we would never be able to figure it out. Pride might have been possible, too. There were players in online games that valued their level above all else and looked down on anyone that was a lower level. Ren seemed really proud, or at least the way he seemed to romanticize his lone-wolf tendencies spoke to a sense of pride. I guess Itsuki was a better fit for that one.

"Eclair, aside from the seven deadly sins, there's also the eight cardinal sins. It's possible that it could coincide with one of those."

"Oh! I've heard of those."

Rishia spoke up while raising her hand hesitantly. So those existed here, too? The previous heroes must have really been into all this sin business. Probably some escapist fanboys.

Anyway, the seven deadly sins were a revised version of the older eight cardinal sins, which included gluttony, lust, greed, sorrow, wrath, acedia, vainglory, and pride. So envy was missing, but sorrow and vainglory were included. Acedia was basically the same thing as sloth. Later on, sorrow and acedia were consolidated into sloth, vainglory was merged with pride, and envy was tacked on, resulting in the seven deadly sins.

"If the older eight cardinal sins are included, then it

might be vainglory, or being concerned solely with superficial appearances."

"You think so? I can't really say for sure, but . . ."

"Is the Sword Hero that concerned with outward appearances? I can see the connection, but it seems a bit weak."

Raphtalia and Eclair expressed their doubts about the possibility of vainglory.

"Well, this is just based on my understanding, or shall I say the unique understanding of someone from another world. Let's see if I can make it easier to understand . . . Eclair or Rishia, do either of you know of a game where people play with cards on a table or something to mimic battles with monsters?"

"Yes, I do. There are similar educational materials used to teach people how to fight monsters and get stronger," Rishia replied.

"Educational materials? Whatever, that will work. To put it simply, people from worlds like Ren and I play with educational materials like that a lot. But just playing with those educational materials doesn't actually make a person stronger, does it?"

Rishia and the others all nodded. Rishia knew that better than anyone.

"Those educational materials—I'm guessing they're only used by several people at once here in this world—but people all around the world can play together in similar games in the worlds that the heroes come from."

"Fehh . . . Did you all play these games with that many people?!"

"Itsuki's case is a bit different, but for the most part, yeah."

Itsuki had played a console game back in his world. I hadn't asked him about the details, so I wasn't sure if it had elements like those you would find in online games.

"I see. Now I understand why the heroes are so knowledgeable about this world. The importance of prior knowledge cannot be underestimated," said Eclair.

The power obtained in online games wasn't true power, and it was vainglory that created attachment to that power. Of course, the experiences gained from playing online games were real, and I'm sure there was value in becoming powerful. Back in my world, there were people that had gotten jobs as a result of relationships built in online games. In fact, someone I knew from online once offered to set me up with a full-time job at his company after I'd graduated from university. It was a guy I'd met in real life, too. He told me that his company could use someone fearless like me that had the charisma I displayed as the guild leader. I'm not sure how honest he was being, but it felt good to hear, anyway. Thinking back on it now, he was probably just flattering me in an attempt to make me his errand boy or something.

But judging from Ren's personality and relationships with others, I couldn't even begin to imagine him being able to build a relationship from which he could expect anything like that. It was easy to imagine him being the kind of solo player whose interactions with others wouldn't extend far beyond flaunting a rare drop he'd gotten from a boss or something. Managing a guild had made it painfully clear that being the strongest wasn't everything and going around flaunting items like that was not only pointless, but also super annoying. But there were people that got off on that kind of thing in online games, and you could probably even say those players were the reason the game companies did so well.

"If he persisted in believing that transient power was true power and neglected his inner development . . . That would be vain power, right?"

Although, if we were talking about vainglory, would Ren really be the best fit? It probably corresponded to Itsuki more than anyone else.

"It's hard to say one way or the other, since the conditions required to trigger a curse are still a mystery. And I don't know which sin it would be, but . . . he's definitely guilty of blatantly committing several of the sins."

"Hmm . . . So the fact that you are guilty of several sins that haven't appeared as a curse series serves as counterevidence to the theory, making it even more difficult to determine the curse," Eclair replied.

She was right. If being a bad person was all it took, I'd

committed plenty of sins. But wrath was the only curse series that I had unlocked. If they triggered based on behavior patterns, I'd have to be worried about greed more than anything else. Even I recognized just how greedy I was. I wasn't afraid of the wrath series, since I'd started to understand how to stay in control lately, and I had companions that helped me do that.

Maybe the kind of emotional outburst that almost shattered a person was a condition? Hmm . . . I probably needed to spend some time determining the conditions that triggered a curse or I could end up in trouble. But the love of money was greed, right? Thinking about the pile of treasure behind me, I couldn't help but feel like I was just a big mass of desire. And then there was insatiable desire. But I hadn't been consumed by greed. There had to be a reason why.

Anyway, the curse series most likely to have tainted Ren was probably gluttony, greed, pride, or vainglory. We'd narrowed it down to a certain degree, so now we could further refine our line of thinking. I had a feeling that it could be dangerous if the curse remained unchecked for too long. The curse series included skills that required the user to pay a price. There had to be a way to get Ren under control before he used those skills.

". . . ?"

"Rafu?"

Raphtalia and Raph-chan were blinking and looking behind me, in the direction of the entrance to the bandit hideout.

"What is it?"

"Umm . . . I'm not sure, but it felt like a hidden presence."

Raphtalia and Raph-chan could use illusion magic, so they had increased resistances to the effects of concealment skills and magic. Raph-chan had detected Ren earlier, for instance. I guess it was because they had gotten stronger, but lately they had even started to detect concealed shadow lookouts.

"Is someone there?"

"I'm not sure. They were really well hidden, and I think they'd already fled by the time we noticed."

"I wonder if it was Ren. That would just make things worse."

"I think I would know if it was the Sword Hero. It was probably someone else."

That meant that someone had been watching us seize the hideout from the shadows. If it had been Ren, and now he had fled to a completely different location, that would only make things even more impossible for us.

"Mr. Iwatani, I think it would be best to report this to the authorities."

"I guess we could report it and have them cast ceremonial magic to interfere with attempts to escape."

"Yeah."

It was a reasonable strategy. Chasing him would be pointless if he just used his portal skill to flee every time we found him. He'd gotten away this time, but if we found him again, we would need to jam his portal skill before he could run. Seriously, it would have been so simple if all we had to do was defeat him. Capturing him alive was a real hassle. And then I suddenly remembered something that happened in Zeltoble.

"S'yne."

I called out to Murder Pierrot, a.k.a. S'yne. She was keeping tabs on me, after all, so I figured she might come if I called. In the blink of an eye, S'yne was standing before me.

"What?———"

Having a conversation with her was difficult, but it seemed like she could hear what we were saying reasonably well, so I guess that was all that really mattered. The real problem was that I didn't want to rely on her too much.

"Sh . . . she just appeared out of nowhere!"

Oh yeah, I hadn't told Eclair about S'yne.

"You've seen me use portal to teleport somewhere and appear out of nowhere, right? Don't be so surprised. Just think of her as . . . my own personal shadow."

I didn't want to bother with explaining about heroes from other worlds and all that mess. This explanation should do for now.

"She doesn't seem to be our enemy, so you don't have to worry."

Raphtalia told Eclair what we knew about S'yne. I wasn't

sure if I could trust her, but I couldn't deny that she seemed to be trying to protect me. It probably wouldn't hurt to rely on her a bit. Hmm? There were two stuffed dolls floating next to S'yne. One was a life-sized replica of Raph-chan. The other one looked like it was based on Sadeena's therianthrope form. I stood there staring at the stuffed dolls and S'yne pointed in their direction as if to ask what I was staring at.

"Yeah, that. I want the one that looks like Raph-chan later."

"What kind of request is that?!"

"Rafu!"

There was Raphtalia with another sharp retort. What was wrong with wanting the doll? Just seeing it next to my pillow at night would be sure to make me feel all warm and fuzzy inside.

"I'm Miss S———familiar. Pleased to meet you."

The Raph-chan stuffed doll gave a quick bow. Aw, HELL naw. Raph-chan squealing "rafu!" is what made her cute.

"Fail! You don't understand what makes Raph-chan cute at all. A Raph-chan that speaks human languages can't be called a Raph-chan. Change the design."

"Fine. I'll———so that it doesn't talk."

And the other doll was Sadeena, of all people. S'yne tinkered with something for a moment and the Raph-chan stuffed doll stopped moving.

"Why are we chatting about the stuffed dolls . . . the familiars that S'yne made?!"

Raphtalia had a point. We needed to get back on topic.

"You used some skill that interfered with our skills, right?"

"Yes. Skill————al can block skills."

"Since you've been watching us, I'm sure you know what I want you to do, right?"

S'yne nodded.

"You want me to capture————he flees?"

"Yeah. Can you do that for me?"

S'yne nodded vigorously as if to say, "Leave it to me!"

"You better not kill him. Even if he has a cursed weapon, I'm guessing he's still so weak that he can't even begin to compare to us."

"He's really that w————?"

I looked away from S'yne and nodded.

"It's really kind of sad, isn't it?" said Raphtalia.

"Let's not go there . . ." I mumbled.

He'd used a finishing move on me in a surprise attack and it didn't even scratch me. Then he used an attack that was the equivalent of my Iron Maiden skill and the only reason it stung a bit is because I was still weakened from a curse. Now I understood how Glass felt when she fought us. The fact that Ren was weak hadn't changed. It was just that capturing him without killing him or allowing him to escape was a hassle. Things would be a lot easier if this were a certain monster tamer RPG, where all we had to do to capture him was weaken him and then throw a ball at him.

"Okay———go now?"

"Yeah, if you don't mind. He likes to use surprise attacks, so I'm sure he'll attack you if you just walk around by yourself for a while. Will you be okay?"

"Yes."

S'yne skipped out of the bandit hideout . . . and then immediately returned.

"What is it?"

"That———!"

I looked over in the direction S'yne was urgently pointing toward.

"What are you still doing alive?!" I blurted out.

The man from another world that S'yne had only recently slaughtered casually strolled up along with one of his friends.

Chapter Sixteen: The Merits of Invading Other Worlds

Was he a ghost or something? No, he certainly looked alive. Maybe it had been a stand-in that S'yne had killed. He could have used some spell to create a double or something. That would be really troublesome.

"It's the Shield Hero! Eeehehe! Now I can take revenge on you for killing me!"

"Oh? We heard that there might be a holy hero around here. Looks like we hit the jackpot."

The friend of the man we killed was a large, tallish man that was carrying what looked like a kusarigama, or chain sickle. Paired with the small man, the two looked like a real odd couple. Judging from what he'd said, they must have been searching for the bandit hideout to find and kill Ren and ended up running into us by coincidence. But what the hell did that dimwit mean by "revenge," anyway? He's the one who attacked us!

"Mr. Naofumi!"

Atla yelled out to me with a serious look on her face.

"Are those enemies?!"

Sensing the tense atmosphere, Fohl prepared himself to go to battle, but Atla held her hand out in front of him as a sign that he should stay back.

"No, Brother. They are far too strong! We are no match for them right now!"

"B . . . but—"

"If you don't stay back you'll just get in Mr. Naofumi's way."

Impressive. It seemed like being blind had given Atla a really strong sixth sense or something. To be honest, even I was probably going to have a tough time fighting these enemies. If that was the case, Atla and Fohl joining the fray would more than likely just drag me down.

"I think our best course of action would be to take the captured bandits away from here so that they don't get hurt," Atla said.

"Good call. That's exactly right. You two stay back. We'll deal with these creeps."

"Understood!"

"Raful!"

Raphtalia drew her katana and Raph-chan jumped up onto my shoulder.

"Are these the enemies you mentioned, Mr. Iwatani?!"

"Fehhh . . ."

Eclair and Rishia prepared themselves to be able to attack at any time.

"We're not really interested in killing the rest of you, but eeehehe . . . doing so shouldn't be a problem by the looks of it."

Right now I had Raphtalia, Filo, Raph-chan, Eclair, Rishia, and S'yne with me. I was genuinely thankful that Atla and Fohl had backed down. That would make things a little bit easier on me. We were only facing two enemies, so the odds seemed to be in our favor. But that man had used some peculiarly powerful magic. He'd also been able to keep up with Raphtalia's movements . . . and now there were two of them. I would have preferred to be able to take care of them somehow with just me and Raphtalia fighting, but . . .

"Your goal is to kill the holy heroes, right?" I asked.

"Eeehehe, more or less."

"And that has something to do with some legend in your world or something . . . right?"

If they were willing to listen, we might be able to avoid fighting. We could form an alliance of nonintervention to prevent fighting between our worlds, like we had done with Kizuna . . . perhaps.

"Ah, I see. So that's about the extent of your knowledge, I guess."

"These———won't listen!"

S'yne swung her scissors up high into the air and swiped them at the taller man.

"Ha!"

The taller man blocked her scissors and then struck at her hard with his kusarigama. S'yne leapt backward and dodged the attack, but the airborne kusarigama wrapped around her scissors.

"Sorry, but this one's nonnegotiable. We're going to kill the holy heroes of this world."

"To delay the destruction of your world?"

Glass had come from Kizuna's world to try to kill us because of some legend she had believed. By my analysis, these guys were sure to be after the same thing. I didn't have a solution, but surely it was still worth trying to talk it out with them. If nothing else, I could get them to share some information that we didn't already know.

"Delay the destruction? There's no doubt our world will be the one to survive. Or do you guys not know?"

The small man's eyes twinkled, and his voice was brimming with confidence, as if what he was saying was completely obvious.

"Eeehehehe! Well, I guess you're going to die before the next wave comes, anyway, so I might as well tell you. When you destroy another world, you get crazy amounts of experience and all kinds of new abilities. The vassal weapon holders back in our world call them bonuses."

What a shitty excuse. The hell if I was going to let someone destroy this world for an excuse like that. But it did pique my curiosity.

"And those bonuses are how you're still here despite us having killed you?"

"Eeehehehe, of course!"

"That's enough small talk. There's no point in pretending like we're going to be friends," said the taller man.

"You're right. We've seen holy heroes like this guy before. Eeehehe!"

I really doubted that. The pair shouted out in unison with smug looks of confidence on their faces.

"Our world is the strongest world!"

"Wh . . .what?! Strongest world? What are they talking about?"

Eclair was clearly confused. So were Raphtalia and Rishia. But from what these creeps were saying, it was clear that there were people intentionally going around and destroying other worlds. Destroying other worlds could get them huge bonuses. And these creeps weren't holy heroes or even vassal weapon holders. Now that I thought about it, those bonus abilities were probably the reason Eclair and the others could understand them.

Judging by the determined expression on S'yne's face, it was safe to assume that these creeps had destroyed her world. In that case, settling things peacefully wasn't going to be an option. Just like it was easier to kill a person the second time around, if these guys had destroyed another world before, they were probably going to do it again.

But with rewards like resurrection, things were starting to

sound exactly like an online game. What kind of impossible game was this?! If we died that would be the end, but if we killed them they could just resurrect! There was a strategy in online games back in my world where people would just keep resurrecting to slowly whittle away at a powerful boss. But the boss didn't get to resurrect, and right now we were the boss! This wasn't really a solution, but . . . going off of my knowledge of games and our experience so far, there was probably some kind of save point or something that we needed to destroy. Otherwise they would just keep coming back.

It was undeniable that these guys were even more of a hassle than Kyo had been. Actually, this is probably exactly what Kyo, the other vassal weapon holders, and the supposed genius scientist had been trying to achieve. Destroy another world to get tons of new abilities. That sure sounded nice. It was immoral and not something I wanted to do, but I might have to consider it an option, considering the kind of battles we would be facing in the future. Only while the waves were still occurring, of course.

" . . . "

S'yne was staring at me. I guess the reason she had ended up being a drifter was because someone had destroyed her world for a reason like that. *"Look at her! There's no way you can say that's acceptable!"* I could hear Kizuna saying it now. I had to agree, though.

"Eeehehehe! Here I go!"

The small man pulled out his shamshir and quickly leapt toward me, coming only inches from my chest.

"Die!"

He thrust the shamshir at my throat. But Raphtalia's katana suddenly blocked the shamshir's path as Eclair jabbed her short sword at the small man.

"Oh!"

The man dodged the attack by a hair's breadth and formed a seal with his hands. I grabbed his hands as quickly as I could to thwart him, but he cast the spell immediately.

"Explosive Shot!"

An explosion occurred with the small man at its center. It must have been one of those really convenient spells that didn't harm the caster.

"Ahhh!"

"Ugh!"

The blast from the explosion sent a heavy shock wave coursing through my body. Raphtalia and Eclair were both sent flying several meters backward from where they had been standing behind me. Luckily they managed to take a defensive stance and soften the blow, but they had still suffered heavy damages. Mere moments into the battle and it was already vividly clear that our enemies were adept fighters.

"Yah!"

"Aiyah! Bound Thrust!"

Meanwhile, Filo and Rishia were helping S'yne fight the large man. Because of the man's large size, Filo was using her filolial queen form.

"Haikuikku!"

Filo's movements sped up and she was about to give the man a swift and powerful kick. Nice! I'd help her out with some support magic.

"Zweite Aura!"

I held my hand out toward Filo and boosted her stats. Her speed skyrocketed.

"Rafu!"

Then Raph-chan backed her up with some illusion magic that made it look like Filo had split into multiple copies of herself. Only one of them was the real Filo, but would he be able to tell which?

"Hrm? Hey!"

The large man called out to the small man.

"Nullify this support magic already!"

"Eeehehe! These twits get a power boost if we do that!"

When we first fought the small man, he'd attempted to nullify the support magic I cast on Raphtalia and ended up nullifying the effects of her curse along with it, after which she'd backed him into a corner. He must have been referring to that.

"Oh? So there's an ability for that? Intriguing! Then how about this?!"

A split second before Filo's kick made contact, some kind of barrier appeared and blocked the kick, sending ripples across the surface of the barrier.

"H . . . huh? That's different than Master's! It felt like kicking the ocean!"

"My attack . . . It should have done some damage. What is that thing?!"

Filo and Rishia both cried out. What was up with that defense? S'yne was trying to attack the man along with her familiars, but none of the attacks were making it through. Were those familiars a redesign of those creepy puppets she'd used at the coliseum? Talk about fancy! The Raph-chan look-alike moved similarly to the real Raph-chan, swiping its tail and scratching at the man, but without success. The Sadeena stuffed doll was swimming around in the air and charging at the man repeatedly.

"Not even knowing what blocked your attacks is just sad. This is Absolute Shield. It absorbed all of your attacks."

"Huh?!"

Damn it! These creeps sure had some convenient abilities. He was protecting himself with a defensive barrier that absorbed attacks.

"You better pay attention!"

The small man held his shamshir out and came charging at me while spinning around in an attack similar to Filo's Spiral Strike. Shit! This guy was an annoying little bugger. I tried to grab him with all my might, but he kept spinning away in an attempt to drill through my defense.

"Eeehe! I guess that's the defensive holy hero for you! Damn you're tough!"

"Now it's my turn," I said.

Like usual, I had my Demon Dragon Shield equipped at the moment. It had a counterattack effect called "demon bullet" that shot magical bullets at the enemy when the shield was attacked. It must have been because the man had made contact with the shield so many times, but a ridiculous number of bullets went flying at him. The barrage of bullets shot out from my shield and straight into the small man while I held him firmly in place.

"Ow! Ow! Ow! Damn! Are you telling me multi-hit attacks work against us?!"

Before I could catch him, the small man skipped the laugh and tried to put some distance between us.

"I won't let you run! Hiya!"

Raphtalia swung her katana in a diagonal downward cut.

"Eeehe! You again! You're a bit of a pest, aren't you?!"

"Don't forget about me!"

Eclair thrust her sword sharply at the small man and the blade grazed his cheek.

"They're weak but they have some skill, it seems. We shouldn't underestimate them. The Shield Hero's defense seems pretty solid, too. Maybe we should call you-know-who to take care of them."

"Eeehehe, that's probably a good idea. Someone with abilities to counter defensive heroes is just what we need."

"You're full of holes!"

Eclair caught the small man off guard and . . . hmm? She launched an attack that was far more powerful than any of her previous attacks and plunged her sword into the man.

"Oh! Not too shabby!"

Eclair's sword stabbed deeply into the small man's shoulder and he grimaced in pain . . . or at least I expected him to, but the part of his shoulder that had been stabbed began to waver like a mirage and the man stepped to the side. Was that part of being able to resurrect? What a pain in the ass!

"Yah!"

Filo launched a kick with all of her might right smack-dab into the large man's face.

"Hmph, not bad. But not enough to beat me."

The man swung his kusarigama in a counterattack, but Filo dodged instinctively.

"Jingle-jangle!"

Filo pulled out the morning star that she'd been keeping hidden in her feathers and flung it at the man. That was Filo's toy. We'd gotten it while we were in Zeltoble! It made pillars of fire wherever it hit. Where the hell had she been hiding that thing?! Did she not think that would be dangerous?! I figured she'd lost it, since I hadn't seen it lately. But apparently it had been hidden in her feathers. That said, I couldn't deny that it was a pretty clever tactic. In fact, it sent a huge wave across the watery surface of the large man's barrier, causing it to burst open.

"Aiyah!"

"Take this!"

Filo launched a sharp kick and Rishia flung her throwing knife through the opening and straight into the man.

"So you managed to break through my shield, huh? You're tougher than I thought. It's been a while since we got to really enjoy ourselves!"

"Right? I said they seemed weak, but I'll take that back."

What was with these guys? It was almost like they felt no pain and were coming at us like it was all a game . . . but that wasn't quite right, either. It was more like they knew this was a real fight to the death, and yet they were still completely relaxed. They were enjoying the fight, and I could tell that they were confident they would win.

"Eeehehehe! Well, things are just slowly going downhill as it is. It looks like we'll need more people to get the job done properly."

"I won't let you es———"

"I'll be damned if I let you kill me again!"

Thread shot out of S'yne's ball as she launched a follow-up attack, and the small man began to cast another spell.

"Alright, in that case . . . I guess I might as well cast support magic on everyone," I said.

It was true that the situation was gradually getting worse. But that didn't mean that our attacks were completely ineffective. Raphtalia had the most powerful attacks among us. If she used her strongest attack along with my Attack Support, we might be able to finish these creeps off.

"Zweite Aura!"

I cast my support magic on Raphtalia. I needed to concentrate so that I could cast multiple times. Our enemies were getting a good idea of what we could do. We'd be at a disadvantage if we didn't finish them off before they figured out exactly what we were capable of. There was a world where people wanted to kill holy heroes to get stronger and they couldn't be negotiated with. It was becoming clear that this was a fact.

"Raphtalia, you know what to do, right? I'm going to use Attack Support."

"Yes."

Raphtalia gave a big nod and sheathed her katana. She was preparing to increase her speed and launch a powerful skill at the enemy.

"Filo and Rishia. Sorry to split you two up, but when I give the signal, each of you launch your most powerful attack at one of the enemies. Eclair, you follow up Raphtalia's attack. S'yne, you know what to do."

"Okaaay!"

"Understood!"

"Got it."

"——y."

With this many people, carefully splitting up our attacks wouldn't be necessary. The enemy had some really annoying abilities, but it wasn't like our attacks were ineffective. I didn't know if they were just impervious to pain or if it was because they were something similar to Glass's spirit race. But their bodies almost seemed to act like smoke at times. I was impressed that S'yne had managed to kill one of them. I didn't know what their weak spots were, but we needed to finish them off either way. I didn't really like the thought of outright killing them, but they were trying to kill us, after all. There was no turning back now.

"Eeehehe! I'll kill you next time for sure, Shield Hero!"

The small man leapt over next to the large man and began to cast a spell.

"That's not going to happen!" shouted Raphtalia.

"Eat this!"

I threw my Attack Support dart and it smashed into the

rippling barrier protecting the large man.

"Jingle-jaaaangle!"

"Hyah!"

I don't know when Filo had retrieved her morning star, but she flung it just as Rishia threw her knife and their attacks pierced the rippling barrier.

"Instant Blade! Mist!"

Raphtalia's katana went straight through the opening toward the small man . . . but just before it hit, the large man reached out to protect him. Blood sprayed out from his arm.

"That's sharp . . . That must be a vassal weapon!"

"Eeehehe, it would seem so. Your coordination is fitting for a hero's party, but—"

"You're not getting away! Four Cross!"

Eclair's short sword flashed brightly as she struck at the enemy. The rippled barrier had begun to regenerate, but her attack pierced through and hit both men! But they must have realized that they wouldn't be able to dodge it, because they both took defensive stances to reduce the impact. Damn . . . This was tough.

"Later! Transloca—"

"Not———pen!"

S'yne used her Skill Seal and thread shot out of her ball and wrapped around the men's bodies.

"Damn, it's interfering with the skill!"

"It's just thread! Rip it off!"

"I know that!"

S'yne glanced over at me. She was trying to tell me to finish them off before they got away.

"Attack Support!"

I threw a second dart. Now someone just had to attack! Nice! Attack Support hit the large man!

"Hiya!"

Raphtalia struck out with her dual blades.

"Triple Thrust!"

Raphtalia's skill generated three successive thrusts instantly, and she had skillfully launched it from both hands. In other words, she'd fired off six rounds straight into the enemy. That is, if things went our way.

"Hmph!"

The large man swung his kusarigama adeptly and formed a large X-shape with the chains while taking a defensive stance. Raphtalia's attack was thwarted as it crashed into the chains and sparks flew everywhere.

"Harumph!"

S'yne's thread snapped with a loud pop.

"Eeehe, I guess we were just a little bit too hasty. Translocating Light!"

As soon as the small man uttered the words, the two men disappeared instantly.

"Shit! They got away!"

Damn it! That was not how I wanted things to end! Not to mention, this was not where I wanted to run into them again!

"What was that? Who were those men?" asked Eclair.

"Judging from what S'yne told us and what those creeps said, they're basically assassins from another world. On top of that, they have ill-willed intentions to destroy this world."

There were benefits to destroying worlds. Glass and the others hadn't actually succeeded, so they probably didn't know that. Destroying a world could give someone powers that included the ability to resurrect . . . It was like the worlds were practically being coerced into fighting with each other.

"It's a clash between worlds separate from the waves. Basically, the heroes from different worlds can kill each other, and those creeps want to prove that they're the strongest."

What a ridiculously lame excuse. Not to mention, they weren't even vassal weapon holders or holy heroes, so it was like my companions . . . it would have been like Filo and Rishia sneaking into another world to fight, for instance. Considering how strong those creeps were, if their boss—holy heroes couldn't invade other worlds, so it would probably have to be a vassal weapon holder—showed up, what then? There was no doubt someone like that would probably be strong enough to kill us.

"In any case, we can't have Ren running around out there

with people like that roaming around. We have to get him somewhere safe."

I was treating everyone's wounds while I spoke.

"I'd heard about the truth behind the phenomenon of the waves, but to think there were enemies like that, as well . . ." said Eclair.

"It's hard to wrap your head around. On top of that, they can return from the dead, even if we do kill them."

"They almost seemed to be fooling around, but they were incredibly strong. And now you're telling me they're immortal, too? Mr. Iwatani, we need to formulate a strategy quickly. We must figure out how they're returning from the dead."

"I know that. But we need to take care of the other heroes first."

"He's right. We need to get the other three holy heroes somewhere safe as soon as possible."

I had to agree with Raphtalia.

"They were super-duper strong. But I don't think they had leveled up much yet," said Filo.

She might have been right. Judging from past experience, I had a feeling they had probably crossed over to this world and been in the middle of leveling up when they confronted us. So it was either smoke them out in a hurry, figure out how their resurrections worked, and finish them off. Or get the heroes to safety first . . . It was a hard decision. It certainly seemed like the longer we waited, the more we'd be at a disadvantage.

Raphtalia, Filo, and I had reduced stats at the moment because of the curse, and we were still a long way from complete recovery. S'yne wasn't all that strong, and Eclair had learned the Hengen Muso style, but I really didn't know how much potential she had. Rishia was still developing. It was hard to say before we got her to level 100, but I had big expectations for her.

Even if we figured out how the enemy's resurrection abilities worked and came up with a plan to kill them for good, it was unclear if we'd actually be able to pull it off. Either way, securing the heroes had to be the priority. I wouldn't have to worry so much if we got them as strong as I was. And if we could get the seven star heroes together, too, we'd be all set.

"Mr. Naofumi."

"Oh hey, Atla."

Atla and Fohl approached, having decided that it was now safe.

"I . . . I've become painfully aware of just how weak I am. I want to get stronger."

"You don't need to worry about that kind of thing, Atla! Leave the fighting to me!" Fohl interjected.

"Brother, you need to be more realistic."

Atla furrowed her brow and gave Fohl a stern look, like she was about to lecture him.

"We are far too weak to fight at Mr. Naofumi's side in our current condition. You say I don't need to fight, but right now you're nothing but a hindrance to Mr. Naofumi. You need to think about how you're going to get stronger."

"A . . . Atla?! Ugh . . . You're saying I need to be even stronger?!"

Being told off by Atla seemed to have gotten Fohl fired up. The hakuko were considered to be superior, even among the demi-humans, and had the potential to become incredibly strong. Considering what was coming, I couldn't deny that I wanted to see them develop quickly.

"Mr. Iwatani, I'll do my best to be useful, as well. There is no way I'm going to let someone like that destroy our world!"

"Good, that's the spirit. Anyway, our task for the time being is to get Ren to safety fast. S'yne, go see if you can lure Ren out, just like we originally—"

And then it happened, just as I was giving the order. I felt something rush by at incredible speed. Sheesh . . . It was just one problem after another and it was starting to piss me off.

Chapter Seventeen: Temptation

"What is it this time?!"

Had our enemies returned already? Or was it Ren?

"Ugh . . . What was that?"

Raphtalia was holding her head and shaking it while looking all around.

"Hmm? I have a weird feeling in my tummy!"

Filo must have sensed it, too.

"Ugh . . ."

It had felt like some kind of shock wave, but we hadn't seemed to take any real damage. But a few of the others were reacting strangely.

"Atla!"

"Mr. Naofumi! Let go of me, Brother! Let go!"

"Atla! Atla! Atla!"

"Fehhhhhh?!"

"I . . . I don't know what happened, but . . . Ugh, what is this feeling?"

I turned around to see everyone acting really odd. Umm . . . I was just going to ignore the hakuko siblings. Rescuing Fohl would be a hassle, and rescuing Atla would probably be a hassle, too. As for myself . . . I wasn't really sure. Rishia and Eclair didn't seem to be affected all that much. They were squirming around a bit, but that was about it. What had happened? There was too little to go off of to even begin to know how to respond.

"Master . . . huuu . . . huuu . . ."

Filo was, uhh . . . She was staring at me with bloodshot eyes. I wasn't sure if I should run. Judging from the way Fohl and Filo were reacting, it must have been some kind of status effect.

"Rafu!"

Raph-chan smacked Filo on the cheek. Filo blinked a few times and then returned to her normal self.

"Huh? What happened?" she asked.

"Rafu!"

Raph-chan jumped up onto Filo's head and started doing something. I'm sure she was creating some kind of protective barrier or something. Raph-chan sure had some convenient abilities.

"————over there."

S'yne was pointing her finger.

"What is it?"

"You should probably go look for yourself."

Just then, a cloud of dust shot up from in that direction.

"Mr. Iwatani!"

"Mr. Naofumi!"

"Yeah, I guess we better go see what's going on."

I had no idea what was happening, but we dashed out of the hideout to go find out.

"Brother! Let go of me!"

"Atla!"

Umm . . . yeah, I'd just leave them to their own thing. Considering their levels, it was probably too dangerous for them, whatever it was. If it was those men, they were after the lives of the heroes, so the siblings would be safer if they weren't near me.

"Aiyaaaah! Yah, I say! You're weak! Too weak!"

"D . . . damn it!"

We arrived and there before our eyes was—

"Motoyasu?!"

"Oh! Father! I shan't let you down!"

I had a feeling Motoyasu was sounding even stranger than before. He was pushing Ren's sword back with his spear while waving at me with a big toothy smile. Damn, he was annoying. Who the hell was he calling "father"? And who waves in the middle of a fight?!

"Uhh . . . what are you doing?"

"You said you wanted to capture Ren, Father! So I lured him out and made it so that he can't run!"

"Mr. Naofumi! I think perhaps it was the Spear Hero that was hiding outside of the bandit hideout earlier . . ." Raphtalia suggested.

"You're probably right."

So he heard us talking about capturing Ren and went out ahead of us to try to give us a hand without even asking! And just as we missed him, our new enemies showed up at the hideout. But anyway, did Motoyasu not realize we were trying to capture him, too?! This was all starting to make my head hurt.

"Transport Sword!"

Shit! Ren had noticed us and was trying to run!

". . ."

Ren and I stood there staring at each other silently. But his skill must have failed to activate, because nothing happened. Could it be that the strange shock wave from earlier was interfering with his skill?

"Ha! Ha! Ha! You won't be able to escape from the power of my Temptation!"

It must have been Motoyasu's doing, after all. But . . . Motoyasu's spear seemed to have some kind of black mosaic-like design on it now. Was I seeing things? Judging from the skill name—and the way Fohl was responding earlier—it must have generated a field that triggered some kind of allurement type of effect. That fit Motoyasu perfectly.

Huh? What was that? Motoyasu was suddenly looking really handsome. He was surrounded by brightly glittering strands of gold on a background of pink. Oh lordy . . . what a hunk . . . I'd be happy to bend over for a man that handsome . . .

"On a cold day in hell!"

I shook my head vigorously and pulled myself back together. That was close. I'd been on the verge of passing a point of no return. This field produced a truly formidable status effect.

"Is everyone okay?!" I asked.

"Y . . . yeah . . ."

Raphtalia didn't seem to be affected. Her resistances to illusion-type magic and skills were high, so she had probably been able to block the allurement effect, too. That would have been really depressing if Raphtalia had been attracted to Motoyasu, even if it was because of a status effect. Thank goodness for her illusion resistance. I guess being a racoon-type made her as tricky as a tanuki. Hooray for racoons!

"Uh . . . huh . . ."

I couldn't help but wonder about Eclair's response. I wanted to believe she was fine, though.

"I . . . I'm in love with Mr. Itsuki! I can't!"

Rishia was acting a bit strange. It seemed like the allurement skill was forcing her to decide between Itsuki and Motoyasu.

"I'm fiiiine!"

"Rafu!"

Filo was only fine because Raph-chan had been sitting on her shoulder. She must have already forgotten that she was about to come at me with bloodshot eyes just a few moments earlier. As for S'yne . . .

"————fine."

She seemed fine. I wasn't really sure how to feel about this field that triggered a status effect, but Motoyasu had created an opportunity for us and passing that up would be a waste.

"Ahem . . . So anyway, Ren. It looks like your game of hide and seek is over."

I wasn't really sure how to respond, but Ren not being able to escape was a good thing. I'd just have to let the whole freaky skill thing slide, since it seemed like Motoyasu was genuinely trying to help.

"Filo-tan!"

"Nooo!"

Filo looked at Motoyasu and began inching backward away from him before turning and fleeing.

"Filo! Stop! Where are you going?!" Raphtalia called out.

"Rafuuuu!"

"Hey! Leave Raph-chan behind!" I shouted.

Raph-chan was still sitting on Filo's shoulder . . . What the hell? Our numbers were dwindling fast. Right now, I had Raphtalia, Eclair, Rishia, and S'yne with me. Capturing both Ren and Motoyasu at the same time with this lineup was . . . still possible, maybe?

"Your time has come to pay the piper, Ren!"

"Pay the piper? That's my line!"

They'd already started arguing without me, damn it. Well, it looked like Motoyasu was cooperating, anyway, so that should make capturing Ren a lot easier. Ren was still refusing to face reality, like always.

"Looks like I'm surrounded by a bunch of weaklings who have to gang up on someone to do anything."

"Say whatever you want, you friendless loser. Don't think I've forgotten about before."

Ren pissed me off, so I insulted him back.

"I'm not going to lose to a bunch of cowards that have to gang up to fight one person!"

"Concealing yourself and using a finishing move on someone who doesn't even have attack capabilities isn't being a coward?"

"It's your fault for not being able to detect me."

"Like hell. I did detect you, thanks to my companion. Yeah, I have companions, unlike you, loser."

Ren had gone off the deep end. Everything he did was right and everything anyone else did was wrong. He was talking and behaving strangely, almost as if his unconscious mind had risen to the surface or something. He was acting kind of like . . . No, he was acting *exactly* like one of those people in online games that was completely obsessed with being the absolute strongest player. Honestly, I wanted to rub it in his face that having no friends was the whole reason he was a failure, but it wasn't like he'd actually listen.

"Prepare yourself!"

"Listen to—"

Before I could finish my sentence, Ren thrust Motoyasu away and came charging at me.

"Ah! You wait, I say!"

I'd just block his attack for now. Then I could give Raphtalia and Eclair the order to attack. The two of them seemed to understand, because they backed down. S'yne was using me as a shield, too. Rishia was . . . still shaken up, damn it. Prepare to fight already! Jeez. I couldn't help but be a bit worried, but it looked like we would be able to coordinate well enough.

Ren raised his sword and rushed at me . . . No, wait. He suddenly switched his target to Rishia and rushed at her. Oh, come on! Just like I thought, Ren wasn't right in the head. He lacked coherence. Or maybe direction was more accurate.

"Feh?!"

Rishia squealed when Ren suddenly changed the direction of his attack. If I had to guess, the bastard was going after the person here that looked the weakest. Taking out the weak ones first was a basic rule of warfare, but what the hell happened to "fair and square"? The thing is, Ren had made a big mistake. This wasn't the same Rishia he knew.

"Hi-yaaahhhhhh!"

Ren howled as he swung his sword down at Rishia.

"Fehhhhh!"

But Rishia instantly shifted into a crouching position, and before I knew it she had launched her throwing knife at a nearby tree and then used the attached rope to swiftly pull herself out of Ren's reach. When pulling herself away, she had simultaneously launched four or five iron spike things in Ren's direction.

"You surprised me!" she said.

"No, you surprised me," I replied.

Talk about a speedy escape. What the hell was that ninja evasion? Her reaction had basically been instantaneous. It's like she was fighting on a completely different level than the rest of us. But no, I could see her moves, so it wasn't like I wouldn't be able to defend against them.

"Rishia, you really are something."

Right? With moves that flashy, of course even Raphtalia would be impressed. And where had she been hiding those iron spikes in the first place? That was probably some kind of Hengen Muso concealed weapon or something.

"Grr . . ."

The spikes hadn't hit him, but Ren groaned with irritation when things didn't go his way.

"You had best not forget about me!" shouted Motoyasu.

"I'd really rather I did, though," I retorted.

I couldn't let Motoyasu set the pace. I really wished he would just stand down, actually. I had several things I wanted to ask Ren about right now while he couldn't run. Like who was behind . . . behind Ren . . . No! I wasn't talking about Motoyasu!

"Hey! Is Witch not going to come help you?"

". . ."

Ren grimaced when I asked about Witch, and the sinister power emanating from his sword intensified.

"It looks like you said the wrong thing, Mr. Iwatani," Eclair observed.

Hmm . . . I guess asking the wrong questions would end up working against us. That would make getting any information out of him tough. I wanted to find out where that skank was off hiding, if nothing else.

"Anyway, Ren, I'm not your enemy. Nothing good can come from taking orders from that bitch and playing bandit chief—"

"Rahhhhh!"

Before I could finish, Ren went into a rage and swung his sword high into the air as he came rushing at me.

"You're nothing but a demon pretending to be a hero! I shall bring you to justice!"

This guy was completely off in his own world. He obviously didn't realize it was him that was backed into a corner.

"Power within me! Awaken! It is in battle that I become stronger!"

Stop it! It hurts! I felt a chill run down my spine. He was taking the fantasy world geek performance to the next level.

"Perish!" shouted Motoyasu.

"Don't kill him!"

Motoyasu raised his spear in preparation to finish Ren off, but I stopped him. Ren's sword smashed into my shield with a loud clang. Hmm . . . Just like I expected, his attack wasn't very powerful. I probably could have grabbed his sword with my bare hands. Should I try it? Maybe he would surrender if he saw just how big the gap between us was.

"I will become strongest of them all! Yes! There is no limit to my desire! I shall awaken new strength in this very moment and defeat you! There is no limit to my desire! My desire feeds my rise to the top! I will awaken new power! I will triumph! I will get the best equipment, all of the money, and all of the power! I will become the strongest across all worlds! I shall be the envy of all worlds!"

Umm . . . going a bit bananas, aren't we, Ren? He kept repeating the same thing. Desire this and desire that. It was annoying. Awaken power? He'd already awakened as the Sword Hero . . . I guess being consumed by a curse would make someone that bonkers. He'd completely gone off the deep end.

Thanks to those other two we fought earlier, the whole thing about becoming the strongest across all worlds really hit a nerve. But . . . I had a feeling I knew which curse Ren had been consumed by.

Greed.

But something seemed off. It felt so miserably trivial for greed. I didn't know if I could actually call that greed. Greed was supposed to be insatiable desire, right? Limitless desire that made someone want anything and everything. But Ren was just focused on becoming stronger. Of course, I wasn't trying to say that wasn't desire. But people that were truly driven by greed were far more despicable, and they wanted to have everything.

But in the end, all Ren wanted was strength . . . Ah, so that was it. I finally understood why. If I had to spell it out, I'd say it was the *process* that he was chasing. With greed, you desire something, and so you obtain it. Once you have it, you want something else, and so you obtain that, too. That's the basic premise. But with Ren, his objective was the *act* of getting stronger. It wasn't that he wanted to get stronger because he wanted some *thing*. The process and the result had swapped places.

It made all the more sense having experienced something similar myself. Back when I was spending a lot of time peddling wares, I'd originally set out to make money so that we could get better equipment. But before I knew it, my goal had become the act of making money itself.

So I guess even something as petty as that could unlock a curse series. But that was also why he wouldn't be able to win against my wrath. No matter how much stronger his curse grew, that pathetic greed of his could never overcome my wrath. It was transient, two-bit greed.

His weapon was part of a curse series. I was confident of that much. Which meant there had to be a reason for the curse to trigger. For me, Witch interfering with my duel against Motoyasu is what sparked it. The curse series hadn't actually triggered then, but later on when I thought Filo had died during our fight with the dragon zombie, the Shield of Rage first appeared.

The weapon that Motoyasu was using looked like part of a curse series, too. Hmm . . . Maybe the curse series were something that triggered when a legendary weapon user experienced extreme psychological stress or something. Motoyasu and I had both been in really bad situations. Our psychological states had been bad enough that suicide wouldn't have been unthinkable. But the heroes couldn't be allowed to die in this world. If the heroes died, it could mean the destruction of the world itself. Suicide was unacceptable.

I think I'd hit the nail on the head. Put simply, the curse series was a defense mechanism that manifested when a hero was suffering from some psychological issue. Still . . . Even if that were true, what was it that had driven Ren this far? At the very least, he had still been calm enough to have a civilized conversation when we'd met before at the tavern. Even if he had been making excuses like blaming his companions' deaths on their own weakness.

"I am the strongest hero! I am the one who will save the world!"

Ren's words pissed me off, interrupting my thoughts. All the bastard cared about was something so insignificant! He needed to get a grip! I didn't care about what had caused the curse anymore. I just wanted to shut him up.

"Save the world? Then go save it, you goddamned fool! Do you really think you're going to save the world by running around playing bandit chief here?!"

The strongest? Save the world? By running around here playing bandit chief and ambushing anyone he didn't like, going on and on about who won or lost? If he could save this rotten world by doing that, then he was welcome to keep it up! But that wasn't going to save the world, and it wasn't going to stop the waves.

"I'm tired of listening to you drivel on about being the strongest! I don't have time to be dealing with an insignificant brat trying to be king of the mountain out in the middle of nowhere!"

"Wait! This isn't over! Let's see if you can withstand my maximum power!"

Ren's sword transformed again. Had it evolved to the next stage? My Shield of Rage had transformed into the Shield of Wrath. It was safe to say that Ren's current situation was similar to the one I had been in when that happened. In that case, it was highly possible that Ren's sword had just transformed into a superior version of itself.

"Yes! A new skill just came to me! Maneater! Shooting Star Sword!"

He'd used that on me last time we fought! He was acting like he'd just come up with a skill that he'd been using all along. Using the same skill repeatedly wasn't going to work even in the most cliché of manga. Seriously, what the hell?

"*Let this foolish sinner pay for his transgressions with his being crushed in the name of a god! Take my riches and unleash a godly assault upon him!*"

"Gold Rebellion!"

Ren raised his sword up to the heavens and golden treasures began amassing from out of nowhere to form a human image in the sky. It was a sinister and unbelievably gaudy sculpture made out of gold. Taking the attack head-on would probably leave a scratch, but I had my companions with me, and I was guessing that not all of them would be able to avoid it. Goddammit. I guess that meant I had to eat this lame-ass attack. That would make anyone want to sigh.

What happened to Maneater Shooting Star Sword, anyway? This was obviously a completely different skill. His tricks were becoming more and more cowardly. Could this still be called greed for victory? That skill . . . I'm guessing it was the equivalent of my Blood Sacrifice. There would most likely be consequences for using it. Ah, so that must have been why Ren's equipment was so shabby.

"Eat this!" he shouted.

"Back up, everyone!" I yelled.

"O . . . okay!"

"Will you be okay, Mr. Naofumi? Right now your stats are . . ."

"We don't have time to get away."

Maybe we could have run if one of us could fly or something. It would have been nice if Filo could still fly like when we were in Kizuna's world. She was big enough by the time we'd left that I probably could have ridden her. I was imagining it as the idol came crashing into me. It sent a heavy shock wave reverberating through my body that felt like it might dislodge an organ. Damn . . . Being weakened by the curse made me feel that one a bit, after all.

"Raphtalia!"

"Understood!"

Raphtalia sheathed her katana and took a quick-draw stance before springing toward the statue that I was holding off.

"Instant Blade! Mist!"

An exquisitely clean whishing sound filled the air as Raphtalia drew her katana. She then landed firmly on the ground and returned her katana to its sheath. A loud crash rang out and a fissure tracing the path her blade had traveled began to open on the surface of the statue before it crumbled away and disappeared.

Sheesh . . . I really wished this guy would come to his senses.

"Mr. Iwatani . . ."

"Yeah, I know. I may be tough, but even I have my limits."

If Eclair and the others had been able to get away, then it would have made sense to just dodge an attack like that. Even so, this was just part of the job. As the number of people involved grew, our ability to respond swiftly would continue to decrease. I wanted us to be able to respond just a bit more quickly. Looking at it from a different perspective, though, you could take it as a sign that our military power was increasing, like in Kizuna's case.

I guess I should be focusing on Ren right now.

"Grr . . . It's not over . . . I can still become stronger . . . I have to give more . . . I have to win, even if it means sacrificing everything!"

"Get a hold of yourself!"

Intent on cutting me down, Ren raised his sword and struck from overhead, and thrust at my chest, and made a diagonal downward cut . . . and just kept slashing away using all sorts of attacks. I evaded, blocked, and parried, and not a single one connected.

I didn't have time for this. He would trust some bitch that told him what he wanted to hear, but he wouldn't trust me.

And now he was in a place like this, swinging around a cursed weapon and going on about getting stronger. It had been the same with the Spirit Tortoise. It was the same with everything. It was all a game to him! He gave up on the Hengen Muso training because it was boring. He didn't even try to believe what I told him about sharing power-up methods.

I was all out of patience. Maybe it would be best to just cut off his limbs and keep him locked up somewhere, so that he didn't end up getting killed. It would only cause problems if he died, after all.

"Shall I off him, then?"

"Didn't I say not to kill him?!"

Motoyasu was really itching to kill Ren. Or at least that's the way he was making it sound. Why was he pretending to be on our side, anyway?

"S'yne, you keep Ren from being able to use any skills. The rest of us will incapacitate him and then we can take him with us. And if he still won't cooperate after all of that . . ."

I stopped in the middle of my sentence, but everyone seemed to understand what I wanted to say.

"I guess it might be unavoidable, after all."

Raphtalia nodded regretfully.

"No, please. Wait a moment."

A single person seemed to take exception to my suggestion.

"Mr. Iwatani . . . Please allow me to duel the Sword Hero," Eclair pleaded.

"Why?"

"It's something that occurred to me when we fought before. I have a feeling that we may be able to use swordsmanship as a means to get through to the Sword Hero."

"You realize only some musclebrain who lives and breathes training would say something like that, right?"

"I do. Regardless, my patience is running thin, too. I'd like to give the selfish Sword Hero a good shaking. Let me fight him one on one."

"At least that excuse is a little better. I'm going to intervene if things start to look dangerous, though. You good with that?"

That might not agree with Eclair's knightly ideals, but she was a valuable military asset . . . It didn't sound right coming out of my mouth, but she was a valuable companion that I couldn't afford to lose. I wasn't going to be naïve and say I wasn't prepared to accept any sacrifices in the fight for this world's peace. But at the very least, her life was not one I could afford to sacrifice for something as stupid as this. Plus, even if she did have some skill, I didn't really feel comfortable pitting Eclair against a hero.

"I'm going to cast my support magic on you to make up for the fact that he has a legendary weapon. I'm not going to approve of the duel unless you're okay with that. It would be unfair, otherwise."

"That's fine. I thank you for your consideration in making things as fair as possible."

I cast Zweite Aura on Eclair. If Sadeena were here, we could cast Descent of the Thunder God on her, but whatever. This was as good as I could do in these circumstances. After all . . . casting Sacrifice Aura on her would surely be going too far.

Once my support magic took effect, Eclair turned to Ren and readied her short sword! Ren was already preparing to chase after Rishia, but Eclair stepped in front of him and blocked his path.

"Mr. Amaki the Sword Hero! This will be the second time that we cross blades."

She swiftly pointed the tip of her short sword at Ren.

"If you wish to fight Mr. Iwatani or Mr. Kitamura the Spear Hero, then you must defeat me first!"

"Hmph! It doesn't matter who you are—you're no match for me!"

"Our fight was interrupted last time, so let's finish it here! Sword Hero! My name is Eclair Seaetto, and with this sword presented to me by the queen, I shall cure you of your selfish ways!"

Eclair finished her declaration and the duel began.

Chapter Eighteen: Flash

The two clashed, and the rest of us backed away to watch the duel. Motoyasu looked like he was just waiting for a chance to stab Ren to death from behind.

"Don't interfere, Motoyasu."

"As you wish!"

He was being helpful for the time being, but . . . it seemed like I still needed to set him straight eventually. He did seem to be listening to me, which was more than I could say about Ren, but he had a really bad habit of running away.

Eclair's sharp thrust nailed Ren right in the shoulder. It hadn't actually pierced his skin, but that was a point for her.

"Hmph, is that all you've got? You weren't this sluggish last time."

Upon hearing Eclair's provocation, Ren's eyes opened wide and he squeezed his hands tightly around the grip of his sword.

"I . . . will not lose. I . . . am the strongest and . . . to become stronger . . . I will . . . gain all and . . . devour . . . all!"

Ren's speech became fragmented and his sword—what had been a sinister, single-handed sword—transformed into a soot-black long sword. On top of that, the black aura that it had already been emitting intensified.

Would Eclair really be okay? That sword . . . I wouldn't have been surprised if its stats had risen enough to overcome my defense now. Looking more closely, I noticed that there were lots of little decorations on the sword. There was a dog-looking animal on the guard . . . a fox, maybe. I could see something that looked like a pig on the hilt, too.

But Ren's speech had gotten even stranger when the sword transformed. Gain all and . . . *devour* all? If he'd meant "devour" in the literal sense, then it was possible that he'd awakened the curse of gluttony, too.

"I . . . will become the strongest! Even now . . . in this very moment, I am evolving and . . . I will harness . . . an unfathomable amount of strength . . . and defeat you all . . . and devour the experience!"

Ren swung the long sword up into the air and dashed forward. His movements were awkward, but they were also quite fast.

"Raahhhhh!"

Ren began swinging the long sword around furiously. There was absolutely no rhyme or reason to his attacks. Eclair was crouching, bending, and maneuvering her body to dodge all of the attacks.

"Your swordsmanship is dull and simplistic. No matter how much your abilities increase, with swordsmanship like that you wouldn't be able to hit me, even if I hadn't improved a single bit since our last encounter!"

Oh, nice! She was right. His movement was quick, but it was also haphazard. I guess if someone had been swinging a sword around as long as Eclair, they would be able to dodge that much. I had a feeling the situation was similar to when Raphtalia and Sadeena had fought. Sadeena had completely read all of Raphtalia's attacks and dodged every one by a hair's breadth. It was an incredible feat. So now Eclair had become strong enough to do the same thing to Ren.

"Grr . . . Stop missing! Each of my attacks should be strong enough to destroy anything it touches!"

Stat and ability-wise, Ren was most likely well ahead of Eclair. The reason he still couldn't hit her was probably due to a vast difference in the levels of their swordsmanship.

"Why?! Why am I missing?!"

"There's no way you could hit me. Not with that languid blade. With haphazard attacks like that, it's as if you're not even trying to hit me."

"Shut uuuuuppp!"

I wondered how Raphtalia or Filo would dodge if it were one of them fighting him. They probably wouldn't dodge by a hair's breadth like that. They'd probably just use pure speed. It was probably because she had always fought by my side, but Raphtalia tended to fight really aggressively. I guess that only made sense, though. In all of our battles, her job had been to try to land the most fearsome attack possible while using me as a shield instead of dodging. Perhaps it was time for us to undergo some serious training, too.

To get a better idea of Eclair's skill, I decided to ask her fellow Hengen Muso pupil Rishia what she thought.

"Hey, Rishia. What do you think so far?"

"Fehh? Umm, the Sword Hero's attacks are all rather monotonous. I'm sure anyone experienced at combat would be able to dodge them."

"Hmm . . ."

I guess so. Ren was fast, but even I would probably be able to dodge those attacks. That's how repetitive and tedious his attacks were as he swung his sword around. For the most part, they were either cuts straight down or slices to the side. Every now and then he would make a right-angle turn or something, but it was always completely obvious when he was going to change his path.

Technique-wise, L'Arc and Glass were probably far more advanced. Compared to them, these attacks of Ren's were like a child's sword-play. The strength gained from a curse was basically a stat boost. I had a feeling Ren had actually fought smarter and been stronger before he had been consumed by the curse.

"Alright, I guess that's all you have to show me. In that case, now it's my turn."

"Grr . . . I'm not finished! My victory will be one-sided!"

What a line. He was saying it was all about his attacks, and the opponent shouldn't even get to counterattack. Oh yeah, Ren had mentioned that shielders had died out in the VRMMO he used to play. Maybe that's why he was so caught up on defeating his enemies before they could counterattack. He'd also said something about expecting them to evade, though. It didn't add up.

Since even the earliest online games, it was usually in PVP where the existence of defensive classes really made a difference. It seemed to me like Motoyasu, Ren, and Itsuki were all total noobs when it came to fighting against other people. Of course, things probably worked just like they said in their own games. But that's not how it worked in this world. That much, I was sure of.

"Eat this!"

Ren swung his sword down hard and recklessly. The instant the tip of his blade touched the ground, the earth shook and split open. Oh man, so it was one of those earth-splitting attacks. It seemed pretty powerful.

"You're full of holes!"

Aiming for Ren's shoulder, Eclair unleashed a sharp jab just like the last time they had fought. With a dull thud, her jab bounced off of Ren's shoulder, ineffective. It was clear that Ren's defense had risen even higher than it was several moments ago.

"Mu-ha-ha! The sword that I am currently using features the highest level of automatic self-repair. Your measly attacks are meaningless. Quietly accept your defeat!"

Ren's eyes twinkled as he laughed sinisterly. I guess he was laughing because he'd realized that Eclair lacked a decisive blow. But what was up with the explanatory narrative? Actually, the armor I'd been wearing before had automatic self-repair functionality, too.

"Hmm . . . So he's not as tough as Mr. Iwatani, but he rejuvenates as soon as I cut him. That makes things difficult."

Eclair mumbled while looking at the tip of her sword. She must have still been pretty relaxed, because there wasn't a single bead of sweat on her brow.

"Quietly accept defeat and give me my experience points! Maneater! Shooting Star Sword!"

That skill again! I guess it's because it was a long sword now, but the cloud of black stars dispersed over an even larger area. Eclair's appearance began to . . . blur as she went about dodging every single one.

"That . . . that's the Hengen Muso evasive form Shimmer!" Rishia cried out.

Umm, yeah. Rishia had the fantasy world geek thing down pat, too.

"Rishia, stop playing the narrator character. 'What?! It was?!' Is that what I'm supposed to say? Because you know I have no idea what you're talking about."

"Well . . . You're right about that much. But seeing Rishia and Eclair fight makes me think we need to do some training, too," Raphtalia said.

Raphtalia was absolutely right. I was starting to feel like I was lagging behind those two, from a technique perspective. And it seemed like it was only recently that they had just suddenly pulled ahead, too.

"Yeah . . . I have a feeling we need to get serious about learning this stuff."

If it meant being able to move like that, it probably wouldn't be a bad idea to prioritize learning the style. The heroes' weapons made mastering it more difficult, apparently. But it couldn't hurt to learn how anyway. Maybe we should go hole up deep in the mountains for a while. For the sake of being able to survive what was coming.

"I'm not finished! Chain Bind!"

"Hmph!"

The chains that Ren had called forth went flying toward Eclair, but she swung her sword and they shattered into pieces.

"What?!"

"Just as I thought. Even strong chains or tough defenses shatter easily if you take advantage of their weak point."

"I'm not finished! Try my finishing move on for size! Hide Sword!"

Ren began to waver and then disappeared. That idiot. He just kept using the same attacks. What happened to Hundred Swords? Or Thunder Sword? It didn't matter how many attacks he had. If he wasn't going to put some thought into how he was using them, he wouldn't be able to beat Eclair.

"Parlor tricks. When Raphtalia disappears in front of me I can't detect her life force."

Eclair swiped her sword to the side. That's all it took for Ren's concealment skill to be canceled out, revealing him once again. Nice one. That was pretty impressive.

"Is she telling the truth?" I asked Raphtalia.

"What do you expect? I specialize in that kind of magic."

I guess that would be depressing if Ren had outdone her specialty magic. I'm sure I would have been annoyed if he'd outdone my defense.

"Now then, how about you try another one of mine."

Eclair crouched down low before springing toward Ren, thrusting her sword at him. Ren didn't feel it necessary to defend. No, he suddenly jumped backward away from Eclair.

"That won't work."

Eclair moved even faster than Ren could retreat and leapt right up against him.

"Four Cross!"

Her short sword flashed brightly as its path traced the form of a cross. It was one of those magic sword techniques. Those were in a category separate from both skills and magic. Eclair had used that on our enemies earlier, too.

"Ugh . . ."

Eclair's attack was a direct hit. I could see some kind of light cut through Ren's body. But in the same instant he took damage, the wound began to close. Ren stood there grinning like nothing had happened.

"To think that one of your attacks could actually touch me. Not too shabby. I guess you're worthy of seeing what it looks like when I start to get serious."

What the hell was he saying? That bastard had been having the struggle of his life, and now he was saying that it had all just been an act? Get a grip! If we'd been serious, I'm pretty sure defeating him would have been easy as pie.

And anyway, what happened to the aftereffects of the curse series skills? Was he not feeling the effects of the curse? He seemed to be moving around normally. I wanted to make a witty remark about it, but I kept my mouth shut. I figured he'd just say something like "no curse can touch me!" or "curses can only make me stronger!"

"Hogwash! Nothing is more insulting than holding back against an opponent in actual warfare! Stop pretending like you're not struggling, you fool!"

Oh man, he went and made Eclair mad again. These two were as incompatible as it got. Even so, Eclair had seen right through Ren's act. He was fast, but that's all he was. Eclair could read his every move. If that was the case, being fast was pointless.

That said, Eclair's attacks lacked power, too. Even if she'd mastered the old lady's defense rating attacks, they wouldn't be very useful unless the opponent had an extremely high defense, like I did. I'm sure her swordsmanship was superb, but being pitted against a hero consumed by a curse put the odds against her.

Those defense rating attacks didn't really make sense in the first place. It was almost as if they were made to be used against the Shield Hero. I didn't know where the Hengen Muso style had originated, but if it was Melromarc, then it was possible that hostility toward certain countries drove them to develop the technique for exactly that purpose.

"My attacks will devour all. Yes, that includes your experience points!"

"It doesn't matter how strong your attacks are—if they can't hit me, they're pointless!"

The fight had reached a stalemate. Ren couldn't land any attacks, and Eclair's attacks were ineffective. A long, drawn-out battle would put Eclair at more of a disadvantage. Ren's attacks weren't landing, but that didn't mean they weren't powerful. Judging by the way things were now, there was a high probability Ren would win this fight.

"What do you want to do, Eclair? If this continues, things are just going to slowly go downhill until you lose, don't you think?"

"Mr. Iwatani, give me a little more time! I've almost reached through to the Sword Hero's heart."

Heart, huh? Maybe she was dealing with something I couldn't understand, since I could only use a shield. I mulled over it as Eclair asked Ren a question.

"Tell me, Sword Hero. What is your objective? Mr. Iwatani says he intends to return to his own world."

"Leave me out of it!"

Ren was obsessed with being the strongest, so she was just going to make him come after me! Sheesh . . . Oh? Ren didn't seem to know how to respond. Hmm . . . Maybe this really was the key to getting through to him.

"I . . . I . . ."

"I'm asking what your objective is. What do you hope to accomplish by becoming stronger?!"

Oh, come on. Asking him a question like that was only going to get an asinine response. You could see the crazy in Ren's eyes. That guy wasn't thinking straight, or even at all.

"I have to become the strongest or I won't be able to bear it! I will become the strongest across all worlds, all times, and all dimensions! This is my greed! This is my gluttony that seeks and devours all experience points!"

Ren finished his spiel and the pitch-black aura emanating from his body intensified. I could tell he was about to use some skill.

"You can help make me stronger! Give me my experience points!"

"Let this foolish sinner pay for her transgressions with her being preyed upon in the name of a god! Accept as an offering the earth's nourishment I have received—unleash its putrefaction upon her and let her be devoured!"

"Strong Decline!"

Ren clenched his fist tightly. His whole body began to glow like a firefly and then the light seeped away into the ground and disappeared. The ground began to shake and then suddenly split open beneath Eclair's feet. Ah, so this must have been some kind of evolution of that other attack that had caused a fissure earlier. The incantation had been similar to the one I used for Blood Sacrifice. Fangs grew up out of the fractures and were attempting to bite into Eclair.

"Your attack is full of holes! If this were Mr. Iwatani's attack, I wouldn't be able to avoid it!"

"Stop comparing him to me! You're going to make Ren come after me!"

"Mr. Naofumi, just be quiet and watch for a moment," Raphtalia whispered.

"But . . ."

"It's going to be fine. I have a feeling this will work. Have some faith in Eclair."

Did it really look like it would be fine? I guess it was just one of those things you had to be a martial artist to understand. But if Raphtalia thought it would be fine, then I'd trust her.

Eclair had successfully dodged Ren's attack, by the way. It looked like it was pretty much the exact same attack as Blood Sacrifice. No, wait, I guess it was different after all. Some gray, foul-smelling substance started spraying up out of the ground like a geyser. The golden idol earlier had been off-putting, but this was just disgusting. Whatever that was, getting hit by it probably would have been bad, even for me.

It had missed Eclair, though. Just like Blood Sacrifice, that meant that the user would have to pay the price of using it without getting anything in return. In my case, that would have been an utter tragedy, considering my current condition. Yeah, if I ever needed to use it again, I'd have to make sure there was no way it would miss. I couldn't let myself forget that the reason it had worked on the high priest was because the queen had kept him in place.

"F-f-fehhh . . . What is that stuff?!"

"Who knows? Probably best not to let it touch you, though."

We were keeping our distance, so I figured we weren't in danger, but the ground near where the attack had taken place started dissolving into a muddy mess. The surrounding area looked like it had been devastated by fire, and an unbelievably rancid odor filled the area as mushrooms and mold began to pop up out of the dirt. The rotten earth had become a putrid sea, and creatures resembling monstrous flies started to form in the muddy waters. That was a cursed skill if I ever saw one. Eclair seemed to be the only target. Before long, the monster flies began to swoop down on Eclair.

"Take aim before attacking! Your attacks lack determination! When Mr. Iwatani unleashed his finishing attack while shouldering Ost's final wishes, taking painstaking care to ensure it would not be wasted, *that* was an attack that carried weight. I believe it is that determination that is true strength."

The cursed onslaught of monster flies cannonballed toward Eclair . . . She swiftly leapt straight over the creatures and landed directly in front of Ren. Having lost their target, the monster flies continued to charge forward miserably before crumbling away and disappearing moments later.

I sighed. I couldn't help but feel like the whole area had been horribly contaminated. There was seemingly no end to the damage this bastard did to others.

"Now, let me ask you once again. What is it that you desire after you become the strongest?"

"After . . . becoming the strongest? After?!"

"That's right. You say you're the strongest now, right? Then what will you do with that power?"

"Grr . . ."

Ren didn't know how to respond. Ah, so that was it, after all. Now I understood why something about Ren's greed felt so weak. I'd already noticed that the process and the goal had been swapped. But beyond that process there was nothing more to Ren's greed.

That might have been why I hadn't awakened the greed curse series. I greedily wanted to make money. But to me, the money of this world was simply something I needed to survive the waves, and that was the extent of my interest in it. I would be returning to my own world eventually. So when that time came, giving any leftover money to Raphtalia as payment for everything she'd done was about all I could do with it. Of course, I would be lying if I said I never thought about living a little more extravagantly. But if I had money to spare I was going to spend it on equipment or invest it in facilities.

The same went for Ren's gluttony. It had probably awakened as an extension of his desire to be stronger, but after he'd consumed the experience points of an opponent, there was nothing left. Once he'd become the strongest, he would be satisfied. His gluttony would be satisfied once his stomach was full. It wasn't the kind of gluttony that came from insatiable hunger, where a person could eat and eat and never be satisfied.

My curse was wrath. I was filled with a borderline overwhelming sense of wrath toward injustice. The object of that wrath was this whole world, starting with Witch. Of course,

I had hopes that my wrath might disappear when I returned to my own world, but . . . most likely, I would still become unreasonably angry at times even after returning to my own reality. I would just have to do my best to control it.

So between being constantly consumed by unremitting anger and an unfulfillable desire to be the strongest, which would be more agonizing? Maybe the reason I had been able to withstand my wrath increasingly more lately was because I had been able to take revenge on Witch and Trash to a certain degree. It might have been that the power of the curse series would change depending on the intensity of the hero's emotions.

"I . . . I will . . . I will become the strongest and . . . s-s-save the world!"

"I don't want to hear about some mission you've been given by someone else! There's nothing at all convincing about that!"

Eclair discarded his response without hesitation. His eyes and voice had both completely lacked conviction, after all.

"If it's so hard for you to admit it, then let me spell it out for you directly. I'll tell you exactly what it is that you want."

"What?!"

Ren began trembling violently, and Eclair finally delivered her berating verdict.

"You don't want to become strong. You just want to get back what you've lost!"

"Ugh . . ."

"Like a fool, you went charging in thoughtlessly and you lost your companions, numerous others, and the trust of the people. All you really want is to get all of that back and becoming the strongest is simply a tangible goal that you think can make that happen! Nothing more!"

"Sh . . . shut up!"

"But even if you were a god . . . No, as a hero you are a god. But even so, getting all of that back is impossible. Do you really think becoming the strongest is what you should be focusing on right now?!"

"Shut uuuuuuppp!"

Ren swung his sword wildly at Eclair. I wondered if I should step in. I started to take a step forward, but Eclair held her hand out as a sign that I shouldn't interfere. She then went about reading and narrowly dodging each and every one of Ren's attacks. Man, she was good.

"The truth is you already know this. You know you don't have time to be rotting away in a place like this!"

"Shut your mooooouth! I don't want to hear what you think!"

Ren showed no sign of stopping and just kept swinging at Eclair.

"Your companions believed in you until the very end, and for that they are but dust in the wind. It is on their behalf that I now swing my blade!"

Eclair held her sword up in front of her chest and then launched a skill directly at Ren.

"Hengen Muso Sword Technique! Multistrike Demolition!"

Eclair unleashed a string of attacks that poured straight into Ren. I could see a flow of magic . . . or was that life force? I wasn't really sure. It looked kind of like a special effect, but I guess it was probably life force. Anyway, some kind of light started swelling up inside of Ren. It was as if the technique was destroying him from the inside out. It must have been one of the old lady's specialty defense rating attacks. It looked similar to one she had used on me before. Taking a string of that many defense rating attacks would be hell. And since I was particularly weak to such attacks, just watching sent shivers down my spine.

"Gah!"

"Sword Hero, you are weak. It is by accepting this that you can become stronger."

Eclair paused and returned her sword to its scabbard.

"The people that you lost are never coming back. But starting now, you can live with enough purpose and fight with enough vigor for yourself and all of them, too. I will assist you in any way that I can."

She was making herself look good, but Ren hadn't actually taken that much damage. But then again, he was a hero, even if he was a lame one, and he had unlocked two curse series. For Eclair, that was probably one hell of a close fight. If she had eaten even one of Ren's attacks, she'd probably be split clean in two right now.

"U . . . urgah . . ."

And then Ren collapsed. Oh man, that kind of defeat was straight out of an anime. I mean, come on, he'd clearly had plenty of stamina left.

"Don't run from your sins. Every time you try, I will be there standing in your way. For the sake of your deceased companions."

"Urgh . . ."

Ren was still collapsed on the ground, but he was crying. Was it involuntarily? He was completely still otherwise. His long sword had changed back into a normal sword, and the sinister aura had vanished. When Eclair finally turned around, I called out to her.

"I never knew you were so skilled at psychological attacks."

Praising her too outright would be out of character for me, so I masked the compliment as sarcasm. Putting it like that was probably a safe bet.

"It sounds so horrible when you put it like that."

Eclair responded deploringly, but it was true that she hadn't actually physically defeated him.

"This was supposed to be an emotionally moving scene! It was supposed to be a communion of two hearts, via the sword, guiding a troubled soul to harmony. But you just completely ruined it, Mr. Naofumi."

Now Raphtalia was giving me the evil eye.

"Did I?"

But seriously, it was basically a psychological attack, right?

"Oh, looks like we have a little scrap going on here. Eeehehe!"

And then with the worst timing possible, the same pair that had fled only minutes earlier faded into view. What the hell were they doing here?! This was not the time for them to show up again! They were supposed to be running away!

"We were going to run away, but then we noticed a cloud of smoke and decided to check it out. Is that one of the other heroes?"

"Shit . . ."

This was bad. Ren and Motoyasu were so weak that they couldn't even begin to compare to me. Not to mention, Ren had passed out and couldn't even move.

"Who might this be?" asked Motoyasu.

For some reason, he was over by Ren and Eclair just standing there looking confused. He obviously had no idea what was going on.

"Judging from the power of his attacks and that flurry of skills, he must be a weakling, unlike the Shield Hero."

"It wouldn't make sense to pass up an opportunity like this. We might as well finish him off real quick."

"I won't allow that!"

Eclair pointed her short sword at the pair and readied herself to protect Ren. I couldn't just let Ren and Motoyasu be killed, either. That would only make things a lot harder on me, after all.

"Die, holy heroes!"

The small man began to cast a spell and the large man started spinning his kusarigama around and running toward us.

"Not on my watch!"

"Not happening!"

"Please make it in time!"

Raphtalia and I swiftly broke into a sprint, and Rishia threw her knife and was trying to obstruct the men by getting them caught in the rope. Should I use Attack Support and fire off a skill? I was almost close enough for Ren to be in range of Air Strike Shield. The large man was headed toward the collapsed Ren and it wouldn't be long until he reached him. Neither Eclair nor Motoyasu had an attack strong enough to deliver a decisive blow.

"Blast it! I didn't want to use that technique before I had mastered it, but it appears I have no choice!"

Eclair crouched down low and readied herself to perform some kind of technique. What was she going to do?

"Mr. Iwatani! I won't be able to fight after using this technique, but it will buy you some time. I leave it to you to protect the Sword Hero!"

"Got it!"

I guess she still had an ace up her sleeve. Eclair was going to buy us some time so that I could protect Ren.

"I'll help, too! Muso—"

Rishia was focusing in preparation to use some kind of technique, too. I wanted to jab her about not waiting until the last second to play her trump card, but I guess this wasn't the time for that.

"Are these your enemies, Father? They shan't defeat me!"

Motoyasu sprung forward and stood next to Eclair.

"Stay back, Motoyasu! You're no match for them!"

His efforts were commendable, but frankly, him jumping into the fray would just make things messier. What the hell was I going to do if Ren and Motoyasu both died on me here?!

"Outer Hengen Muso Secret Technique—"

"Looks like we win this one!"

The large man grinned and swung his kusarigama at Motoyasu and Ren, while the meteorite summoned by the small man appeared in the sky above them. I just had to hope that Eclair's and Rishia's attacks would make it in time. I was concentrating while running to prepare to cast my support magic on Raphtalia and the rest of us.

Finally! Ren and Motoyasu were finally in range of my defensive skills!

"Air Strike Shield! Second Shield!"

That should buy us a little time.

"Eat this, I say!"

Motoyasu thrust his spear at the large man out from behind the shield that had appeared in front of him. The enemy had some mysterious rippling defensive barrier. Motoyasu's attack wouldn't be able to touch him! Even if he did have a cursed weapon, just like Ren, his attacks wouldn't be powerful enough to—

Pop!

A sound like a balloon popping echoed out. I'm pretty sure it was louder than when Filo and Rishia had just barely managed to break through the barrier.

"Gah!"

Motoyasu's spear had pierced through the barrier effortlessly and straight into the large man's chest. The spear went clean through the large man, and Motoyasu started swinging the spear around like it was a toy, with the large man still skewered on the end.

"Wh . . . what?"

Both the large man and the small man were flabbergasted.

"Ugh . . . gah . . . stop . . . damn it!"

The large man was struggling to free himself from the spear while being flung around.

"There's a meteorite coming this way. You needn't lift a finger, Father."

Motoyasu was looking up at the sky and staring at the meteorite rushing straight toward him.

"How long do you intend to be stuck to my spear? It's unsightly!"

Despite being the one that had skewered him, Motoyasu reprimanded the large man while looking at him like he was a piece of trash.

"G . . . go to hell! Urgah . . ."

It was everything the skewered man could do to squeeze out a response while he continued to struggle. Blood spurted out of his mouth. He had almost managed to pull the spear out of his chest.

"It seems that you two are Father's enemies. Death to enemies, I say!"

Motoyasu gripped his spear tightly.

"Burst Lance!"

The tip of Motoyasu's spear began to glow a bright red.

"Wha . . . urgaaaahhhhh!"

The skewered large man was screaming while trying to free himself from the spear, but a loud blast echoed out and a massive explosion occurred at the tip of Motoyasu's spear.

"Gaaahhhhh!"

Still stuck to the end of Motoyasu's spear, the large man exploded into pieces right before our eyes. Luckily it wasn't one of those disgusting scenes where chunks of flesh went flying.

The explosion had reduced him to atoms.

"Wh . . . wha . . . You're kidding, right?"

The small man was dumbstruck. But he must have pulled himself together quickly, because he flashed a vulgar grin before making a comment.

"Eeehehehe . . . I never expected he would get killed. Resurrecting him is going to be a pain."

He was laughing flippantly about his own companion's death. These creeps really did have a game mindset. They were even worse than Ren.

"Translocating Light . . . doesn't seem to be usable, I guess. This has turned out to be a real hassle."

"You're next, I say!"

"I'd like to see you try!"

The small man pulled out his shamshir and readied himself to engage at any moment. Then he turned to Motoyasu and just as he was about to dash forward . . . Motoyasu was already standing directly in front of the man. When did that happen?! Aside from defense, all my stats were currently reduced by more than half due to a curse, but even so, surely he couldn't move so fast that I couldn't see him, right?!

"M . . . Mr. Naofumi?! Do you think the Spear Hero . . ."

"Spear Hero?!"

"Fehhh . . ."

Motoyasu had just blown a man to smithereens and yet

he was acting completely unaffected. Something about his expression seemed crazy. Oh, that's right. Motoyasu was using a cursed weapon, too. I'd forgotten since he had actually been listening to me, but Motoyasu obviously wasn't in his right mind.

"Rah!"

"Too slow! Death to Father's enemies, I say!"

Motoyasu swung his spear to the side. It sliced clean through the small man's shamshir . . . and his neck, too.

"Wha . . ."

Blood spurted out all over Motoyasu. Red had been one of his favorite colors to start with, and now he was covered in blood. He was red from head to toe. Having just seen two seemingly formidable enemies effortlessly killed in a single instant had left us speechless.

"Motoyasu . . . You . . . How did you get so strong?"

"Your words can never be wrong, Father!"

"In other words, you used the power-up methods I told you about?"

Motoyasu nodded without hesitation, as if to imply such a thing was only natural. That meant that the Motoyasu here with us had implemented all of the power-up methods of the four holy heroes. On top of that, he had probably powered up his curse series weapon, too. It was probably at stage IV, like my Shield of Wrath, or perhaps even stage V.

That shield had made a huge difference when fighting the Spirit Tortoise and Kyo. It was ridiculously tough and had some powerful abilities, but what about in Motoyasu's case? It only made sense that his weapon equivalent would have extraordinarily high attack power. In other words, Motoyasu now possessed a colossal amount of power. It would be a far cry from the mediocre strength that Ren had displayed. That was certainly reassuring.

Crazy. To think that he'd been able to so effortlessly and brutally annihilate enemies that I'd had such a difficult time with.

"That takes care of all of the enemies," he said.

"Yeah, it does."

The enemies had appeared unexpectedly, but we'd narrowly managed to protect Ren, thanks to Motoyasu. The completely unanticipated turn of events had thrown me for a loop, but now we needed to focus on Ren.

"Anyway, let's get Ren out of here."

"Got it."

Out of the corner of my eye, I looked at the fallen corpse of the small man as Eclair and I hoisted Ren up off the ground.

"Let's put him in the carriage and take him to the village," I said.

"That's right, we left it back by the bandit hideout, didn't we?" Eclair replied.

"Yes. We'll need to find Filo, too," said Raphtalia.

"Yeah, since she ran off somewhere with Raph-chan."

"Fehhhhh . . . What have we doooone?!"

Rishia was just now noticing the state of things and making a commotion. Curious, I gave our surroundings a quick once-over. Headless corpse. Putrefied earth. It would have been hard to describe the fierce battle that had occurred here in only a few words.

But wait a minute, the men's corpses hadn't turned into light. I wondered why. It would have been nice if they could give us a clue about how to prevent our enemies from resurrecting.

"Alright, Motoyasu, you come with—"

I looked over to where I expected Motoyasu to be standing, but there was no sign of him there. Then I heard a high-pitched sound, so I looked over in that direction. A short distance away, Motoyasu was walking off whistling, for some reason.

"Motoyasu!"

I was about to call out for him to stop, but he turned around and replied.

"The hero should always make his exit upon saving the day! Farewell, Father!"

"There will be no making exits! Stop screwing around!"

He was using a cursed weapon. It would be a problem if he just went and disappeared again at a time like this! I don't know what the consequences were for using it, but I was sure they wouldn't be pretty! But before I could tell him that, something came speeding toward Motoyasu from behind. Was that . . . Filo's carriage?

"Noooo! My carriaaaage!"

Huh? Filo came running up from a short distance away.

"Gweh!"

Filo's carriage was being pulled by . . . huh? It was three . . . . filolials—one red, one blue, and one green.

"Farewell, I say!"

Motoyasu went running away alongside the carriage while holding on to the side as if he were preparing to leap into a speeding vehicle.

"Filo-tan! Father! Should you ever find yourselves in a predicament, know that I will come running!"

"Give me back my carriaaaage!"

Filo went chasing after Motoyasu with her cheeks puffed out and fury in her eyes. I sighed. But I guess I'd be mad, too, if someone just went and used something of mine, like it belonged to them. I could understand how she felt.

"Rafu!"

As Filo ran past us, Raph-chan jumped down off of her and onto my shoulder.

"Welcome back, Raph-chan," I said.

She'd probably had a rough time, with Filo carrying her off somewhere like that. Filo had gone chasing after Motoyasu, so if everything worked out, maybe we would be able to capture him, too. Although, judging by the way he was now, that wasn't going to be easy.

"Rafu! Rafu rafu!"

For some reason, Raph-chan jumped up onto my head and pointed at something just like she had done when pointing out Kyo's soul before. I was suddenly able to see the souls of the pair of men we'd just defeated.

"Oh? It looks like the Shield Hero can see us. Eeehehe."

"Oh yeah? Whatever, that's fine. We lost this time, but we're going to kill you and your friends next time! I'm going to make you pay for doing this to us!"

Hmm? Something about this situation . . . It seemed like we should be able to do something.

"S'yne, I can see those creeps' souls over there."

"Yes. The souls will resur————"

Her speech was breaking up like usual and I couldn't understand what she was saying. But! I knew of an attack that would likely be effective on an opponent like this. Indeed . . . The situation was exactly like when we had defeated Kyo.

"Raphtalia, see those spirits over there? Use Spirit Blade to . . . mince them."

"U . . . understood!"

"Wh . . . what?!"

The pair's voices cracked when they cried out. They'd

probably thought we wouldn't be able to do anything to their spirits, but they were wrong. We couldn't be sympathizing with enemies that were trying to kill the heroes. If we didn't do anything right now, they would just come back for revenge. We needed to take action now while we had this chance. If we managed to kill them, it'd be like hitting the jackpot. That would mean we had figured out a way to keep enemies from resurrecting.

But in online games, whenever you resurrected, you would return to some kind of save point. So why were their souls just hovering around over there? And then I remembered what had been going on here just a few moments ago. Now it made sense. Motoyasu and Ren had destabilized the Earth's magnetic field here. Their souls must have been stuck here for the same reason teleportation skills couldn't be used.

"Eek! S-s-stop! Stay away!"

"Wait! Listen! If you let us go, we'll make a special exception just for—"

"Unfortunately for you, I'm not willing to trust anyone that talks like that. Raphtalia, snuff 'em."

"Understood. Spirit Blade! Soul Slice!"

Raphtalia used the katana that had been unlocked by the soul eater materials and sliced through the air where I was pointing.

"Gaaahhhhh!"

Her soul-slicing skill cut through the pair's souls, which then dissipated and vanished. It would be a real feat if they somehow still managed to resurrect. I looked back over at their corpses, but they showed no sign of turning into light. I guess they were honest-to-goodness dead now.

"We beat them————we beat them? To think you could————"

S'yne's voice broke up as she whispered. A look of relief was on her face. I wasn't sure exactly what she had tried to say, but I'm pretty sure I understood how she felt. We'd finally defeated an enemy that kept coming back to life, no matter how many times they were killed. Of course she would be relieved.

"We ended up having to take their lives. It leaves a bad taste in your mouth," Raphtalia whispered as she returned her katana to its sheath.

"The creeps were going on about their world being the strongest. It wasn't like the sense of purpose that Glass and the others had. They were sickening. There's no need to feel sorry for them," I told her.

I could tell they weren't the type that would listen to reason. It felt like we'd been fighting against children in adult bodies. Mortal combat was a game to them. I'm sure the reason they had been talking like it was all a game while we were fighting is because they were confident they would be fine even if they died. It was a setting where we had one life, and they had infinite lives . . . No thanks.

I had the urge to complain about how our problems always suddenly piled up all at once like this, but . . . I guess right now I should just be happy that we had won.

"There might still be some of their companions around. Let's be cautious as we head back. Don't let your guard down."

"Understood."

We waited for Filo to return and then headed back to the village.

By the way, Filo had gone chasing after Motoyasu but ran out of steam before she could catch up with him. Sheesh . . . Motoyasu was nothing but trouble. Still, I wanted to think that the fact he'd been acting on our behalf was a sign that he'd changed. If he was that strong, I was sure he wouldn't end up dying easily, anyway.

Epilogue: Making Peace with the Sword Hero

When all was said and done, we took the unconscious Ren with us back to the village.

"Ugh . . . huh? Where . . . am . . ."

"You're awake. This is the village I'm overseeing. That area you were causing trouble in is part of the territory the queen gave me."

"Oh . . . I see . . ."

Upon awaking, Ren was calm. He was looking at me and Eclair with regret in his eyes. Raphtalia was staring at me like she was keeping watch, to make sure I didn't try anything. Oh, and Fohl had returned to normal as soon as Motoyasu left, by the way.

"Sheesh . . . Becoming a bandit? You know better than that."

"I messed up . . ."

Ren remained calm and listened to what I had to say without protest. It seemed like Eclair's chastening had been effective.

"For the time being, why don't you tell us where Witch is?"

"Sorry, I have no idea."

"Bullshit. Witch is the one that told you to play bandit, right?"

"No. Ending up as a bandit . . . was my own fault."

Ren began to tell his story. Apparently, the same day the two of them fled, Witch told Ren she wanted to meet someone and took him to a certain town. It had been near where Ren had teleported them to. There, Witch introduced him to a man. He'd recognized the man's face but couldn't recall from where. The man had pulled out a sword and asked Ren to teach him how to use it.

"Sure. I can show you a few things," Ren told him.

Ren happily obliged and did some light sparring with the man. And then the man began discussing something with Witch off to the side. It was hard to make out what they were saying.

"Honestly, [. . .] than expected. In that case, [. . .]"

"If you think [. . .], then."

"But he's [. . .], right?"

"Yeah, but [. . .] stubborn, so taking advantage [. . .] tough."

Something was uncomfortable about the way they had been staring at him at first, but Ren trusted Witch and then she smiled at him, so he decided not to let it bother him.

"Alright, Mr. Ren, I'm sure you're tired after all that's happened today. Let's go rest at an inn."

Witch took Ren to a somewhat expensive inn and they got some rooms.

"We've really been looking forward to traveling with you, Mr. Ren," said Witch.

"Indeed! We always admired you much more than the Spear Hero, Mr. Ren," Girl 2 added.

"Oh . . . really? I'll . . . do my best to save the world . . . for you two."

Ren made up his mind to fight once again for the sake of the people that believed in him. He was fed up with the people of this world and their sudden change of attitude, but even so he'd fight for the people that believed in him.

That was, until the next morning, when he realized that Witch had stolen everything except for his sword and run away. She'd left a letter behind on the inn table.

"This is the letter," he told me as he showed me the letter.

Had he been holding on to it as a keepsake? Ren handed me the letter. It was full of wrinkles like he'd crumpled it up before, but I was still able to read it.

"You're no longer of any use to me, so I'm taking everything that is and leaving. I'm grateful that you helped me escape from the Shield and the Spear, but I'm afraid neither your looks nor your personality is my type. I guess I'd be willing to love you if you ever became strong enough to defeat the Shield. Of course, judging from the way you are now, that will never happen. Ha ha ha!"

Damn, she was annoying! Without even thinking about it, I ripped the letter up and threw it away. That Witch bitch! She was beyond redemption!

But to think she'd already ditched Ren by the following day . . . Damn, she worked fast! Bloody hell. It made me wonder if the real reason she'd approached him was to get her hands on his equipment and money. But I guess she probably just decided that keeping Ren in the dark for much longer would be too much of a hassle.

"I think something probably snapped inside of me at that point. Everything went black and one of those curse series you'd told us about appeared on my status screen," Ren said.

He'd decided to believe in someone again and they immediately betrayed his trust, after all. I could understand how he must have felt. If Raphtalia had betrayed me the day after I'd realized she believed in me, I'm sure my wrath curse series would have evolved much quicker, too.

"After that . . . things just went into a tailspin. I left the inn and walked around looking for anything of value . . . I decided if people were going to steal from me, then I'd just steal back from them. But I didn't want to reveal my identity, so I got a mask and . . ." he went on.

I guess that was when he ambushed the bandits' carriage, made them his underlings, and formed his own gang of bandits. It was a perfect example of a life spinning out of control.

"Naofumi . . . I know it probably sounds disingenuous, but I hope you'll forgive me for everything."

"Yeah, whatever. Regardless of whether I forgive you or not, my objective has been to protect you from the very start. I'll let it go as long as you don't do anything like this again, so heed my advice and just focus on getting a little stronger."

There were people sneaking around in this world that wanted to kill the holy heroes. Considering that and what was coming, the heroes needed to get every bit as strong as they could. I was sure Ren had the potential to be stronger than me at the very least, and that's why I wanted him to learn how to power up his weapons properly.

"Okay. I'll do my very best to follow your advice and get stronger."

Ren had been a huge mass of pride obsessed with maintaining his suave image, but now he was bowing his head meekly and apologizing to me. He seemed genuinely regretful. If he was going to apologize this much, I felt like forgiving him might actually be an option. Did that make me a softy?

"I never imagined Witch would be that horrible. I mean, I did have my doubts. But . . . she was kind to me, so I made the mistake of trusting her. It was foolish and unforgivable. I ruined what may have been your last chance to capture her!"

Ren got pretty fired up as he badmouthed Witch. He'd gotten played, after all. He probably hated her almost as much as I did. In that sense, I could sympathize with Ren. It felt kind of like . . . we were connected by a common enemy now.

"Well, the bitch is a waste of good looks, and she's a pro at pretending to cry, too."

"You're maligning the former princess, now? Well, it's not

like I can't understand how you feel, but . . ." Eclair mumbled while scratching her head.

But where had that woman run off to, anyway? Based on what Ren had said, she seemed to have an accomplice. A man that Ren had seen before somewhere . . . That meant it was someone that Ren had come into contact with at some point. Who in the world could it have been?

I had no idea. Anyway, if we wanted to go after Witch, we probably needed to find Itsuki. Witch had targeted me, then Motoyasu, and then Ren. It was highly likely that she would go after Itsuki next. I didn't know what her plans were, but they certainly didn't seem to be well-intentioned. Seriously, that bitch brought nothing but trouble. It was possible that there were still more enemies like the pair Motoyasu had killed lurking around, too.

"Which leaves . . ."

Now the question was whether I should tell Ren how to get stronger again or not. He seemed genuinely regretful, and it wouldn't hurt to have him on our side. After all, the heroes were supposed to work together to fight the waves, like Kizuna, Glass, and their companions.

"You were using curse skills one after another, so we need to figure out what kind of condition you're in right now. Other than that . . . actually listen to what I say and get stronger. It's really not that hard."

"I will. Naofumi . . . Thanks in advance."

"Don't worry about it. All I want is for you three to get stronger. You need to recognize what kind of situation we're in now, too."

"Yeah."

All I could do was defend. I had to rely on my companions to attack. The reason I could put up such a good fight now was because Raphtalia just happened to have been chosen by the katana vassal weapon. In other words, the other three heroes were supposed to be the foundation of my offense. If I could get Ren on board and if he really made an effort to get stronger, then that would be just about the best companion I could ask for.

"I . . . I'm going to face up to what I've done. Welt, Bakta, Tersia, and Farrie . . . My companions died trying to bring peace to this world. I want to fight to make sure they didn't die in vain."

It seemed like Ren was finally ready to listen to what I had to say. I was still a little worried, but it looked like things might work out.

"Sword Hero, try not to worry about things too much. We . . . Me, Eclair, and the village children that I grew up with are all here to help."

Raphtalia was trying to comfort Ren, perhaps because she sympathized with his newfound purpose. Ren nodded meekly in response.

"Thank you."

"Mr. Amaki the Sword Hero."

Eclair faced Ren and stepped forward. Ren stared at her.

"Yes?"

"You understood what I was trying to say during our duel, right?"

"Yeah . . . Thank you . . . for stopping me."

"Of course. I, too, will do everything I can to help. Let's fight this battle together. What do you say?"

Ren closed his eyes and nodded quietly.

"I don't want to be a bother. But if I start heading down the wrong path again, please stop me."

"Certainly. If you ever start to go astray again, Mr. Amaki, I will be there standing in your way, no matter how many times it happens."

"I'll count on it . . . umm, Eclair. And please, call me by my name."

Ren held his hand out to Eclair.

"Mr. Ren."

"You can drop the honorific. There's a lot I'd like to learn from you, Eclair."

"Of course. I must warn you, Ren, my tutelage is exacting."

"I was counting on that."

There was bromance in the air as Ren and Eclair firmly shook hands.

"Mr. Naofumi, you're thinking about something rude, aren't you?"

"I was just thinking about how it seemed like a nice bromance."

"Eclair is a female!"

"Mr. Iwatani . . . Good grief . . ."

"Naofumi."

Ren looked at Eclair's face and then addressed me.

"What?"

"I'm sorry I didn't trust you."

Wasn't it a bit late for that? But whatever. We'd both been tricked by Witch. I wasn't looking for a support group or anything, but I felt like we could sympathize with each other. Another member had joined the Victims of the Witch Bitch Club.

"Anyway, just take it easy for today. We have a lot to do starting tomorrow. Later."

I left Ren with Eclair and exited the room. Raphtalia followed after me.

"That was a big step forward. The Sword Hero seemed to have a positive attitude."

"Yeah. So far, our force to fight the waves . . . and the next guardian beast—the Phoenix—is steadily increasing."

Other than that, we would have to deal with those enemies looking to kill the holy heroes. I couldn't imagine those two men being the end of it. Thinking about the fact that there may still have been others lurking out there somewhere just made me feel sick. Kizuna's world had its share of problems, but we had heaps of our own here in this world, too. Knocking them out, even if only one at a time . . . was our only choice, I guess.

"Alright, Raphtalia. We've got plenty of headaches ahead. We don't have time to be taking it easy. We have to be ready to deal with any enemy that stands in our path."

"Understood! What will we do now?"

"Reconstruction and building up our offensive capabilities are both important, but after seeing the rapid improvement of Rishia and Eclair, I think it may be time for us to do some serious training."

"I agree. Sadeena keeps telling me I don't know how to use a katana, so I've been feeling like my technique is lacking lately."

Our stats were reduced at the moment. I could have just used that as an excuse, but I think we needed to go back and do a thorough reassessment of our technique. Our enemies this time had only been the vanguard. They weren't holy heroes or even seven star heroes. They had been the equivalent of hero companions. Struggling with enemies like that was unacceptable. We would continue with our usual tasks, but I was going to add training to the schedule, too.

"Alright, in that case, let's do this!"

"Understood!"

Looking out over the village, well on its way to returning to its former glory, Raphtalia and I both went back to work.

Character Design:
Atla

アトラ

フォウル